# BLAKELY HIGH

## AND THE

# VOODOO
# PHANTOM

*By*

*Dot Jay Gomez*

*"Fiction is real life with a twist."*

Blakely High-Voodoo Phantom is a work of fiction. Names, characters, places and incidents are the products of the author's imagination or are used fictitiously. Any resemblance to actual events, locales, or persons, living or dead is entirely coincidental.

Published in the United States of America.

Quail Harbor Productions
P.O. Box 8185
Cave Creek, AZ 85327

ISBN 978-0-615-66907-6

Printed in the United States of America.

Library of Congress Cataloging applied for.

Cover design by Shaun Wawro.

*A special thanks to*

*Grant the Great,*

*and 'Marketeer'- Andy.*

# BLAKELY HIGH

## AND THE

# VOODOO
# PHANTOM

### Fiction

**Also** by Dot Jay Gomez:

## Blakely High Photo Play

A young teacher, Gina McHenry, becomes entangled with danger as she searches for answers to a kidnapping, a terrorizing car chase, and a mountain trail ride shooting. Qwest for answers to hidden secrets take you from the CAVE CREEK desert to the high country of the RIM and into the BLUE RIDGE forest.

### Mystery- Romance - Action

About the Author:

- ➤ Dot Jay Gomez
- ➤ Retired high school teacher.
- ➤ 24 years at Paradise Valley High School.
- ➤ B.A. and M.A. from Arizona State University.

Favorite Mottos:

- ➤ It's not what you know; it's what you do with it.
- ➤ He who is bored, is boring.

# CHAPTER ONE
## October 14
### Friday

Gina McHenry sat in class shaking her head periodically to stay awake as the old graying English professor droned on and on in an abscessed monotone. His incessant robotic reading of notes, a verbiage that allowed for no classroom interaction, was a mind sleeper.

An evaporative cooler hummed in unison adding to the monotony of this second Friday night class in October. She pushed back pale-yellow-curls limp with sweat and re-adjusted her up-do with a simple hair clip.

Loudly, she un-wrapped her favorite dark chocolate bar as she knew the professor would not bother to look up, continuing reading from his notes, "How to keep your classes motivated."

Irony! She snickered as she sneaked a peek at others around her checking what they were holding. Most were slurping drinks, eating candies and chips and tucking empty wrappers into their pockets. Some were dressed casually in tees and shorts while others squirmed uncomfortably, decked out in their after work attire of heels and ties.

She was one of the lucky ones who had a few minutes after teaching to run home and change to a casual attire of white short-shorts and her favorite soft purple tank with the comfortable built-in. None noticed her tiredness as they too shuffled their feet with a few in the far back row nodding off occasionally.

Fifteen terribly tired professionals sat attending a four hour lecture for pay scale incentives…..a class that demanded attendance for credit.

She needed more credits toward the next step on the increment scale to tag "on top" of her Masters; it's called 'climbing the pay scale'; they all agreed.

The recorder was set on high trying to catch the professor's voice, as promised, for her best friend Nancy Lopez who was sick and could not join her.

"You tape the lecture and I'll type the notes."

"Deal!"

Friends since starting their teaching career five years ago, they were now collecting notes for a book on "Teaching Tricks" that they had experienced or gleaned from others whom they admired.

Gina looked at the large round clock on the wall above the tall gray haired man and groaned.

One more hour.

After a grueling week of teaching one hundred and seventy bouncing students daily, FRIDAY night was Gina's least favorite time to do something unpleasant like sitting in a classroom in an old rambling building on the far eastern side of the towns of Carefree and Cave Creek.

She knew that Creekers would be at Tumbleweed's dancing and her crew of friends and family would be laughing away the week's stress while sitting at Greasy's drinking cold tea, beer, and eating mounds of nachos.

She sighed too loudly.

This time the professor looked up, raised his eyebrows at her, glared, than smashed his eyelids together before continuing.

She limply stared back.

She pretended to write notes as her mind drifted. Doodling pictures on her note pad was a plus. It had been a disheartening second week of October and deviations were all negatives.

Her dad whom she called Pop, cranked all week because the popovers he baked at his newly opened bakery, flopped, flattened and saucered every time he took them out of the oven. "What am I doing differently? Last week they were perfect."

She doodled puffy cream balls.

He had commissioned his cycle group of four retired buddies, THE FAMILY FARM, and they were immersed nightly up to their elbows in flour. They too were perplexed over the unfortunate situation of his prize pastry. They were a pudgy-balding-whiskered group of retired professionals and shadowed each other in support of everything. However, they didn't want to make decisions, only follow orders.

Deviation number two: Heleena, the English Department head that was too old to teach but too young to retire, had told her to prepare for a "surprise" professional observation sometime this month; Gina was always queasy during observations. Much to her embarrassment, her tongue would suddenly get thick and her old childhood lisp would come back as the 'observer' wrote down every word and movement made by her, the 'observee'.

She doodled a face with an upside down smile.

Deviation number three caused her to frown with depression as she thought about Rick Del Rio. Was he her boyfriend or not? Where has he been all week? He has not returned any of her messages. Was he out checking on crime scenes or was he just OUT?

It wasn't her fault he couldn't find the dead body out in the desert two months ago…it had simply disappeared. Now he was obsessed and seemed to drift away every time she talked too him.

She doodled a heart with a crack in the middle.

A nine o'clock bell buzzed in the old hollow building reverberating against the wall, vibrating the desks and causing Gina to jump.

The classroom emptied within ten seconds; people hurried and pushed to the entrance.

All except Gina. The thirty-two ounce bucket of iced tea she drained during class necessitated a trip to the bathroom up a flight of stairs to the second floor and at the far end of the hallway.

After slamming everything off the top of her desk into her bag, she was the last to leave.

Clicking along noisily, she hurried, echoing in the now empty building, pinching herself for not having taken advantage of the ten minute break earlier....when she was sitting in class pondering problems....doodling.

The old bathroom door with an opaque pane above the handle swung open noisily then closed with a bang. It was late and she was thankful for the bright lights hanging down from the middle of the ceiling.

Outdoor lights filtered eerily through the four rows of glass cubed windows set about two feet above the sinks. The old bathroom glowed with bouncing light.

After shutting herself in a metal stall near the end of the room and finding no place to hang her shoulder bag, she opted to set it on her lap after sitting down.

Instantly, the bathroom door opened with a loud bang as it hit the adjoining wall.

Gina bristled!

Heavy booted feet shuffled slowly...slowly along the floor. Each metal stall door slammed open purposely with a loud annoyance.

Gina sat there too numb to move. Her heart pounded aggressively as she tightly clung to her bag unknowingly holding her breath.

Fingers started scrapping and scratching then tapping at the top of each stall door...monotonously.

Shuffling feet stopped outside her door and fingers began to tap--tap--tap at the top.

One, two, three, four.

Knees creaked and within seconds a masked face peered directly at her from under the door.

Spurred by a calamity of fright and anger, she sped into action. Her hand had been clutching a can of pepper spray which she now used spraying the mask furiously.

Next, she threw the can on the floor violently, pulled up her lacies and thrust the door open with such force it hit the man's mask, smashing it in his face where he now sat on his rear groveling and screaming in pain.

"Hey! Hey somebody," she yelled loudly as she ran the length of the hallway pummeling down the stairs skipping every other step. Now puffing and panting, she ran out of the building and into the empty parking lot. Occasionally, she spun around looking for a follower.

Up ahead her Jeep Wrangler beckoned where she had left it under a night light. Again turning quickly, she made sure that no one was following as she jumped in the unlocked Jeep with keys already in hand.

While driving out of the lot she saw no other cars. No Security Guard. Nothing! The parking lot had emptied within minutes of the bell.

Ghostly!

She spun around in her seat anxiously looking about for her own safety. She shook and shivered while checking her rear view mirror. Nothing!

Where was the peeking pervert? What was he driving? In her speed she thought about the mask and could she identify it to Del Rio when necessary?

Driving away in a fury she added this night to the top of the list of 'downers' and feared the future.

Mentally she doodled a big grade of "F" for the night.

## CHAPTER TWO
Friday


Driving west as fast as she could on Cave Creek Road towards town, Gina soon discovered flashing lights in her rear view mirror. Pulling over on the right hand shoulder of the road with relief, she turned off her Jeep Wrangler and reached for her purse with her driver's license. Although she was still shaking, she was somewhat relieved of fear.

Out of the unmarked car stepped Rick Del Rio. She lost her composure seeing him so handsomely suited and foolishly started sobbing uncontrollably. Her inner strength diminished further when he opened the Jeep's door, pulled her out, and hugged her tightly.

"Ok, what's going on?" He patted her back hoping it would stop the shaking. After she explained everything he held her at arm's length and asked, "Masked?"

"African mask." Stammering, she tried to gain some composure. While still holding her in one arm he radioed for backup. "Meet me at the old studio east of town," he ordered.

Cupping one hand under her chin, he wiped away tears with a small handkerchief he kept tucked in a pocket.

"Now I know what to do to get your attention," she said breathing deeply. "Where have you been? I haven't seen you lately."

"I've got you on my radar…always." He ran his thumb around her mouth tickling her lips, and kissed them softly.

She wavered. "Aren't you proud of me though, the way I handled it?" She mustered a meek, smeary smile, her infamous crooked one with a side of her mouth tilting up and rubbed the tip of her nose with the back of her hand.

"I'm impressed!" As his eyes gleamed a bright emerald green, his hat and face changed colors to multi soft yellows and reds with the rotating light still flashing on top of his car.

"Come with me. We need to go back there now to fingerprint the correct stall door and cordon off the bathroom until a forensic team finishes their investigation."

After locking her Jeep she jumped in the car with Del Rio and felt more relaxed and secure until nearing the old building.

"Of course the security guard is there now! Where was he earlier," she complained.

"That's for us to find out," he stated with disgust.

The old building was now lit up like a Christmas tree. In the parking lot were cop cars, rotating lights, men in brown uniforms and cycle groups circling about.

Gina explained in detail what had happened and with great reticence showed them the stall where she had been. To her embarrassment, several cops gathered around and surveyed the stall closely.

"You realize the enormity of the situation," Rick said to everyone. "A peeking pervert is among us!" Looking around the floor he plucked a four inch reddish-brown feather from a corner.

"Look familiar?" He twirled it between gloved forefinger and thumb before bagging it.

"That was on the mask!" Gina gasped, stepped back and covered her face for a second. Then she explained further. "The Arts and Crafts classes are constructing African masks as part of our month of October African studies.

"What?" Three officers in cowboy boots simultaneously questioned with a startle. "African studies?" Officer Colt turned around and chuckled.

"Yep! Talk to the principal." Raising her eyebrows, she punctuated her remark with a wave of an arm.

"Gina," instructed Rick, "first thing Monday morning go to the art department and describe the mask as accurately as possible. I'm sure the teacher can tie it to a student. And tonight when you get home, write as many notes as you can remember."

She squeezed folded arms together and shivered.

The officers milled around being careful not to touch anything as they secured the area with yellow tape. Earlier, the door had been gingerly opened but now stayed propped with a wedge.

"I'll be right back," Rick told the men. "Watch for forensics."

"Let's go," he told Gina after taking her by the hand. They walked quickly out of the building to his car. "I want you to go straight home and not make stops at Greasy's, Tumbleweeds, or Screaming-Ice Cream."

"Are you trying to be funny?" Then added, "Are you coming by tonight?"

"I can't. I have too much to do here. I'll talk to you tomorrow."

"Crap! So much for Friday night!" Her shoulders drooped from an accumulation of tiredness and fright.

"Hey, no droopy mouths! I'm calling Pop to tell him that you're on your way home. He's to call me in twenty minutes to let me know you made it. Be sure and tell him and Dixie everything."

At her Jeep he kissed her lips softly before opening her door. "I'm coming over for breakfast.

Explain more detail then, and I also want to hear about the African studies." He muffled a smirk.

"Waffles?" She asked.

"Waffles." He smiled.


She locked the door as she got in waving to Rick who was watching her before he drove off. An arm waved high in the air as he hurried away after making a u-turn on the now empty Cave Creek highway to head back east. Looking in her driver's side view mirror she watched him leave and started the engine.

Before accelerating, she screamed and flopped back in her seat. A mask was stuck on her windshield with a wiper protruding out of one eye socket. It was 'the' mask. She dialed Rick on her cell.

Within minutes his car with lights and siren full force was behind her Jeep.

"Good deal," he said with too much delight. "Now we have the evidence!" Pulling a plastic bag from his car, he bagged the opulent mask without touching it.

"A-hah," he exclaimed looking at the contents holding it up in the dark night. Flashing lights added to the mystique of the colorful mask. White highlights exuded a cold iridescence, an ominous glowing that gave it life.

"Eerie," Gina said. The mask appeared both grotesque and real through the plastic bag as she stared at it, imagining that an hour ago it hid a face.

"Devilish!"

"I'm calling for help here. You're going to be followed home by one of my officers."


Pop and his long time girlfriend, Dixie Hoot, were anxiously waiting by the kitchen door when she walked in.

They all hugged. Dressed in his comfortable baggy shorts and loose tee, he was comforting to her eyes, looking extra strong to her tonight.

Now, he ran thick fingers through his dark wavy hair which was his habit when he was upset or anxious. "What's going on? Del Rio called us briefly to make sure we were home and the tone of his voice was upsetting."

"Let's sit at the table; I'll open a bottle of wine, and you talk to us about tonight's episode," demanded Dixie. "You look bewildered!" Her long loose shift covered her rounded figure and bobbling top as she brought wine, glasses, and a large bowl of fresh popcorn to the table.

Their pet greyhound danced a few turns when she saw the bowl.

"Just a little bit Nellie," said Pop as he put a handful into her bowl.

She ate the corn in ten seconds, did a few more turns, than rested her head on Pop's slippered feet. He and his cycle group, THE FAMILY FARM, had rescued her two years ago from extinction where she was left to die in a south of Phoenix river-bed. Now she was forever humble and always by his side.

Gina explained her terrible night, not leaving out any details, and Dixie took notes on a long yellow tablet.

"I'm so thankful that you make me carry Pepper Spray."

"It's a deterrent all right," declared Dixie. "We have a peeking-pervert in town. We'll find him!" With scowling eyebrows she adamantly pounded a fist in her palm a couple times.

Gina sat at the table dazed, leaning on an elbow.

"It's late." Dixie yawned. "I want to hear all about this African mask stuff in the morning."

Pop turned off the lights. "Gina, are you just going to sit there in the dark?"

She didn't move. "What if I can't sleep?"

"Nellie will protect us." She wagged her tail at the mention of her name and they both patted her head. "We'll figure it out. Del Rio's coming in the morning for breakfast. Stay calm."

Gina went to bed, still shaking every few minutes as she thought of the earlier encounter. She knew that in the near future, she would find the masks in the Arts and Crafts room to be repulsive rather than artistic pieces of beauty.

And she was supposed to judge them.

# BLAKELY HIGH VOODOO PHANTOM

*He moved freely among his friends with an extra bounce in his step. Shuffling his booted feet, he kicked at a few rocks in the parking lot; so proud of his accomplishments tonight, he knew that he would continue.*

CHAPTER THREE
Saturday—October 15


Gina got out of the shower the next morning to the scent of bacon. She scrunched her curly hair making a 'do' that would dry well. After looking at her tired selection of end-of-summer white short-shorts, she chose black. It would be a few more weeks in a hot October before she put the stack away for another year's heat. Next, she pulled on a form fitting V-neck tee and felt happy, sort of relieved after last night's ordeal.

The kitchen was busy. Dixie was turning eggs, Pop was toasting bread, and Rick was standing there holding a full plate of crispy bacon while chatting.

"Just sit down," Rick told her promptly while looking at his watch. "We want to hear all about what's happening at school." He pulled out her usual chair from the table.

"What's this---queen for the day? Where are my flowers?

"Don't get pushy" said Pop as he started putting platters of food on the table. Then he placed a small jar of wild Yellow Desert Marigolds near her plate. "I'm always one step ahead," he said grinning his wide ear to ear smile. "You need to recuperate a bit." He pulled up his comfy elastic waist shorts that were sagging a bit in the back, his at-home costume.

"Where's the waffles?"

"Waffles on Sunday. You make the best," said Dixie.

"Where's the mask?"

"I've got it. I'll take it to the Arts and Crafts teacher," said Rick. "What's her name?"

"Becky Painter."

"Hah! How appropriate. I want to find out who made it." He got up, refilled his coffee cup and checked with others before putting the pot back on the hot plate.

"I have a dilemma," said Gina after adding handfuls of ice and then milk to her glass of coffee. "Nancy and I are to judge all of the African masks and I don't think I want to see another one."

"Just how do you judge them? It sounds exciting. Call me. I'll be there in two minutes," said Pop.

"Becky's giving us a list of criteria and it should be easy. Fortunately, we don't have to grade them. The thought of looking at all of them is creepy."

"It's art," offered Dixie clearing a few plates from the table, "like Pop's jewelry making. The

17

important things to look for will be authenticity, coloring, workmanship, and a whole lot more. I heard in the front office that there'll be a grand showing at the end of October of all the things that the kids have done."

Rick looked at his watch. "Ok, start. What's going on at school?"

"The principal, Mr. Shieter, became Dr. Shieter over the summer completing his degree in African studies. So, he called a faculty meeting two months ago to announce that he wanted us to incorporate African studies in our curriculum for October."

Gina rolled her eyes and sipped on her iced coffee. "Across the curriculum, means entire school involvement and ALL of the classes need to learn something. 'Sort of a Halloween special', he joked."

"That's hard to do," said Pop leaning back in his chair and putting his hands behind his head. "But it could be interesting."

Dixie added, "He's always been a flamboyant dandy, prancing around in his three piece suits, not remembering anyone's name. We laugh at him in the front office because he's always in his room with the door closed…escaping."

Rick grimaced and motioned for Gina to hurry on. "How did the faculty react?" Now being impatient, he flipped his straw cowboy hat end over end.

"Everybody came unglued, at first. We all griped. The older teachers complained loudly. The younger ones sat stunned. Then he told us to get into our specialized department groups and start brainstorming. Most importantly, he had dozens of fresh doughnuts and hot coffee delivered. We were happy."

"Feed a teacher and it all goes to hell," Pop stated with a smile folding his arms and leaning back.

"Teachers from a comparable school in West Africa are coming to visit us and he wants to put on a show for them, to make them feel at home."

"So, how's it all working?" Dixie asked. "I feel vibes in the front office but really don't know how to read them." She sipped on her hot coffee.

Rick interrupted briskly. "What's everyone doing? How did they all react?"

She sighed and took a deep breath before listing. "Social Studies' teachers bounced in their chairs with excitement of units on travel, geography, culture, politics and more. There's a lot that they can do. The math group stuck up their noses and sat silent; the Physical Education Department is studying African-tribal games and long distance running; home-economics teachers are cooking African regional foods; Arts and Crafts are creating paintings and masks."

"And, what are you doing?" Rick asked.

"My Science Fiction classes are learning about Voodoo. They have to write poems based on the lecture material---and cspccially a limerick. Nancy and I will have a limerick contest soon and we need help. Anybody here want to read them and be a judge?"

They all shook their heads and roared "NO!"

"Jeesh, you sound like barking dogs."

She continued. "Also, my Western Literature classes will be writing letters to African students telling them about our culture and their personal daily lives. Students really like writing auto biographies when I give them an outline to follow. I have a list of pen pals' and teachers' names from West Africa who are eager to write to our school."

Dixie asked, "How's the December trail ride going? It's too bad the Africans won't be here for the ride."

"My max is thirty---that includes sponsors. Too many riders and the accidents begin. Because the students wanted to secure a spot early, I already had the permission slips signed by the parents and sealed by the District. They're now hidden away in my desk drawer."

"You riding in the Cave Creek Mountains?" Rick asked.

"No, the Superstitions out at Apache Junction."

"Ahah! Maybe Pop and his cycle group THE FAMILY FARM and I will meet you there." He looked over at Pop teasingly. "I get a kick out of saying the name of your cycle group."

They all smiled a bit.

Dixie stood up and stretched. "Before everyone leaves, what's going on tonight? Let's all meet at Tumbleweed's for dancing." She put her hands on Pop's shoulders and shook them hoping for a positive reaction.

"You know I don't dance. Plus, we at the bakery are going to be extra busy preparing the Sunday specials."

"Let's go just for an hour to listen to the band and then I'll help you tonight. Maybe we can figure out why the popovers are flat? That's your signature pastry." She rubbed a little harder on the shoulder joints.

He grimaced and lowered his bad shoulder. "I am so out of patience. But, ok it's a deal. I sure could use you tonight. It's the teenage girl's night off you know, the one who's always texting."

"I have a sweet-tooth so I have to ask. What are you baking tonight?" Rick put two hands on the table to push away.

"Cream rolls filled with a mix of powdered sugar and whipped cream; Cream Puffs filled with Satin Chocolate Mousse, and dozens of Chocolate Eclairs filled with a French Vanilla Custard---and of course, we're trying the Popovers again."

"I'm on duty later, so I'll stop by."

Everyone got up and began cleaning the kitchen.

"Sorry to go from something pleasant to something unpleasant," said Dixie, "but whatever happened to the man's body out on the desert—two months ago."

Rick shook his head. "That's my crutch. We have no leads whatsoever. We know that he was a middle aged man who died from venomous bites and we were too late getting there after the tip. Recently a new forensics group has been working on identification.

"I can't fathom why anyone would want a dead man's body." Pop shook his head.

Dixie added, "It doesn't make sense. What about the main man, the chief of the whole photo-play business? What happened to him?"

"Scary," shivered Gina.

They all shook their heads.

"I need to pay a visit to Dickie out at Blue Ridge near Hannagan's Meadow. He told us that the chief of the organization was his cousin, and he was quite sure of it." Rick was adamant as he declared loudly to everyone, "I'll solve this puzzle. I've been working on it night and day."

"Oh we know," declared Gina. "Just write me a letter when you have time."

"Do I note a touch of sarcasm?" He put on his hat that he had been tossing around. "Our first fight! I'll make it up to you tonight. We'll have dinner at the dance."

Gina walked him to his car which was parked next to her Jeep in the free standing carport. Then noticing with shock she complained loudly, "Why is my Jeep lop-sided?"

Rick walked around to the side and ran his hand over the tires. "Two tires have been stabbed," he noted after looking closely. "It was a slow leak because I would have noticed something when I parked here earlier." He bent down to examine the other two. "This was done very early this morning by someone with strength."

Pop and Dixie were furious when hearing the news. "I'll take care of this," Pop said to Rick. "You do what you have to do to find the culprit, or culprits."

"I'll get my team out here to look at tire prints and footprints. Try to stay away from this area," and he pointed to specific places.

"Since we're on the edge of a huge wash, anyone could come up through this area and hide behind the creosotes and mesquites then climb through the barbed-wire fence and get in." Pop shook his head in disgust.

"Someone is after me with a vengeance," blurted Gina with mixed emotions of shock and anger.

"Now, we all have to pay attention," declared Rick. "Notice all that's going on."

"On our toes," Dixie squinted with an angry snap of her fingers.

"I'm going to have a meeting with my cycle group so they can help look for suspicious activity here and there. We'll do our own secret police work."

"From now on keep me informed," Rick said. "And just who are the guys in your cycle group THE FAMILY FARM?"

"We call them the four B's: Bing, Bob, Brad, and Blake. They're retired professionals from different lines of work. Bing is a retired cop from New York. He's especially knowledgeable."

"Let's just all work together. Gotta go! See everyone tonight." He gave Gina a quick perfunctory kiss on the cheek and drove away.

"All of this won't do," Pop began. "Dixie, Gina, I'm calling a kitchen meeting with the four B's and you two.   Dixie, have your long yellow note pad ready. We're going exploring."

Pop headed to his tool shed to retrieve the tools needed to un-mount the punctured tires. "This mystery is getting expensive."

CHAPTER FOUR
Saturday Night

Rick Del Rio called to tell Gina that tonight he had new tasks to take care of and couldn't make it to the dance. "Don't go alone. There's a pervert or stalker out there, so make sure that you stay close to Dixie."

Nancy was still sick. Dixie and Pop were not leaving the house until much later, so Gina decided to go early, get a good table and "the heck with everyone!"

She put her feet in her tight fitting jeans and stretched out on the bed to zip them completely. After tucking in her black tee with the gold sparkles at the V, she belted choosing the one with her favorite hand made silver buckle with her dad's logo, 'Quail Harbor' inside the small rectangle.

After Gina paid her fee and walked into Tumbleweed's, she felt less secure and hesitated before selecting a table in a dark corner. She chose a table for two along a glossy grizzly-brown wall where she could see the entrance, the dance floor and the bar. A football game was playing on one television above the horse shoe shaped bar, while local news and soccer were being watched on the other two.

A ruby red glass vase housing a lighted candle sat in the middle of the table adding ambiance to the area with a subdued light on the red and white checkered table cloth.

The place was moderately full. The band was new and a few couples were out on the floor, dancing to a downer, Gina's least favorite tune. She groaned.

HE WALKED UP TO ME AND ASKED FOR A DANCE
I TOLD HIM JUST MAYBE HE MIGHT HAVE A CHANCE
WITH HIS ARM AROUND ME HE CAME SO NEAR
I COULDN'T TELL HIM WHAT HE NEEDED TO HEAR;

DON'T YOU KNOW I'M A BRIDE TO BE
I PROMISED I'D LOVE FAITHFULLY
DON'T YOU KNOW I'M A BRIDE TO BE
SO MISTER QUIT SMILING AT ME

"Hey why the long face?" Guy Wagner, head of the Physical Education Department, teacher and coach of many sports, slammed his hand loudly on the table and abruptly sat.

"Jeesh!" Gina jumped back about a foot from the table and knocked her head on the wall behind.

"Oops sorry." He patted the back of her head and played with the curls surrounding her face. "Where's the big guy? Where's little red? That's one hell of a tee you're wearing." He flashed one of his famous flirty smiles showing model teeth—white on a perfectly tanned face.

The red plaid 'Cowboy Hardware' shirt he wore was a starched 'fresh press' from the dry cleaners. Clear blue eyes crinkled in the corners under thick eyebrows specked with gray. A cowboy's straw sat on his head perfectly in lieu of the daily coach's cap.

"You look great," she said as simply as possible trying to hide the full body flush she now felt from toes on up and leaned back in the wooden chair eyeing him. "Ok town flirt. Del Rio's working and Nancy's sick."

"So? You're too serious tonight. Lighten up!"

A busty middle aged waitress wearing tight denim short-shorts and a red V neck tee belted in with a thin circle of leather came by to take their order. "You two decided?" She placed napkins on the red checked oil clothed table unhurriedly and smiled.

"Onion rings and beer," said Gina

"Ditto here," Guy said. "Give us the 'shovel-full' order and make that a pitcher of beer."

"You got it!" She gave Guy an extra lingering look before turning away.

"Where's the smile?" He moved close to Gina's face and looked into her eyes. "And I'm not the town flirt." He smiled wolfishly. "At least I won't take that while standing up."

Avoiding his remark, she leaned her elbows on the table and rested her face on her fisted hands. "Guess what happened to me last night." She then narrated the full episode; knowing that Guy was familiar with hundreds of students and parents, perhaps he could have some insight.

"Since the pervert knew what I was driving, he has to be a local. You're the town gossip king; maybe you can stay aware and listen to the teens."

"Teens know everything that's going on!" Guy remarked. "Good or bad, teen gossip spreads faster than digital." He leaned back from the table as the waitress placed two ice-cold frosty beer mugs down on napkins followed by a misty pitcher of beer and an actual shovel, minus the handle, stacked with steaming onion rings.

He poured beer into their clouded mugs, picked up an onion ring and squinted at her. "I'm not the town gossip---it's just that I know large groups of people because of sports. Small town folks love sports!"

"This song needs to end," Gina complained as she drank and ate. "It's a crappy song."

## I TOLD HIM GOODNIGHT

THAT I HAD TO GO
HE SAID, 'I KNOW' AS HE WHISPERED
LOW
I'LL GIVE YOU MY CARD FOR SOME
OTHER TIME
WHEN YOU'RE FEELING LONELY
AND WANT TO BE MINE

"We need to dance. You need to get cheery." He pulled her up from the chair and out on the floor.

"But it's a slow tune!"

"Still complaining? These are my favorites. With the fast ones, my feet fly all around the floor un-attended."

Gina laughed at his remark as he clung to her tightly. She decided not to push back and they danced cheek to cheek. He was comforting and after all, they had been friends through these few five years at Blakely.

She admired the way he cared about his football players by frequenting her room after school to check on their progress in her English classes. If a player was performing poorly in her class or others, that player was promptly benched for the next game. Guy supported the academics.

They went to their table and he ordered another pitcher.

"What's new around town? Give me the scoop." Gina circled her ring finger with two onion rings and chewed on them.

"We have two new eccentrics, very interesting people. They're newcomers and settled in this year sometime…I think around February. A Mr. Hollywood likes to flaunt his affluence by driving around in expensive convertibles. The other person is a gargantuan Russian woman who drives a dually-truck with a minimum of four dogs in the back seat or in front."

"Sooooo," while dipping her onion ring into sauce, "sounds like ordinary 'Creekers' to me."

Guy leaned forward in mysteriousness as he continued. "Mr. Hollywood drives a different convertible each week, is shirtless and dripping with gold necklaces and thick wristbands." He indicated the area around his neck as he spoke with animation. "When he stops to shop somewhere, usually at Janie's Coffee Pot, he throws on a short sleeve shirt, unbuttoned, exposing a deeply tanned gray-hairy chest."

"Jeesh! You sound like a writer."

They snickered and started laughing loudly, smacking the table…. feeling their beer for a good five minutes.

Gina turned away to wipe at her laughing eyes and lightly blow her nose. "And the big Russian?"

"She claims to be an antique collector and scours the desert and back alleys for treasure. In reality I think she's a hoarder…like they show on television."

"How do you know all this?"

"Remember, I'm out and about with my sports teams, my cross country runners, other sporting events.

Plus I live close to town. You're about four miles north, aren't you?"

"Lazy Lizard Lane. It's about that."

"Also," he added, "you're glued to grading papers at your school desk or probably at home too, right?"

After smirking a negative she did a slow 'yes' nod.

"I'll keep you informed. Just ask me the 'town gossip'. Come on. Let's dance."

Again he held her close to a 'slow one'. She absorbed his earthly clean scent and moved closer as he held her tightly. *Ok, we're just friends. Where is Del Rio and why would he be working on Saturday night.*

"Hey, Dixie and Pop are supposed to be passing by for an hour. Have you seen them?"

"Don't break my mood. I'm swooning."

"You're very comforting considering all that I've been through lately," she sighed.

"Oh? Like a brother or a lover." He pulled her closer to him in a tighter cuddle.

"Always a brother. We work too closely together to be anything else."

"Ridiculous!"

The music stopped and they went to their table. "How about coming to my place?"

"Sure, if you dip your stick in bleach first!" The middle-age waitress in the denim short-shorts, who happened to be passing by, gasped and hurried on to the next table.

By this time, Gina and Guy were laughing so loudly, and slapping the table with such fervor, others turned to look at them, smiled and resumed chatting.

"Now that's an original," Guy said lifting his straw hat and running his fingers through his thick rusty brown hair before putting it back on, still widely smiling.

"Uh oh!" He warned while looking towards the entrance and over Gina's shoulder and losing his smile. "It's the big guy."

Gina turned around to look and quickly lost the merriment of the night. Ducking, she half hid her face in disappointment. Del Rio and a woman arrived at the front entrance, both smiling contently. Del Rio was too 'slick' looking for a work night, and the woman was too 'movie-star gorgeous' to be a cop.

CHAPTER FIVE
Saturday night

Since the entrance was an upper deck, Del Rio saw Gina and Guy instantly after entering before they saw him, and winced. He had an aversion to confrontations.

To Gina he seemed gutsy as he smiled boyishly—sheepishly when he saw them, then walked towards their table with a possessive touch to the back of 'movie-star gorgeous'!

She sipped on her glass of beer to hide spasms of anger, and took three deep breaths in-and-out-slowly, a trick learned from counseling classes on how to communicate with angry parents and complaining students. Tonight it was to hide her disappointment. She thought his walk too swarthy and hers too wiggly as they strolled over.

During introductions, she sat glued while Guy stood salivating, dumbfounded, hooking his thumbs into his front denim pockets like a cowboy.

"Ms. Delilah Mallory, this is Gina McHenry and Guy Wagner." Avoiding direct eye contact with Gina he continued. "She's in charge of a forensic team from Phoenix and is actually Dr. Mallory."

Gina managed a tight lipped greeting. Extending her hand too quickly she knocked over a tall mug of beer spilling the contents on the table and "oops" on Delilah's pale-blue-form-fitting designer jeans.

"Sorry," she blurted out with scorching embarrassment.

The two men paled.

"Oh, I've had worse." Delilah gorgeous waved it all away with a flip of her hand and a small laugh as she grabbed a table napkin and dabbed away.

A very small laugh thought Gina who wanted to apologize profusely but was too tongue tied. Her chair seemed to sink into the concrete floor like quicksand.

"You sure you're ok?" Del Rio asked, trying not to look at her pale-blue-form-fitting designer jeans.

Gina lifted her eyebrows, then squinted her left eye. He was soooo attentive to her sopping jeans—getting tighter by the minute.

Guy didn't move but stayed standing, shuffling back and forth from one foot to the other. Thumbs hooked.

"We're actually working," Rick explained quietly. "We're going over there to a corner table to finish our discussion." He nodded his head to the left.

They made a hasty retreat with no "happy to meet you" salutation from Ms.Gorgeous.

"It's getting late." Guy threw money on top of the bill lying on the table. "I have an early morning schedule."

After noting the subdued lull he added, "Come on. I'll walk you to your car." He put his arm around Gina's drooping shoulders.

"Pop and Dixie must have gone straight to the bakery for an all night bake-a-thon. Go find them….and cheer-up," he added loudly at the exit squeezing her tightly, both hands around her waist.

They stepped outside to a starry sky and a surprisingly cool temperature of seventy five. The half-empty parking lot contained a sprinkling of couples here and there pasted to the sides of their trucks, embracing. The few remaining patrons inside, danced and drank until curfew, the last hour offering free coffee, water, and sodas.

After opening her Jeep door, Guy took her in his arms and kissed her gently.

She felt nothing.

"You always have me blondie," he said while in a bear hug.

"Friends?" He held her at arms length.

"Friends." Nodding, she managed a small smile.

At the bakery Gina's mood changed with the busy scene of hustle and bustle with pots and pans and scents of fresh baked pastries and bread. The four B's were busy washing pots at the sink, rolling dough into small rounds, whipping creams and tending to the oven.

After stowing away two cream puffs, two cream horns, and four chocolate éclairs in the bakery's fridge, she said, "For Monday."

"There go my profits," Pop said jovially. He was in the land of love and showed it with his long white apron tied around his massive middle and hands full of flour as he dusted a work table.

"Catch," laughed Dixie tossing a large, puffy popover to Gina.

"You guys have all the fun. These are great! What did you do differently?"

"Nothing! Absolutely nothing! When Susie comes in, I need to watch her more closely. She's doing something wrong. I'm putting her cell phone in the oven."

"She's putting a HEX on your popovers," Gina said.

"Huh? Wh-What?" Dixie purposely stuttered, as she almost dropped a pan of apple turnovers.

"It's Voodoo. We're learning about it in my Science Fiction classes."

"Well, Voodoo your body over here and help out. We can finish earlier," suggested Pop as he took sheets of popovers out of the oven. "My helpers, the four B's, are wearing out."

"Speak for yourself," said Blake the retired restaurant owner. "I'm in home territory."

By one a.m. Gina fell asleep leaning on a sack of flour and awoke to Pop shaking her shoulder.

"We're leaving. Come on, we'll follow you home." After drying his hands and hanging the towel on a horseshoe screwed into a rack, they walked to her Jeep.

"My desserts in the fridge! I can't leave those."

"I'll bring them. Go ahead. We'll be following you shortly."

Late Saturday nights' business traffic was usually light but continuous. Local bar hoppers, out-of-towners from the Phoenix area, and 'Snowbirds' here for the winter, were out and about until early Sunday morning. The October weather was perfect for convertible top-down time, and there were plenty of them.

Cycle groups convened at a hide away beneath and around tall Salt Cedar trees. Many were moving together smoothly east and west on Cave Creek Road in both directions. Some went south out of town down

Scottsdale Road, while others chose the only other route south, Cave Creek Road.

Thanks to the local town mayor and his group of followers, there were noise ordinance signs throughout Cave Creek and Carefree. Because the cycle riders were respectful and content with it, they were treated like royalty by the community in general and flocked to the area in droves from all over the valley. Most riders were teams of retired married couples, here from the cold areas of Chicago and St. Louis.

But--- it was a new model, glassy-black Camry with dark tinted windows that pulled next to Gina in harassment as she drove west on the four lane highway towards home. At first the Camry was on her right, moving along with her Jeep. Because she was in an inside lane watching on-coming traffic she didn't notice it. Instantly, it pulled in front of her and slowed. She braked, missed it by inches, and pulled to the right lane. The driver pulled in front of her again and slowed--- purposely.

She braked instantly. With an oncoming adrenalin rush, she lost her tiredness.

"What the heck!"

Heading towards a four way stop intersection, she was ready to get the license plate number of the mystery car that was playing cat and mouse--at least a couple more times--but instead of stopping, the driver floored the accelerator, ran through full speed and barely missed Mr. Hollywood in his 1946 lime green Willy's Jeep convertible.

Extremely pissed, Mr. Hollywood flung his hands in the air and added loud expletives into the early morning.

With its extreme speed and a few more turns, the black Camry became a mystery car too quickly out of sight.

Considering the Friday night peeking-pervert episode and this morning's punctured tires, she was shaking. Determined not to head home down the dark long road alone, she pulled over at the edge of town to a side opening and grabbed her cell.

Before she could make a call, a plain undercover car with cop lights whirling pulled behind her instantly, and she powered down her windows to a cool October early morning breeze.

Walking toward her, Del Rio became an instant illuminating silhouette in her rear view mirror as cars passed slowly in trepidation, drivers gawking.

He leaned on the open window frame with both hands.

"Three," he said quietly.

"Yep." She sat with both hands on the wheel looking straight ahead with squinting eyes.

"Your third harassment." He paused then added, "Did you get the license plate number?"

"Nope." Avoiding him, she looked in both of her side view mirrors at the slowly approaching cars.

He looked down at the sandy ground and moved some rocks with the toe of his boot, hands still possessing the open window. "We finished our notes and Dr. Mallory left right after you and Guy Wagner."

Gina looked at her nails and started pushing back her cuticles.

"I'm following you home. I have new info to tell you that you might find interesting. Also, I called Pop and Dixie right after you left the bakery and told them that I was out and about."

She shook her head up and down slowly and mumbled, "Ok," still working on her nails.

She didn't see his mischievous grin nor hear his slight chuckle as he reached his hand in the window, rubbed her neck gently for five seconds, patted the window frame and said, "I'm right behind you."

Driving home, she powered down all the Jeep windows and let the fresh early morning air re-arrange her hair. It was a new awakening after a fretful late evening, and she was extremely relieved that Rick was following her home.

October welcomed a slight seasonal change. Desert nights of ten to fifteen degrees cooler than the scorching summer's, were invigorating. More than anything, positive weather changes refreshed her psych.

Always doing her best thinking while driving, she was determined to figure it all out and could hardly wait to talk to her closest teacher friends, Nancy Lopez and Richard Cloud....better known as R and R for Richard/Raquel. Their rooms were in the same row. The three were always on the same page about everything and covered each other's back. Nancy Lopez was the most creative teacher on 'earth' and R and R was a walking encyclopedia of knowledge. She was in the middle.

They walked in the house to kitchen-accent lights suffused and glowing. Light shadows hovered here and there and danced around to their entrance as a fat vanilla scented candle glowed in the center of the six chaired round table. Shadows of the night enticed a trance like splendor.

"I can't stay," he said as he put his arms around her back in a V pulling her close. "I'm sorry for the misinterpretation but gathered some very interesting new information from forensics."

"You mean Ms. Delilah Mallory." She retorted.

He raised an eyebrow then smiled. "What's this dip your stick business?"

Not answering she started walking backward toward her bedroom subconsciously; he followed easily, clinging.

"I didn't know that you had my table bugged!"

They entered her bedroom; she closed the door. He touched her chin and lifted her face to his. Hot, passionate, long and liquid was the kiss that came next as she remembered it again and again while teaching so gallantly on Monday.

"You're always on my radar," was the last thing he said as they helped each other undress. They turned down the coverlet of denim and white lace and quickly met in the middle.

*The large gates to the private housing development swung open in the dark near the base of Blake Mountain. He drove the glassy black Camry home and into the private garage. A touch of the remote shut out his guilt of the night, and he smiled in triumph.*

# CHAPTER SIX
## October 16
## Sunday

Ralph McHenry, a popular permanent fixture around Cave Creek, is always known as Pop by everyone, his real name long forgotten. His long time girlfriend Dixie, describes him as a stocky 'Mac Truck'. Otherwise, everything about him is medium: medium height, medium dark brown rounded eyes that twinkle forever, medium smile that travels across his lower face, medium dark brown curly hair, (It's the Welsh, he says), and medium appetite.

However, to the townspeople he is a man of many talents; known first and foremost as "the best jewelry maker south of the Navajo Reservation", he always has a stack of requests to complete, both from locals and out-of-towners. Combining silver and multi-colored tumbled rocks that glisten like real gems, he creates winning originals; the Arizona bola tie adorned with turquoise is his permanent trade mark.

He milks rattle snakes on occasion when the demand is high and sends the venom to the medical labs out at ASU to be manipulated into anti-venom; often he is invited to play the bass fiddle in the band at Tumbleweed's when needed; but now, he owns the best bakery in town and can decorate cakes to perfection. "This is where I want to be," he has said lately to everyone....much to Dixie's satisfaction.

To most people, he seems to know what is going on, before it happens.....until now.

Normally, he can entice a wealth of information from his brother Father Al McHenry, but he is out of town for the month.

So being upset and worried by all the happenings threatening his daughter, he is pleased to be with his friends at the round table this morning eating waffles and thinking of solutions. They were his comfort group.

"We have Guy and Rick working at the bit," added Dixie to the Sunday morning round table discussion.

Rick, the four B's, Dixie, Pop and Gina were filling the long yellow note pad with clues. Dixie with pen in hand, waved it around as she continued.

"Guy tactfully quizzes the teens as Rick works with forensics."

Gina grimaced at the thought of 'movie-star gorgeous' being 'forensics'.

In the center of the table was a stack of left-over home made buttery waffles. A candle lit chafing dish held a server of hot maple syrup which was now gaining a slick topping.

"Ok," said Pop as he blew out the candle. "Here's a plan. How about the four B's selecting a particular part of town to watch---subtly?" He looked at them for support.

They each nodded.

"Bing, take the west end of town to Spur Cross Road.

Bob, you watch the middle of town, the heaviest part to Screaming Ice Cream.

Brad and Blake, you two watch the saloons and bars, especially Tumbleweed's.

The girls and I will watch the east end of Cave Creek and into Carefree. We see something strange—or out of place—we call Rick."

At the mention of his name, he pushed back from the table and laughed hysterically. "I AM SO LUCKY".

Gina gave him the squinted eye look pursed her lips and frowned

Blake, the youngest trooper, got up retrieved the coffee pot in one hand, the ice tea pitcher in the other and filled mugs and glasses. "Remember, I used to own a restaurant," he grinned. Looking at Rick he added "Now, what info do you have?"

He and everyone else gave him their full attention.

"New stuff! The bathroom fingerprints belong to a middle aged man. We've been trying to get a connection. Delilah—uh, I mean forensics, has identified the body that has disappeared as belonging to a decadent photographer named Jack Malone, better known by the mob as Scruffy. We just need to find him, or it."

"The new black Camry," mentioned Bob the retired construction worker from Indiana, "we see one, we make note of it."

They all nodded in agreement.

Gina started gathering dishes. "Tomorrow I'll talk to Becky Painter about the mask. I have a pretty good description in my notes."

She rinsed dishes briefly in the sink and started to load the dishwasher. "Incidentally, what do we know about the two new-comers in town, a large Russian woman and an eccentric older man who drives expensive convertibles?"

Over at the table Dixie said, "They're not new. They've been around for about a year."

Others started to help clean the kitchen.

"She grooms dogs," said Bing wiping the table.

"She cleans the streets of left-over trash as a measure of good will, so she says," added Brad rinsing the coffee pot. "As an ex-marine, I'm always skeptical."

"He wants to finance a new brick sidewalk from Cave Creek to Carefree," added Blake while rinsing the coffee pot.

ACTION STOPPED.

Pop asked, "How do you know that?"

"I go to town meetings."

"Well, where's the sidewalk," asked Dixie putting both hands on her hips after throwing a towel over her shoulder.

"Truthfully," continued Blake, "they can't decide whether it should be straight or curvy."

'FIGURES', they all chimed in and started moving about continuing their cleaning.

"It's Bicker Creek at its best. This could go on for months." They all mumbled in agreement.

Gina put her arm through Rick's bent elbow. "I want to go see where the body used to be. Is it a problem?"

"It's a date. I can't think of anything more romantic," he said putting his arm around her.

Everyone departed: Pop and Dixie to the bakery store, the four B's on a cycle excursion to Bartlett Lake twenty miles east of Cave Creek, and Rick and Gina to the desert site.

## CHAPTER SEVEN
Sunday

End of October brings 'snowbirds' by the dozen to Cave Creek. Cookie stamped, pudgy smiley men in khaki shorts keep hands in deep pockets protecting something—money or vitals—who knows? Their mates have short-short lawn mower cut hairdos, wear baggy clothes and friendly grins. Always in sandals and short sleeved tops, they are walking neon signs compared to the regulars wearing long sleeve shirts and denim pants.

The mates hang on to the smiley-khaki-shorts protecting THE wallet in THE pocket. Pearly smooth facial complexions add to their positive appearance which 'leathered beyond repair' Creekers find envious.

The town is hopping with all kinds of activities for this time of year because of the cooling trend, and strangers from neighboring foothill communities like Desert Foothills, Anthem, Rio Verde, and Scottsdale join the locals for fun festivities.

The newly formed detective group will be comparing notes on who's who and the different kinds of eccentric vehicles that come and go. They all agreed that "We have to start with some kind of a plan....until we have a plan."

Each of the four B's was ecstatic about his particular area to watch and its importance.

"Hanging around town with a purpose," was the new motto.

With pleasure, they chit-chatted around from one end of town to the other comparing notes, working their high-tech phones that the youngsters showed them how to use. They would soon become popular personalities at the coffee shops, saloons, dance halls, and numerous hide-away places while meeting with fellow motorcyclists. They paid particular attention to every new blond, redhead and brunette.....comparing notes.

Always on the look out for evil intent of any kind, they felt important as they asked questions in confidence....a clandestine caper of sorts. Most importantly, they were anxious for their meetings with Gina about school happenings, and what information she learns about the African masks.

A dusty four door maroon Ford Dually F350 one ton, with laughing dogs hanging out the back side windows, passed Rick and Gina as they drove north in the Jeep Wrangler.

"That's her, the newcomer dog lady. I'm impressed," said Gina clicking a count with her tongue. "I count six. What the heck!"

"She's a dog groomer, yard cleaner, and everyone likes her!"

"Where's her office?"

"At her house. She bought the old rodeo grounds out at Spur Cross, the entire five acres which includes one big barn, a small artist studio and her home."

"How do you know all this? You don't own a dog."

"I get around."

Turning the Jeep Wrangler from Spur Cross Road, he hung a left and slowed almost to a stop. They now traveled down a narrow dirt trail that ran for about a quarter mile and ended near clumps of desert bushes and a large Ironwood. A small canyon lay ahead.

Moving clouds played hide and seek from the bright sun, relieving the heat of the day in bits. It was a cool eighty-five. The desert site was no longer yellow taped but it seemed quite bare---raped of cactus and desert debris from scouring teams of cops and students of forensics.

"Clap your hands and make a noise," reminded Rick. "October is the busiest month for rattlesnakes out and about"....a fact they both knew.

They each carried sticks that Gina retrieved from her Jeep and started scanning the outskirts of the site, combing through grey brittle bush, prickly pear yellowed and flattened to dried pancakes from lack of rain, and skinny Cholla with their many crooked arms.

They were careful not to brush against the deadly white sticker hooks which come loose too easily, hence, the title of Jumping Cholla. A breeze of any whiff will loosen fist size balls of Cholla, always menacing to horses in particular. They easily get stuck on their heels or pasterns and become quite deadly as they try to kick them off.   The worse scenario occurs when the tiny balls of hooks get stuck under  bellies like magnets.

"Have you ever been stuck by a Cholla?"  Gina wanted to know as she brushed aside the tiny crime balls from their paths.

"Yes, and never again.   It's like a bee sting. And the more you try to fling them off, the deeper they go in."

Approximately fifty yards from the site, they found a pack rat's nest.

"We need to dig through this," she said. "They're famous for stealing and harboring shiny things."

Picking through the dried-dirt 'hard as a rock' mound, they found little pieces of Styrofoam, a twelve inch piece of carpenter's string, a handful of chipped pieces of green bottle glass…and an earring.

"Hey a clue." Trying to gingerly remove the piece without breakage, she dug wide around it with her stick then finished the task with a small pocket knife attached to her key chain.

"We hope."

While pouring water on it from her plastic water bottle, Rick cleaned the dirt away with his fingers. It was one earring intact, a shiny piece of silver with four half inch wires attached, each containing small bee-bee sized glass beads of multi colors.

It sparkled from the afternoon sun, a gem of a piece. Glassy colors of violet, blue and scarlet shimmered on her hand. Turning it, they blended together creating a rainbow, a watering of colors bleeding together.

"A Gypsy's gem!" she claimed.

CHAPTER EIGHT
Sunday

As they turned off the dirt trail and again onto the paved Spur Cross, they talked anxiously about the Pack Rat's nest and their findings.

Eager for more outdoor adventures, Gina remarked, "We need to go Pack Rat treasure hunting more often way out here on the desert where things get dropped along the trails....you know, from hikers, cyclists, and horseback riders." She waved her arms indicating the empty desert surroundings.

"That would be number ten on my list of one to ten, the honey-do list." Now with the windows down, he removed his straw hat long enough for the air to dry sweat from around his ears and shook his head furthering the task.

Chatting on avoiding his sarcasm, she continued. "Once I lost my favorite most expensive pair of sunglasses and searched everywhere. Two weeks later I found them way out in the middle of the yard where I don't usually walk. There they were, unharmed, shining

53

in the sun near a Pack Rat's nest. They must have fallen out of the Jeep's door pocket when I parked and the thief whisked them away."

"Well like you say, they're attracted to shiny things. Not to change the subject, but I enjoy driving your Jeep. Next time, you ride with me on my Harley."

He smiled.

She melted.

"Hey look, a small huboob." It was her turn to be sarcastic while pointing to a cloud of dirt and dust being thrust into the air violently. The new word for an ordinary Arizona dust devil infuriated everyone when first used in the newspaper. "This is OUR dust devil, not an Arabian's," was everyone's quote.

"Someone's stuck out there and probably making it worse. We'll check it out and see what we can do." He noted the distance and looked for a side road.

Plumes of light chocolate dirt spliced with dark sienna sprayed 'non stop' as the driver of the vehicle relentlessly worked to extract it from the perilous sandy ground.

Rick turned on a narrow dirt road and drove for a quarter mile before the road ended at a small turn around. Off the road was the big maroon dually stuck in the middle of the mess. The rear bumper was now resting on the level ground because the back tires were in a newly dug hole.

The truck was not only off road but beyond the limits of careful driving. Both Gina and Rick mumbled about it.

The big Russian woman saw them coming and got out of her truck. A swirl of dust initially hiding her face, faded while coating her from head to toe.

"Hey, my big mistake today!" She stretched giant arms out for emphasis as she spoke. Half of a long white garbage bag hung from her baggy pants pocket, khaki color now spots of chocolate brown dirt. Sleeves were rolled up on her man size shirt exposing blotchy fair skin above her big gloves. She beat a floppy brown hat against one hip.

Six happy dogs ran to greet them with noses out, all different mixes in size and color. Gina noted their well groomed slickness as she patted each one. They twirled and laughed as dogs do, thumping their bodies against each other, greeting Rick and Gina quickly before running around sniffing under Jojoba bushes and Staghorn cactus. Never a boring moment.

"They think this is a play day." Her grin was wide. Thin lips showed big teeth in a soft rectangular shaped face. Light gray hair was now powdered beige as fine dirt clung to its shoulder length thickness. Deep forehead creases pointed down like lightening bolts to ice-blue eyes deep set in a ruddy complexion.

She was an outdoor woman.

Gina thought her eyes were the clearest blue she had ever seen.

Before the waggy-tailed dogs could escape the scene, the giant woman clapped her massive hands, said something weird like "yagu-poogu" or what ever Gina thought she heard, and all six dogs quickly came up to her and sat. From her left pant's pocket she pulled out a handful of bitty treats which they choked-down in seconds and soon hovered around some nearby bushes finding shade.

" 'Eghk' Del Rio. Good to see you." Smiling broadly she covered the one hand he extended with both of hers.

"We need to help you or call for help," Rick said surveying the situation while walking fully around the big double cab dually.

"We should dig and pull," added Gina before introducing herself.

"I have a du long name. Just call me Berty."

Gina thought her name fit her humble attitude as Berty gratefully shook Gina's hand, again clasping it between her two big paws. Considering her demise, she seemed basically good natured, and viewed her problem lightly.

"Such a beautiful day for such a bad 'ting'. In Russia there is now ice."

"Well, the third week in October can be one hundred degrees or a mild seventy-five," said Gina. "Today it's supposed to be about ninety." Looking at the mingling clouds she retrieved her wide brimmed canvas hat from the Jeep and pulled it down low to the top of her brow, hiding the penetrating sun. "Since August, there's only been a spoonful of rain," she added.

Everyone grumbled daily about the desert being exceptionally dry and too hot, long into October.

Rick got all the tools from the Jeep that desert people usually carry for emergencies….. a shovel and a hoe. He checked the winch that was at the back of the Jeep and walked around, hand under his chin thinking and analyzing. "I have a plan to try. We need to take the air out of the back tires to flatten them a little before we try to pull you out." Then after looking at the debris in the truck bed, "But first, we need to unload these crates to lighten the rear end."

Old plastic milk crates contained over powering trash of plastic bags, loose papers, broken toy pieces, smashed cans, and glass from broken bottles. Heavy rocks were on top of the trash to discourage fly-aways.

Berty pulled heavy crates out of the truck easily, making light work of a heavy task. Talking incessantly while lifting, she bragged "I know every back road for twenty miles around." She circled with a large gloved hand for emphasis. "I clean roads, desert lake places and give treasures to welfare and trash to dump."

She climbed into the now almost empty truck bed and handed crates to Rick and Gina. "Careful, careful," she sort of demanded as she looked at each crate admiringly.

Gina noted how the big woman stopped and wiped dirt off colors of glass, opened wads of paper and ironed them on her hip to their original flat shape. As she worked, she seemed to go slower with her analyses.

Rick intervened after he and Gina exchanged wry glances. "Uh, it's getting hot. I'm calling for help in case this pull-out plan doesn't work." He walked away and pulled out his cell phone.

The dogs were impatiently roaming about, nosing into everything, sniffing crates, bushes and all the unfamiliar. As predicted, a Welsh Springer-Spaniel mix took off after a rabbit, yelping hysterically.

Berty took a command whistle from around her neck and used it. "I wait. He come back. Boyfriend's favorite dog." While standing in the truck she pointed to an oncoming small red Dodge. "I call my nephew come and help. He lives with me. He is sister's boy. You know him," she stated as she pointed directly at Gina. "How's he doing in school?" All quickly noted in short sentences and broken English.

At first Gina didn't get the connection. As the truck came closer, she recognized the driver as Cory Connor, a football player on Guy's trouble list. With him was his side kick, Cortez Zander, another troubled troubadour. They were each in one of her Science Fiction classes, one in the morning and one in the afternoon.

"Cory needs to turn in many missing assignments," she hesitantly offered for the moment. She wanted to say more, how she caught him with a very small cheat sheet tucked in his long sleeve during

58

an important exam, but decided that this was neither the time nor the place.

As the boys drove toward them on the narrow dirt road, they stopped a short distance away. It was evident they were trying to turn around, but realized they could not because the area was too bushy, thorny and lined with heavy boulders. Also, going off road meant a risk of getting tires stuck in sand.

The three stared in their direction.

After stopping a short distance away, the boys pulled their caps down low and approached hesitantly. Dark sunglasses hid their faces as they ducked.

"Hey," they each sort of grumbled as they approached with hands in pockets. Not looking at Gina, they moved awkwardly around the debris, dogs, stuck truck and Rick, not acknowledging anyone. They were speechless.

"Hi guys," Gina began cordially.

"Hey!" They nodded without looking at her.

Berty stood in the now empty truck, clenched hands on hips, with a mood definitely without merriment. "Hey, my ass!" Her tone was loud and clear; fly away thick gray hair added to the frightening scene. "Not polite," she added.

Everyone stood still...all was quiet. The dogs pointed their noses back and forth among the people.

And then with extended hand to each, "I'm Rick Del Rio. We can use you boys for my plan."

They relaxed a little.

Gina stood back and stayed out of the way.

Rick asked her to call the 4 B's for their needed help to re-load the thirty to forty crates of 'junk' back into the truck after they get it moved from the deep crevice. "And tell them we need to put air in the tires, to bring a generator."

The four retirees, Bing, Bob, Brad and Blake arrived to help on the uniquely abnormal, hot desert project. Their reaction to the sight of the numerous crates strewn everywhere was laughable; Bing the ex cop, raised his brows and smoothed his goatee; Bob took off his cap, smoothed his hair and "poofed" out a sigh; Brad the ex-marine folded his arms and shook his head in a positive 'I told you so' nod; and Blake the retired 'restaurateur' stood a firm stance with legs apart while sipping on his giant latte and chewing on its straw. He patted his rounded middle in thought.

They all looked over at Rick who had his back turned, hiding a chuckle.

Berty's boyfriend's dog returned promptly to the command of the whistle and jumped into the cab of the truck through doors that had been left open due to the heat.

The group worked at removing the truck with only one problem; the day got longer and hotter before they were finished.

"I'm treating everyone to snacks at Greasy's," said Rick using his shoulder to wipe away sweat after they finished. Since all were filthy, they used generous amounts of hand wipes that Gina had available in the Jeep.

Berty, although extremely grateful, excused herself from the friendly gesture. "I need to get home to my boyfriend and house the dogs." She nodded toward the varied group sleeping under bushes. "Gina, call me. I want you to bring your dad's dog to my place for free grooming. Ehh?" She handed her a business card.

Remembering having told Berty about Nellie the Greyhound, she obliged. Before departing she went to her two students for a friendly "thank's" and "I'll see you tomorrow in class."

Although they had been working vigorously with their backs to her most of the time, she was determined to get into their faces with her teacherish politeness.

She had to follow them to their truck as they seemed to avoid her in their hurriedness. Finally, they were forced to face her as she stood outside the driver's truck door fist on the handle.

She stood there hiding her shock at their extremely scarlet, raw looking faces. One was worse than the other; sun glasses did not hide their discomfort of having to be polite.

"Wow! What happened to you two?"

"Game injuries Friday night," grumbled Cory from the driver's seat.

"Yeah, it was a rough night," Cortez echoed as he ducked and searched for something in the glove box.

Driving out hesitantly as the tired looking group watched them, they did a slow turn around but quickly sped out.

The weary crew followed Berty's dually out of the desert after reloading everything.

A pale sinking sun allowed for no more 'haberdashery' on her part and the crew wanted to make sure she went straight home, positive they couldn't afford anymore Sunday night rescues.

Gina and Rick were quiet on the way to Greasy's, thinking a dozen wild thoughts until she said, "What a strange encounter."

Windows were rolled down when they reached the paved road; the cool breeze erased dirt and sweat but not radical thoughts about the strange events of the day.

## CHAPTER NINE
Sunday evening

At Greasy's, misters were doing their job under the outdoor green tinted plastic awning turning the patio a restful shade of light green. Tired and exhausted, the gregarious group sat quietly for awhile pondering their laborious ordeal that took away half the afternoon. While drinking beer or ice tea, they picked at two stacks of nachos, "the works," as ordered by Rick.

"What the HELL did we just do?" Bing questioned quietly. "Number one, she drove 'off-road' avoiding signs against it; number two, we spent a good hour extracting Cholla stickers from paws of three dogs; number three and most unfortunately, we had to listen to her little speeches of how "valuable" the crates of trash were to her and "Don't lose anything"."

"You mean 'treasures'," added Gina as she palmed her sweating ice tea glass and rubbed the dew on her forehead.

Next, Brad the ex-marine stated adamantly, "She's a hoarder."

"What? You mean like I see on television?" Gina refused to believe it shaking her head a negative.

On the other hand, Brad shook his head in affirmation. "Hoarding is a behavioral disorder. Most people are sentimentalist." Chewing on a chunk of chips with melted cheese, he leaned back tiredly in his plastic chair.

With cold beer in hand, it was builder Bob's turn. "I remember having to clean up the houses of hoarders in my many reconstruction jobs. Let me tell you; it's like a disease. They lose a pet, they store it in the freezer."

All made gagging noises.

He ended with, "I've seen it!"

Slick Rick sat quietly taking it all in.

Gina, sitting next to him, let out a sigh as she put her face down on her folded arms.

It was shoulder rub time as he also pulled loose sweaty hairs into her crystal studded, white hair clip. "We need to show the earring we stole from the Pack Rat's nest."

Gina took the tissue wrapped piece from her pocket, and they all passed it around while listening to the story behind the find.

"You hoarders," smiled Blake while feeling the glass pieces and waving the sparkling earring. "Have this checked out. Are these glass or real crystal?" He rubbed his fingers on the shiny pieces and held them up to the sunlight.

"So, did you find any new clues from the dead body site?" Bing wanted to know.

Rick cringed.

"No. But a dead body just doesn't get up and walk away," said Gina re-wrapping the earring before pocketing it.

"On Halloween Night it does!" Everyone laughed at Bob's stiff joke except Rick.

"I'll find it. I have secrets," he continued. "Exactly two months ago in August, all the 'photo-play' with prostitutes took place." Gina grimaced. "I'm in touch with Dickie out at Blue Ridge on the Rim. We have one more bandit to find, and Dickie's my number one contact."

"Always let us know what we can do to help." Bing pushed away from the table with, "I'm done for the day," got his cap off the table and pulled it down over his balding head.

Others followed.

Bing pointed at Gina who was still sitting there with Rick. "Tomorrow is vital. Find out about the mask from the art teacher. Keep in touch. You have all of our numbers?"

She nodded.

Brad saluted before leaving on his 'cycle'

.        Rick started to get up. "Now, I DO need to go home and gather my thoughts about all of this. I've got early morning duty."

"Hmmm. Did you notice the red faces of the two boys?" She sat there without moving, arms crossed looking ahead.

"Absolutely! A strong mental note! Your job tomorrow is to talk to Guy about last Friday night's game. And don't forget your specific description of the mask that we now have bagged in our possession as evidence."

He walked her to her Jeep with his hand behind her neck.

They had trouble parting.

"Damn, I can't believe I'm sending you to Guy."


Mr. Hollywood drove slowly by in front of Greasy's heading east on Cave Creek Road. With shirt unbuttoned, gold chains sparkled like foil in a microwave. Sitting regally next to him in his 1932 Chrysler Imperial Roadster was Delilah...movie star gorgeous.

## CHAPTER TEN
### October 17
### Monday


Early morning rush hour at the McHenry's started at five as Gina brought Pop and Dixie up to date with Sunday's happenings. Pop was bare-chested in his usual comfy pull on elastic waist shorts, while Dixie and Gina rushed around in thin wrap-arounds. Dixie was applying a pin to her last roll up from her steamed box of rollers, and Pop was combing his fingers through his thick hair.

Toast was toasting, coffee was perking and eggs were frying as the three rushed around in their normal early morning routines.

"There's no way that you're taking my Nellie to that Russian groomer." Nellie wagged her tail and jiggled around Pop at the mention of her name as he handed her a dog treat.

"Heck, I'll go with her. I want to see what that woman is all about and I want to see her place. Make a late afternoon appointment for sometime this week," ordered Dixie while waving the spatula. "I want a cat. Maybe she knows where I can get one."

Pop's smile filled his face as he silently scooted a chair to the kitchen round table. Nellie followed and slumped down at his feet. "You can take her as long as you stay with her!"

Dixie joined him while Gina stood and ate quickly. "Absolutely," and "of course," they each said after patting her head.

The outside morning temperature was an unusual sixty-five degrees at five thirty but was expected to climb to the low nineties. "I'm soooo tired of this heat." Gina grumbled. "Third week in October and it's still hot." She hurried off to her room to get dressed for a busy day.

"Yep, it's Monday." Dixie noted the stressed mood.

From her closet Gina selected a knee length short sleeve black polka-dotted dress with matching belt that tied on the side. The V-neck was embellished with sparkling sequins which she needed to brighten a Monday. After slipping into her favorite black wedge sandals, she grabbed her bag of supplies.

Since her dad had thrown about three full wheelbarrows of Cholla on both sides of the fence near their carport, she didn't fear punctured tires by an invader this morning as she hurried out at six with "see-you-later." Two days ago had been such a nightmare she hoped there would never be a repeat…two tires flattened by an intruder.

Hooked on one arm was a bag of teaching materials, books and essays. On the other was her canvas goodie bag containing coffee thermos, brown bag of lunch, and the box of special pastries to share with her lunch bunch ---Nancy and R & R.

Paper clipped on the handle of her bag was the important "to-do" list for Monday: <u>One</u>, talk to Guy about last Friday's game---did the two boys play? <u>Two</u>, see Becky Painter with mask description the peeking pervert wore; <u>Three</u>, make a contest judging date.

By the time she arrived at school, the faculty parking lot was more than half-full. Teachers were getting a 'kick' out of the new regime and joined others early in the morning for comparisons. It was a sway-away from British Literature, American Government, and numerous other every day regular courses.

Home Economics had explored many African dishes and decided to offer bowls of North African Chickpea and Kale Soup which infused flavors of cumin, ginger, saffron and cinnamon sticks. "Tons of vitamins to be fed on festival day," the teachers excitedly bragged.

Kids in the Physical Education Dance Department were thrilled doing the tribal dances with all their many gyrations. "Very fitting," the teachers acknowledged after watching them dance in craziness.

After all, since the principal had announced that it was for only the last two weeks in October, the culmination of which would be an all day festival the Friday before Halloween, the teachers were excited and willing to welcome the change.

The English Office was 'a buzz' this morning with busy pros going over lesson plans, pecking away at computer keyboards and reading text books. Laughing and chatting around the table while drinking coffee, they compared stories about the students and each other.

A few Social Studies' teachers had joined the gabby group to loudly discuss the combining of ideas. Since it was Monday, the beginning of everyone's two week unit, vim and vigor bounced off the walls.

BUT….it was a two week future that no one could predict….a time entered in the Cave Creek history books as one that all Creekers wished had never happened. It was told later by the town folks that October was the horror month of the decade.

This morning Gina was going to grab Heleena Dunkin, the department head, to discuss the meanings of the many acronyms she periodically put on the chalkboard that hung on the wall in the English Office. Why the text messaging with chalk?

Too late! The board was filled with scribble from Heleena and she was no where to be found. Among the stuff was "B sure 2 B redy 4 surprise observ."

The batch of stuff made her fuse burn a bit.

Since her room was between Nancy Lopez's and Richard/Raquel's rooms, her routine was always a quick chat before classes. It made her day. Nancy was a creative genius and Rich was a walking encyclopedia.

Nancy was busy opening a ten foot long crossword puzzle and laying it out on the desks to check it out.

Gina started the conversation by briefing Nancy on all that had happened to her over the week-end. Then, "How are you feeling?"

"I'm much better but my week-end was nothing like yours. Do we have to judge the masks? And here, help me staple this on the wall near the door where the kids enter." They each grabbed an end.

"Wow, clever idea. You're so thoughtful!"

"Variety, variety, variety!" Nancy punctuated each word with a staple. "This is for that pinch of in-between time when they get antsy. It's a good communicator."

Gina sighed. "Yes, we are judging and it'll be fun because Becky Painter will give us a list of criteria to look for on each mask. It should be easy and I should think positive."

"I'm looking forward to it!" Nancy exclaimed while moving robotically around her room working.

"Definitely, I have to see her today with the description of the pervert's mask that Rick is keeping for evidence because she might remember which student made it."

Before she left, "Good news! I brought some bakery goodies for you, Rich and me. They'll really make you feel better. See you at lunch." She left to quickly talk to Rich.

Because she had been sick and still feeling a bit weak, Nancy needed to look into her hidden mirror to re-apply lip gloss and smooth out her shoulder length red hair. After opening the tall cabinet door where extra supplies were stacked, she looked into the mirror that was attached to the inside of it, shook her head a negative and softly moaned. Someone had taken a red marker and drawn a ghoulish red mask, entirely filling the twelve by twelve inches. Although it was somewhat of an artistic piece, she would tell them at lunch, "The craziness has begun."

Heleena Dunkin scurried through the hallway in velcro strapped sandals wearing a plaid gathered skirt that swayed side to side just above her ankles with each stride. A dark blue long sleeve collared blouse was tucked in at the waist where bulging fabric now puffed above and below the belt.

She frowned and blinked rapidly while giving orders to the kids loitering in the hallway waiting for the doors to open. Turning aside teachers who were trying to talk to her, she rambled on and on to the kids. "If you're sitting on the floor against the wall, keep your feet out of the hallway. Someone could trip." They pulled their feet in until she passed.

"Watch your language;" she reprimanded a small group who were using colorful "F" words and some others that they invented while discussing their past week-end. They hovered tightly together and whispered after she left.

Gina quickly approached her while Heleena speed-walked through the hallway to the steps toward the custodians' office for an early morning smoke.

"Could you explain the acronyms on the board and their purpose?" She tried to be nice and not whine.

"Well! I don't have time right now. The bell is going to ring in one minute. Ask someone who pays attention!" Zoom, she flurried down the steps after checking her watch.

Rich, standing outside his room waving the students in, was amused about her encounter. "It's an African code!" He continued hustling kids in with a swinging arm pointing inside. "During lunch I want to hear all about your episodes this week-end. Sounds like we have another mystery to solve." He did Brad's marine salute and closed the door behind him.

Gina was excited about starting the two weeks' unit in each class. Western literature students were prepared to write their daily biographies using the list of helpful hints that she had given them to review and think about ahead of time.

"Ask your parents for ideas. Remember, in two weeks the African teachers will be presenting their students' biographies to exchange on festival day. You're meeting in the gym like pen pals with individual letters." The students were charmed with the idea.

Science Fiction on the other hand was a challenge. Her plans for the next two weeks, among other things, included a lecture on African Voodoo and a limerick contest involving lecture material.

She began with the traditional organized religion practiced by many including the peoples from coastal West Africa. "VOODOO worshipers believe that individual deities have all the characteristics of the Gods of Ancient Greece. Also, they worship their ancestors and believe that the spirits of the dead live side by side with the world of the living."

"Ooohh"….from the kids wide eyed and entranced.

Gina played a disc with the sounds of soft African drum music in the background and dimmed the lights to enhance the mood of her lecture. A fresh minty plug-in emitted a peaceful scent.

Like the mysterious medieval WITCHES and VAMPIRES from old world Europe, the students were mesmerized by the word VOODOO. They loved the mysterious and the unexplained.

She skipped around touching on the rituals and deities. None blinked when she described the "fetishes" as objects of statues or dried animal parts that are sold for their healing. She refused to tell them about the sorcerers who used "fetishes" to cast spells on enemies....or, how they called upon the spirits to bring misfortune or harm to others.

Keeping on the positive, she ended by explaining how the major deities governed the forces of nature such as streams, trees and rocks.

"Tomorrow, we will start writing limericks about VOODOO'S involvement with nature. Keep it green!"

Knowing that she would have to read about seventy-five of these, she needed them to be pleasant.

During lunch today, Gina briefed Nancy and Rich about all her weird encounters from the week-end. Rich took notes as she talked. WHO was the peeking pervert; WHY the cat and mouse car chase at one in the morning; WHAT was the reasoning behind the two stabbed tires?

Nancy bit into the cold, creamy pastry and closed her eyes in comfort, "Mmmm.... What was used to cut into the tires?"

"Ice pick, according to Del Rio."

"OK," said Rich. "After you cover today's to-do list, check with me before leaving. All of this sounds very close to home---meaning Blakely High."

"You think?"

The sixth hour class started well. It was the predictably squirrely after-lunch-bunch she expected, and Gina needed to use every technique in the teaching book of tricks to keep their attention. Eye contact and lowering her voice helped to calm them. These Science Fiction students voiced their opinions of VOODOO in haunting overtones and made soft ghoulish sounds now and then during her lecture.

"Ok, Ok!! Save it for trick-or-treat night. Tomorrow bring your writing hands."

All were quietly listening until half way through the class when the little brunette Marcie sitting in the row next to the board jumped up with a raised fist and shouted at Tammie two seats ahead of her, "F---you"

"No, F---you"

"You go F---yourself," said Marcie as she took a step in Tammie's direction who had stayed seated.

At least ten students got out of their desks to feast on the fuss before Gina intervened.

"Stop, Stop," she yelled and waved her hands. "Do you each want to be expelled for two weeks? Keep it out of school." She separated them, sending one outside to cool off. "Go get a drink of water." Then she seated one of them at her desk.

She went back to her podium and breathed in and out slowly. "The bell will ring in ten minutes and I'm almost finished with your notes." Everyone quickly calmed down except Gina. Her heart started racing after she now looked all around the room. Seated in the empty desk near the door was Heleena Dunkin, actively occupied writing notes during her unannounced observation.

As the last bell sounded for the day, Heleena was the first one out the door. The students scrambled out next as Gina rushed to her desk to look at her to-do list for the necessary contacts.

Printed in bold, red cryptic letters across her list which was still paper clipped to a big yellow note pad that had been lying there all day, was the word *BLOOD*.

# CHAPTER ELEVEN
## Monday afternoon

During their prep hour and the last period of the day, the three had to meet in the English Office because their rooms were now occupied by traveling English teachers. Each arrived with a stack of papers to grade and hoped not to go back to their rooms for something necessary, only interrupting the other classes.

"Watch out! Heleenas on the loose. She came into my sixth hour during a fight!" Gina explained all as she took the box of remaining baked goods from the fridge and cut a cream horn in thirds.

Rich poured three cups of left over coffee and they sat silently sipping, unwinding for about five minutes.

"The pierced tires, the car harassment, the peeking pervert. Too close to home," said Rich. "You need to see Guy and get his list of football players in danger of not playing at the big homecoming game two weeks from now. It could be a rebellious student. I guarantee the criminal is not anonymous."

"It's on my list. Nancy and I are going to Becky Painter's room after the last bell. She always stays late after school and doesn't dash off like everyone else in the Commercial Arts Department.

Nancy was at the copy machine making copies for tomorrow's lessons. "Guess what I have in my supply closet!" She sat and started counting sheets of paper.

"We're afraid to ask."

"Yeah."

"A very artistically drawn, ghoulish looking red African mask on my mirror."

"What!"

"Just inside the door. The craziness has begun."

The three friends stared wide-eyed at each other, folded their arms and sat back in their chairs in reflection.

"Compare it to my to-do list." Gina showed the cryptic letters written in red which almost completely covered her notes of three items. "Problem is I don't know when it happened. My podium and my desk are in a corner and I would've seen someone come near.....you would think."

"Holy Crapola! We are being targeted. Maybe it's the same person." Nancy finished counting and sipped on her coffee.

"Think it out. There could be a connection to all your harassment. Check with a couple of good students and see if they noticed anything. It could just be a couple of guys clowning around....hopefully," Rich added.

"Jamie Mink and Kim Rose are in my sixth hour. I'll see them tomorrow. Maybe they saw someone loitering around my desk."

The three sat intensely working on tomorrow's lesson's until the last bell of the day rang. They waited until the hallway, dubbed Nascar Raceway, was emptied of shouting kids and until the teachers filed in sighing, rushing around, slamming papers down and lining up for the bathroom. Soda can tabs were popping in unison like revving car engines. The day was done.

Walls along the wide hallway in the Commercial Arts Building contained window lined cubicles of students' works, all themes of Africa illustrated in numerous paintings. Colorful acrylic tigers and lions artfully came alive in different styles of photographic exactness and surrealism. In tall dry grasses of pale citrine, chestnut animals rolled, climbed, slept and stared wide-eyed in a trance.

The two teachers pointed with amazement at the different pieces. "Such talent and skill." They made note of student names for later classroom recognition, if any were their students.

Various gray chalk drawings dramatized the excitement of night time among African landscapes. Lions, tigers, and hyenas crouched in the darkness, hovering under Baobab trees and ready to lurch while lounging on sandy soils. Moods of death and danger lingered, so aptly portrayed in these selections.

"Spooky!"

Becky's door was open and the two teachers had to wait while a couple of agitated students were talking loudly to her.

"I spent hours and hours on that mask," they overheard one girl say almost in tears.

"She turned it in too because I saw her put it on the shelf with the other ones to dry," said another girl pointing to that particular area.

"I believe you; we'll find it," Becky calmly added to their lament as she moved around tightening lids on jars of different colors. Periodically wiping her hands on her white apron which was almost tied twice around her slender waist, she looked like an art piece herself. Short sable-colored hair was gelled back and up complimenting her large chocolate brown eyes. Long black earrings seemed to touch her shoulders in dance as she circled around straightening the room.

"I had about seventy five turned in, so it could be mixed with some that are still drying in the back room."

She spoke with quiet authority. "Remember, there are no names on the masks to allow for impartial judging. Tonight, write a detailed description of your mask and hand it in tomorrow morning so that I can be aware of it throughout the day." Putting her hands on her hips in a finished gesture she added, "Be sure to include all identifying characteristics and colors."

The girls meandered out moodily.

Bingo!! Raising their eyebrows, Gina and Nancy exchanged glances of awareness.

"Hey, hi Becky."

"Phew, I need to sit down. Did you hear everything?"

"You handled it well. I think that we fit in with the conversation you just had. Let's sit."

Gina explained all the events that happened since Friday night's encounter and ended by handing Becky a copy of the complete description.

"I'm going to compare this with Susie Lee's description and I won't tell her that Del Rio has the original mask. See me tomorrow after school. And, how about judging the masks on Thursday so that I'll be able to assemble a display of the winners with their ribbons by Friday? They'll be in the cubicles for everyone to see."

They agreed and walked over to the long counter attached to the wall from one end to the other. An entire row of windows above the counter was aflame with the late afternoon sun, thus illuminating some of the masks in a shocking iridescence. A requirement of 'a speck of white or more' per mask sharpened the patterns and they seemed to glow in waves.

None were comical or clownish. Subconsciously, the three teachers now shivered while looking at the evil, fiendish grins of the masks, all without eyes.

Feeling a decadent vibe, Gina asked, "Are the students supposed to be able to wear these?"

"It is a requirement."

"Be strong," said Nancy while looking at her pale friend. "Don't let the masks dredge up memories of last Friday's encounter."

Becky began standing the masks in their upright positions. "Remember, these are just works of art." While wiping wet paint off her hands from a mask that was not quite dry she added, "Why someone would want to use a mask for malevolence is beyond me."

The three teachers were silent, each reminiscing about the enormity of the situation with the pervert.

"What are you going to do if it is Susie Lee's?" Gina wanted to know. "We need to keep it for later evidence, and I know that it has been finger printed."

"If it is hers, I still won't tell her but give her full credit and help her make a new one." She took off her apron exposing a white long sleeve satin shirt gathered at the cuffs. Her slim black knee length skirt contoured well with her shape. "Perhaps when all of this is over, we can devise a plan of convenience explaining how her mask 'has been found' and she can have the original returned."

"How many winners are we supposed to choose on Thursday?" Nancy wanted to know while helping

Becky set some new ones out that she had brought from the back room.

"And," added Gina, "are we separating them by classroom so each class has an equal amount of winners?"

"Don't worry. I already have them coded per class so that they can easily be grouped. You'll get a criteria sheet and I'm not telling the kids who judged!"

"Good idea! Very important! These are grotesque but beautifully crafted in all their opulence, almost like a diabolical delight." She fingered the holes where the eyes would be. Some were largely rounded. Each was unique. Thin slits above high cheek bones gave one mask the appearance of an aboriginal occult. "Did the students fit the masks to their faces?" Gina felt this was an important question.

"Only eyes and mouth had to fit. They could go wild with the other contours of the face and that's why some seem to have tall foreheads and others very long chins." After looking at the clock on the wall Becky said, "Twenty more minutes and I'm out of here."

"We'll follow you out. Gina needs to find Guy for some questions about students." She carried the last batch of masks to Becky who was placing them on the shelf, pushing them together tightly to make room.

While fingering the masks, Gina didn't notice her shaking hands as she walked along the wall of masks until something glittered and she reached out. As the sun shone on one in particular, iridescent water colors of green, red, and purple sparkled from gems attached on one ear lobe, a small piece containing beads attached to four wires.

"Whose mask is this?" Her voice was urgent.

Becky and Nancy looked at her in puzzlement as she turned ghostly pale again.

"I don't know off hand. I have to look at the code numbers on the back and check my computer at home. I left the list on my desk where I was working last night, but I have to finish recording them tonight."

"I found the mate to this earring out in the desert, half buried in a pack rat's nest." She now played with the wire strings of beads. "It was near the empty spot of the dead body."

The three were stunned!

CHAPTER TWELVE
October 17
Monday afternoon

Nancy Lopez and Becky Painter stared unwavering at the earring while absorbing the significance of Gina's statement. Without talking, the three quietly grabbed a student desk and sat, drinking their water bottles dry.

"The whole town knows about the missing dead body. My students' favorite art project was thematically titled, 'Missing in the Desert'."

"Yeah, Guy remarked the other night that teen gossip is faster than digital."

The three stared moodily, exploring a connection between earrings, masks and a missing body.

"We can only speculate a connection. Maybe there is none. It could be a coincidence." Nancy brought the now empty bottle to her temple. "I'm getting a headache. My mind is blank after a big day of a hundred and seventy teens. Let's go."

They left after exchanging phone numbers. Becky was to find the coded numbers from Susie Lee's mask and check the ownership of the mask with the earring.

Gina was to do the comparison after calling Del Rio for the numbers on the bottom of the mask he had in his possession.

The two discussed the enormity of the situation while walking away. "Why would Susie Lee's mask be staring at me in the bathroom?"

"Someone could have stolen her mask, or it could be a close friend of hers who borrowed it? Let's split the detective work. I'll tell Rich now about what's happened and you call Del Rio."

"Right! First I need to talk to Guy about last Friday night's football game and also get his list of students with delinquent grades."

They parted with, "Call me."

After checking her watch, Gina hurried to catch Guy before he left school for the day; two hours had escaped since the last bell rang while she and Nancy were in the Commercial Arts Building.

First, starting with the gymnasium, she asked several students playing basketball if they'd seen Coach Wagner, to which they replied "out on the football field."

The third week in October meant soft winds still hot and dry due to a lingering summer that refused to leave. She felt the heat in more ways than one. Wearing her shades and ever-ready sun visor that she now took from her large work bag, she stood on the edge of the field and scanned for Guy.

It took her a full ten minutes to realize that among the players and assistant coaches out on the field, there was no Coach Wagner. Young bodies were doing at least three different drills: stopping, starting and dropping, all to the sounds of synchronized grunts, whistles and shouts.

A few sat on the bench near the water station then intermingled with others on the field. It was a well planned exchange of students coming to the bench to cool off and then going out again to sweat in the heat.

"It's a good way to save young lives," said Guy sneaking up closely, well aware of her observation. "In this heat we take no chances. What are you doing out here?" He smiled coyly a skittish grin, his signature in most cases. "You're out of place."

She knew well his mischievous smile with corners that lifted the cheek bones….trying to distract….but she kept on talking.

"I need a list of truant students that may not play in the Friday night's homecoming game two weeks from now, and I have something important to ask you."

"Good, shall we go into my office?" His manly stance of legs split apart, feet anchored and arms folded across his chest seemed beckoning, so she took two steps back. The warm breeze caught a few sandy hairs from under his Blakely High green cap while his tee shirt glued nicely to his physique.

"No! Cory Conner and Cortez Zander.... did they play in last Friday's game?" Cripe, she sounded to hurried.

He took two steps forward and answered, "Negative, they were benched. What's up?"

She explained the encounter with the two on the desert concerning Berty's dilemma with her truck. "Coincidentally, they each had very red faces, but one seemed to be irritated differently, by perhaps a chemical substance. They said it was from Friday night's game." She now walked over to a shade tree and he followed.

"There was a little brawl after the game and maybe they got involved in the altercation. They certainly did not play. Their grades were too bad. Besides," he now spoke quietly in undertones, "neither one could be your 'peeking-pervert' in my estimation."

"Why?"

"They're too sissified. Cory is hen pecked to death by his Aunt Berty, and Cortez is so meek, he stutters and won't look you in the eye when you're talking to him."

"I have no problem talking to either one of them in class."

Lifting his cap for a re-adjustment he said, "Don't you want to go to my office so that we can discuss this thoroughly?" He played with the tip of her sun visor, up and down.

She thought of Del Rio and tingled from waist to toes. "See you later." When she started to turn to walk away he grabbed her hand causing her to spiral into him.

"Stay in touch. I'll have that list of delinquent students in your mail box in the morning. And let me know when you go to Tumbleweed's... alone," he smiled broadly. She felt his 'look' as she quickly walked away.

*What is SHE doing out here on the field? What could Coach be telling her? She alone is the cause of all my problems.*

She hurriedly dialed Rick on her cell and explained all that had taken place today. "When I get home, I'll call you for the code numbers from the mask you have. It might be Susie Lee's."

When he said that he had to retrieve it from forensics, she was irked. Hearing the change in her voice he continued with, "Don't worry. We have saliva samples, hair samples and DNA from sweat mixed with blood. When we have a guilty person, we'll nail him."

Or her, she thought. Considering it was almost five thirty, she now hurried. While walking to her room to get a small stack of papers to grade for the night that she had forgotten earlier, she called Pop at the bakery.

"I need some sweets. Bring home goodies."

He obliged and told her what he and the four B's had accomplished all in one day. "Tonight we'll have to chat about new ideas."

She assumed the new ideas pertained to her harassments.

Only a few cars remained in the faculty parking lot at this time of day; most belonged to the coaches and the administration. After approaching her Jeep, she noted a small piece of paper stuck under the windshield wiper on the driver's side.

The note was brief. "Call me. Tom Shieter." In capital letters and next to a phone number was the word "PRIVATE".


Night time dinner chatter was led by Pop and Dixie while still in their work clothes. Pop's bakery attire of white shirt and pants looked slightly soiled and tired. On the other hand, Dixie's perky denim skirt and silk blouse cinched with a western belt still looked stylishly fresh. "Did you even go to work today?" Pop had to ask as she briskly moved around arranging food, plates, pots and pans, pointing and giving directions to Gina.

"The office was quiet for a Monday. Everyone seemed to be involved with the African studies and I noticed a peaceful hum in the air. I think the school is going to enjoy a two week change of things."

"Hold that thought. You might change it after you hear about my day." Gina was adding chopped onions and tomatoes to mashed avocadoes. Before cutting a fresh lime in half, she waved a small paring knife in the air and continued. "Nancy and I spent almost two hours talking to Becky in Commercial Arts."

"Uh oh, the masks," Pop said with full attention while putting plates on the table.

"Becky and Del Rio are supposed to call me tonight with some very interesting information that might solve a few mysteries. It seems that a student's mask is missing, perhaps stolen, and also we found the matching earring attached to a mask...we don't know whose." Next she explained about the code system Becky used for identifying each mask.

"While I'm waiting for their phone calls, what's going on with your cycle group, the four B's.?"

"They've been busy plotting their surveillance ideas. Bing has his eyes on help from a perky brunette ex-cop from New York. He met her hanging around the police station which is near his watch. Bob has befriended a bleached blond retiree who is helping to remodel "Screamin' Ice Cream with some kind of a painted mural. Brad's working in confidence with a red headed muscular cycle rider who slips in and out of hideaways with the cycle groups, and Blake's new confidant is the hostess at Tumbleweed's."

"Tough jobs," joked Dixie as she slipped two tablespoons of guacamole into her taco.

"After all," added Pop as he chucked a small piece of taco meat to Nellie who was lying under the table with her chin on his feet, "the best way to learn information is to befriend the locals." This was all accompanied with his wide ear to ear grin.

"The principal left a note under my windshield wiper to call him."

"Yuck!" Dixie doused her taco with hot sauce.

"He wrote PRIVATE."

"Double yuck. I need a beer and I'll get you one."

Before Gina could continue, Rick called with the code numbers from the mask "Forensics is finished with it so it stays in my possession for now. Call me as soon as you hear from Becky. I need to know if there's a match."

Next, she told him about her afternoon, including the earring in the mask and talking to Guy.

Pause…."You were out on the field when you talked to him, right?"

"Of course!"

"Just checking."


Later, Becky called with the information and as expected, the mask in Del Rio's possession was Susie Lee's. Surprisingly, the other mask containing the earring belonged to her best friend, the one arguing in her defense earlier.

Dixie listed all new information on her long yellow note pad. She considered herself the note keeper and puzzle solver of the entire group.

With great trepidation, Gina finally called the principal's private number and agreed to meet with him tomorrow afternoon right after her seventh hour prep.

Out front, driving the long stretch of the picturesque Lazy Lizard Lane, was Mr. Hollywood in a 1935 Lincoln Model K Convertible Roadster with the top down. Next to him sat Berty wearing a shiny pink silk blouse and her brightest 'killer-pink' lipstick. A bright pink scarf serving as a head band controlled her grey fly-away hair.

## CHAPTER THIRTEEN

Cory and Cortez knew something was not as it was supposed to be when Berty kept locking the door to the small guest apartment and keeping the key in her possession at all times. Each day she would enter the guest room with a tray containing an ornate blue Russian tea pot, two matching cups, and blue plate of petite sandwiches slathered with cream cheese and whole sardines. The fish were the petite, expensive kind only found in specialty markets that catered to the European palate.

Frequently, the boys watched this scenario while throwing a football back and forth in the very ample space of the courtyard between the main house and guest apartment.

"So small for a grown man," the boys had speculated when discussing the sandwiches for Berty's guest.

"What does he drive?"

"Where does he work?"

Questions between them were mounting daily.

Most generally when Cory would ask his aunt about her friend, she seemed defensive. "Co'y, he works at night and sleeps during the day." She would dismiss further discussion with a rough wave of her hand before stomping away and calling after her beloved pack of dogs.

Such a caretaker she was. The boys were both envious and appreciative as they often saw her walking six dogs at a time, a different pack morning and evening. They were a mix of terriers, hounds, retrievers, spaniels, and others both small and large. "I can't tell a purebred from a mutt," Cortez often said in jest.

Not easily daunted, the two boys were haunted by the mystery of the man locked in the guest house and tried tactfully a few more times to learn more. After all, when they looked through a thickly curtained window lit by an inside lamp, they saw no movement, no shadows of any kind, just stillness.

The last time they approached her with their curiosity she loudly voiced her agitation with such magnitude the surrounding dogs hunkered down or crawled away. Some would lie on backs with paws bent in the air in compliance. "Don't question me again!" Then she would soothingly pet each dog. "You frighten them!"

Baffled and frustrated, they refused to be turned away by the kindly gargantuan. And sadly, Berty was unaware of a teacher's number one declaration of a list of truths: The best way to get a teen to do something good or bad is to tell him he can't."

They made secretive big plans and constructed a list of ideas to follow. The list included words like:

Friday night...

Vodka...a chain with key attached...

Twelve midnight.

"After all, this has been going on for weeks. It's too weird. I want to meet this guy." Cory almost felt that it was his obligation in a strange sort of way to take care of his Aunt Berty. To him, sneaking around was no crime.

"Friday night, we'll have some fun. Coach is not putting us in the game anyway." They relinquished their goal for the time being and decided to get on her good side by offering to help bathe the dogs during her grooming sequences in the barn.

Enthralled by their enthusiasm, she offered late afternoon appointments 'this week only' to all her clients since considering the availability of the boys. "This is trial time because next week you boys very busy with big Blakely High Homecoming Parade; you not have time to help," she uttered in her best English yet.

Little did she know that the energy behind their enthusiasm was spirited by their plot of 'search and discover'. There was such an overload of clients that it necessitated extra help. The boys rallied their girlfriends to lend a hand to the delight of Aunt Berty. "This is Susie Lee and her friend Darlene."

Both girls wore short-shorts, tight v-neck tees and flip flops. "Just show us what to do," Susie said to Berty.

"You four clean the dogs and I'll clip."

Susie assisted Cortez with scrubbing the dogs, while Darlene and Cory dried them with a blow dryer and brushes.

Soon all were up to their elbows in warm, dirty dog suds during the first wash; for the second, they learned to add scents of lemon and mint.

The boys decided not to include the girls in their devious plot of breaking into the guest apartment.

"Too risky."

"It's a private matter."

Daily they connived ways of getting the key without her noticing.

"Does she take afternoon naps? We could quietly make a clay impression of the key while she slept."

"Negative," said Cory. "The key is always on a chain around her neck or in a front pants' pocket."

"Difficult."

"Our best bet is the extra vodka to help her sleep on Friday night."

"You mean deep sleep." The boys planned and re-planned their night of intrigue as they worked late afternoons.

All went well until Tuesday.  It was late in the day when Gina, Nancy and Dixie drove in and briskly walked to the compound with Nellie the Greyhound.

The boys griped and grimaced.

# CHAPTER FOURTEEN
## OCTOBER 18
Tuesday

While driving to school at six Tuesday morning, Gina scanned her list of chores to accomplish before the day ended. Highlighted in yellow on the clipboard she kept handy on the seat next to her, was the meeting with Rick during lunch concerning the earring. Rick wanted to see it first hand and then check with Darlene about where she got it.

Would Rick make a connection to the missing body or simply dismiss it as a coincidence? They had discussed the fact that Pack Rats vacuum the desert of shiny things, and the earring could have been dropped anywhere within a quarter mile radius of the missing body and packed back to the rat's nest.

Everyone in the know about the earring was anxious for more information. Today's answer could be a clue.

Glancing at her lesson plans, today was the day to introduce the limerick to Science Fiction classes and remind them of the due date this Friday for contest judging over the week-end. Fortunately, the four B's had offered to judge since no one else would commit.

Of course, they each volunteered their new lady friends for extra assistance with all the limericks and decided to have a picnic affair during judging.

"Good, because you'll have about seventy of them," she warned. They were ready and felt important.

Today was day two of the two week African units as selected by the school's different departments. Friday, within ten days, an all day African festival involving visitors from Africa would be taking place. So far, everyone around town was excited.

Brochures and pennants advertising the day were everywhere. Storefronts were extra colorful and shoppers bought products to the beat of African tunes.

Color combinations of bright oranges mixed with magenta and canary yellow penetrated the senses, muting Southwestern creams and tans of the old Cave Creek. Cycle riders donned bright African scarves which were the latest hot sale's item.

The four retirees, Bing, Bob, Brad and Blake chose to wear African wooden beads featuring fetishes of popular animals from the African continent. Always, the grayish-brown, white striped African antelope known as the popular Kudu was represented.

Pop had done a little research on his computer and jovially warned them that "Fetishes can be a stimulant you know, like a natural aphrodisiac."

"GOOD!" They approved unanimously.

Volunteers from different committee groups selected African costumes wearing bright long skirts and short sleeve blouses crowned with a variety of the same long wooden beads.

Even the mayor of the 'bicker creek' committee was pleased with the camaraderie taking place in his town and reminded his wife that "we need to dress the part."

Business committees of both Cave Creek and Carefree contributed to the enthusiasm by offering men's tees for sale with the sketch of an African Continent on the front in the non-western colors of purple and mustard. After all, ninety-five percent of the men could not walk around 'African bare-chested' with their milky flesh protruding like pillows over their belts. It was a good plan and proceeds benefited the schools.

Pulling into the large faculty parking lot was difficult because band members were practicing all over the place, circling the entire perimeter while marching to drums. Some were filing out of the band room to the practice field and meandered in and out of parked cars without looking, unaware of cars newly parking.

For next week's special day, a massive parade will convene in the middle of Cave Creek and head to the high school's football field. Participants will parade around the track twice to the delight of those in the bleachers; Cheer and Pompon plan to entertain with special costumed dances.

Most importantly, time is slotted for the Africans to reciprocate with their show for the varied groups of spectators. Reporters from Scottsdale and other neighboring towns 'calendared' their attendance for this unprecedented eventful day.

Gina parked next to Nancy's red Camry, pulled on the small gold lame bolero that fit well over her black dress and re-adjusted the straps to her favorite gold sandals while wiggling her polished toes for comfort. After grabbing the two bags containing her supplies of papers, books and lunch, she hurried to the office.

It was unusually busy this early. Number one, it was still very warm outside and desert people like to get going with their deeds early; and number two, the entire mode of the African atmosphere excited all.

To everyone's delight, soft African drum music played in the background near attendance while teachers, parents, and other classified staff wandered in.

"So stimulating to the senses," someone said while strutting around.

"We should do this all the time," said another jiggling to the beat.

Gina, feeling the vibe, cantered with rhythm over to Dixie who was manning the busiest counter in school. The line included substitute teachers nervously waiting today's assignments, teachers pushing through to key their private mailboxes and impatient parents demanding answers to their many questions.

To Dixie, this was her native habitat. Today she was heavily jeweled 'western' with touches of turquoise here and there. She too chose black, a tunic belted with silver that fit loosely over her black dress jeans. Since she was rounded in the middle but slender in the legs, she could tuck tight pants handsomely into boots or tall moccasins. Today she wore her favorite leather moccasins with silver conchos attached on the sides. "Dress happy, you feel happy," was her motto.

"Hey Gina," she said. "I forgot to tell you last night that I made an appointment for us to take Nellie to be groomed at six tonight. Ok with you?"

"I'm ready." Then in a whispered tone since the line-up of people was listening, "I'm curious about Berty's place!"

Rounding the corner she barely missed running into Dr. Shieter who came flying out of his office shouting, "Turn that music off!" He pointed at the staff quickly with an arm wave and hurried out the glass doors while loosening his tie.

"What's his problem?" Gina asked Dee the attendance dean always in the know.

"He claims the kids are taking too long to get to class in the mornings because they hover too long around the soda machines."

"It's still in the high nineties and we're all sick of it. It's showing on the kids," said Gina. "Good news, a cool November should be around the corner."

Briskly walking to her room, she read her mail. Keeper, keeper, trash, trash....The list of kids with low grades and therefore removed from playing on the team, was in her hand. Cory and Cortez were on the list and Guy had high-lighted them in yellow. She felt bad and knew that she would have to encourage them more and also call their parents.

Passing by the media building, Gina noticed two groups of about ten practicing weird African dances out on the patio. "For the parade," one girl said as she looked their way. "It's a contest between Social Studies and the Athletic Department."

Music was loud and enthusiasm was high. Teens loved competitive fun and seemed engrossed with everything African. Sounds of drums, flutes, and laughter pierced the morning air.

"Hey it's not an Indian dance. You're dancing Indian." More laughter.

She was hurrying along and keeping rhythm to the music when Guy grabbed her from behind, putting his hands almost around her waist. She screamed and wiggled free.

"Did you get the list of truant students?"

"Yep, I did." She moved away allowing space between them as they walked fast toward the English Building.

"Don't feel guilty. The two also have low grades in math. The season is more than half over and I don't see how they're going to play until maybe late in November."

"Do they still practice?"

"We insist. It's good for them one way or another. Hey, keep in touch." He jogged off looking appropriate wearing royal blue sport shorts, and matching Blakely High golf shirt and cap. The latter two a mix of school colors, royal blue and emerald.

She couldn't help but stare after him as he headed towards the gym. To her embarrassment, he turned with his mischievous grin, and waved at her. She turned back around and hurried up the steps to the English Department on the second floor.


*Goofy teachers! Never a worry, no problems, just show offs. That's going to end soon. Chaos is coming.*

CHAPTER FIFTEEN

Stopping by their rooms, Gina asked Nancy and Richard/Raquel to meet with her and Del Rio during lunch.

"Be glad to."

"Sure thing!  Darlene is in my class before lunch. I'll ask her to stay for a chat," said Rich.

"Act like there's nothing wrong.  We don't want anyone getting suspicious.  Make up a story."  Then she added with a big grin, "You're good at that."

The Western Lit classes went well as Gina walked around between rows of students briefly looking over their shoulders at their biographical outlines.  "You may work with a partner sharing ideas but keep a thesaurus and dictionary handy between you.  If you decide to use the computer, I still need a hand written outline turned in with your bios.  Be sure to put your individual brand on the front of your paper and your name on the back.  Papers are due Friday."

She taught them how to make their individual brands at the beginning of the school year, and they used these as their lone signatures on all papers due with the exception of the biographies. "When you meet your pen pal next Friday in the gym, you should be prepared to help him or her make a western brand. I guarantee it'll be a hit." She secretly wished that it would be as simple as it sounds.

All students were well informed concerning the days events. A bus load of African teenagers from a private school in Africa will converge on Blakely High the day of the festivities. They will be a mixed group representing different areas of the large continent. The teachers considered it a good thing because they did not have to specify a particular region when comprising the two week units.

Parents, business sponsors, newspaper reporters and town bureaucrats were ready to join in with a spirit of good will.

Before the bell rang she reminded them about December's event. "Remember, I'm accepting no more permission slips for the trail ride in the Superstition Mountains. The ride is maxed at twenty-five."

Ironically, just after her announcement, in walked an intruder, a parent. He had a "visitor" sticker stuck to the shoulder of his large tee, a very big tee that unfortunately fell about two inches short of his belly button exposing nude fat. "Big Dogs" was written on the front above the design of a foot long hot dog that sort of meandered down vertically to his 'Charlie'. Grey cotton flannel shorts stopped "to close to you know what," as she described the scene later to the group during lunch. Thick hair flopped around on top of his head in a confusion of parts.

Without a hint of shyness, he briskly walked to the front of the class where she was standing. A few girls eyed him briefly then promptly looked away.

"Excuse me for barging in, but here's Cortez's permission slip for the December trail ride. I wanted to hand it in for him because it's been on the counter at home for weeks and I'm sure he forgot about it." He shoved the paper forcefully in her direction.

His fat face was devoid of any expression and he breathed through his mouth with an aggressive manner that caught her off balance.

Asthma, she thought. Good thing Cortez is in my next class.

"Umm—Uh," she stuttered. "The trail ride is currently full, but I can accept this as a substitute spot in case a student cancels."

"Good deal." After he turned to leave, she did a quick glance in his direction to make sure he made it out the door 'pronto' but wished she hadn't. While walking away, his grey shorts were stuck deep in a crevice.

The students were mute and paid no attention to the scene. Nothing surprises them, Gina thought. They've seen it all. She now felt embarrassed for Cortez and hoped his father promptly left campus.

As he walked out the door, Heleena walked in with her eyes almost rolling out of her head. "What the hay did he want?"

Gina told her.

"Well, I hope to go along as a sponsor. As head of the committee for extra-curricular activities, include me in." She walked out with a confirmed attitude and creepy smile.

Holy crapola! Gina was relieved when the bell rang.

During the five minute break between classes, and before the 'just before lunch' sci-fi class arrived, she attacked the little private 'fridge behind her desk, opened a tall bottle of Mexican Coke Cola, and took a long gulp. Next, she broke off a piece of seventy-percent cocoa dark chocolate bar and sucked on it while running her fingers through her hair.

"Ok, give us some." Jamie Mink and Kim Rose came walking in, always first, wiggling their fingers this time for a treat.

Gina found it hard to laugh when she had her mouth full of melting chocolate, so she covered it with a napkin. "Help 'orselves. Just a little piece! I've a long day ahead."

"Don't ever forget your favorites," they said while licking chocolate off their fingers and getting into their desks near the back.

During roll call, and before she started speaking, Dr. Shieter interrupted with a loud announcement that reverberated down the empty hallway and bounced off the walls.

"Because of numerous tardies first hour of the day, I am chaining the beverage vending machines shut all around campus for two weeks starting tomorrow. GET TO CLASS ON TIME!"

Everyone in class grumbled and complained. Cortez, looking angry, slumped down in his desk, the last one in the row and leaned back on the wall.

Moving on, she started class explaining the limerick. "These are due Friday as I have a team of retired people who will judge them for uniqueness this week-end. Everyone gets points for turning in one if it follows the proper pattern. The rhyme scheme is A,A,B,B,A. She wrote a couple samples on the board.

A bikini tan was her dream............A
A day in the sun was her scheme.......A
As the temperature rose..............B
She ran for the hose....................B

But instead of cool water got steam...A

"I don't get it," said a boy drumming his pencil on his pad of paper.

"You know how hot it gets here?" A girl told him.

"Oh yeah."

"Your limericks MUST pertain to the Voodoo notes that I have been giving you."

The students stared into space. No one selected a writing tool to get started.

"Start with simple words like African—Voodoo—religion—spirits—hex—fetishes. Look at your notes. Help each other. Limericks are nothing new to you because you've been writing them since elementary school."

Next she put in a disc of quiet African drums. "Mood music," she said.

They started sharing with others about what they had written in the past.

As Gina walked around through the rows she noticed Cortez was working on his math.

"Do you work on English assignments in your math class?"

He glared at her coldly.

"Spooky!" She whispered almost walking away.

"This is due before the day is over. C-coach worked me late last night preparing me for this Friday's game and I didn't get to finish my math assignment. I'll t-turn in the limerick by Friday."

The glare, his negative tone, his cold stare plus his stutter unnerved her. She moved away to Jamie and Kim who were "having a ball" with the assignment.

Her spirits rose. "You make my day!"

The lunch time meeting went too quickly. Gina, Del Rio, Nancy and Rich discussed the earring on Darlene's mask in the Commercial Art's Building. Not wanting to raise suspicion, they had agreed that Rich should talk to her alone right after class. He retold the conversation with the group.

"She said that Cory gave it to her and he got it from his aunt. She was worried that something could be wrong. I simply told her that someone found the mate to it and we wondered to whom we should return it. I told her that we would get back with her."

Afterward, they grabbed their sack lunches and left for Commercial Arts. Becky was waiting and they all looked at the comparison. The match was exact.

Everyone relied on Del Rio for clues to an answer.

"What are your ideas?" asked Becky.

"How did Berty's earring get into the Pack Rat's nest?" wondered Rich.

"She roams all over the desert clearing trash. She could have dropped it anywhere and the rain could have moved it within the site of the missing body," was Rick's only answer.

"Spooky."

"Too spooky," added Nancy.

They parted with Rick walking Gina back to her class. After quickly closing the door and locking it, they kissed. "I owe you a dance," he said while playing with her hair.

"Don't get me steamy; I have one more class and then I meet with the principal after school." She found it difficult pushing away.

"Oh yeah! I'm very, curious what that's all about." He squeezed one of her legs between his. "What's going on tonight?" He kissed her neck probing at an ear.

"Dixie and I are taking Nellie to be groomed at Berty's." She hugged his firm chest tightly.

His mood changed from passion to serious. "Take notes. I'll get back with you later tonight."

The bell rang and they quickly parted. Gina freshened her make-up, went to her fridge to finish the Mexican coke and whispered loudly, "Cool off, cool off." She put the cold bottle next to her temple.

The 'after lunch bunch' Sci Fi class went by quickly and they were extra excited about their Voodoo limericks. They exuberantly shared with each other. "You people make my day," she always told them. It helped to calm them. The bad wanted to be good and the good wanted to be 'gooder', a word this class coined.

During the last period of the day, her preparation time, she met with Nancy and discussed all the happenings so far especially emphasizing the earring puzzle. "Hey, why don't you go with Dixie and me to the dog groomer's place tonight at six?"

"With bells on my toes! I want to see what she's all about. So far, we see her in her truck of dogs with trash packed high on her dash. I don't know how she can see?"

"And lately she's been seen riding around with Mr. Hollywood! Better her than Movie-Star Gorgeous! I think Berty's lonely."

The last bell of the day rang...a little louder than usual. "Nancy, I have to go see Principal Shieter. Could you possibly do me a favor and knock loudly on his door after I'm in there for fifteen minutes."

"You bet. I'll act naïve and forget about formal protocol. Besides, the secretaries are on our side."

## CHAPTER SIXTEEN
Tuesday afternoon

As scheduled, Gina arrived promptly at the principal's office ten minutes after the bell rang. The door to his room was open and he was busy writing at his opulent cherry wood desk. Two book shelves containing professionally bound classics with titles in gold lettering lined one wall. A broad leafed Golden Pathos with meticulously trimmed trailing vines sat in a small terra cotta vase on a pedestal too close to his desk like a pet. Overall, a musty scent of tobacco lingered from somewhere.

After she walked in, he went into the hallway to tell his secretary, "I don't want to be disturbed," then closed the door.

He smiled nervously at her, more like a short smirk, than asked her to sit down after maneuvering a desk chair next to his. While tapping a pencil loudly, he looked at her a little too long and pretended to shuffle papers. She crossed her legs and put her hands over her knees.

A spiced candle was burning on top of a nearby glass trophy case highlighting his past as a star soccer player. Not one of her favorites, she found the scent repulsive. Having been warned about his physical prowess, she was prepared for anything and simply stared back in resolute calmness, total composure. Echoes of warnings from the secretarial staff were foremost in her thoughts.

"He is a trickster;"

"Look out and be ready."

Then squirming around in his chair he asked, "How's your African unit coming along?" He leaned toward her a little too closely and inched forward so very slightly.

Refusing to succumb to his malingering gaze, she rolled her chair slightly away from his. Now paralleling his desk, she leaned her elbow on it, faking calmness. At least she wasn't shaking. "Everyone's excited and busy." With fortitude, she studiously explained what her classes were doing in preparation for the big event.

Was he listening? She couldn't tell.

Being a task master, as one hundred percent of good teachers are, she planned a hasty retreat while talking…edging away ever so slightly…as he edged closer. Is he salivating?

Simultaneously, and just as she started to get up from her roller-chair, he made a leap for her, missed and caught her around her ankles. The chair rolled out from under and she fell hard on her butt, kicking swiftly up catching him under his chin as he fell to the floor.

At once there was too much commotion. The roller-chair banged on the desk, Schieter yelled after biting his tongue, and Nancy pounded loudly on the door.

"Oops." Gina gasped.

Shieter grabbed a silk handkerchief from his jacket pocket and dabbed away as blood ran down his chin.  After taking a sealed envelope from his desk with Gina's name on it, he shoved it toward her, motioned for her to leave, and slammed the door shut.

She took it and hastily retreated with Nancy at her heels.  "Good timing.  We're a team.  Thanks!"

While walking away, Gina opened the envelope and read her observation evaluation from Heleena.

"I thought you handled the situation well with the two girls who yelled very colorfully at each other.....blah, blah, blah....and I am so excited about the horseback ride in the Superstition Mountains in December...although I have never ridden before, I can hardly wait to go....."

Gina and Nancy moaned.

"Black mail."

"Extortion."

Before parting, Gina planned to pick up Nancy at five forty-five for "tonight's dog grooming adventure".

Much earlier in the day, Bing spotted a shiny new glassy-black Camry with dark tinted windows driving south on Cave Creek Road toward Carefree Highway.  And as planned, he made note of the license plate and called it in to Del Rio for referencing.  "I'll get back with you tonight," Del Rio said.

Bing called his other three friends about his find and they agreed that it was the only one they'd seen so far.  Perhaps the driver of this car was the one who teased Gina last Saturday night as she left the bakery at one in the morning.  Maybe the driver was the pervert and the tire stabber?

The four friends were adamant about solving the crimes and feeling important at the same time.  Tonight while helping Pop in the bakery, they agreed to analyze each other's clues, compare notes. They considered themselves 'justice-minded vigilantes'.

By five p.m. at the bakery, and after the high school teen had been helping Pop closely for one hour, he learned exactly why some of his baked goods were flops. The teen was a texting maniac. Periodically, she would open the oven door while the popovers were baking...they flattened. Ditto with the velvety rich cakes. She not only opened the oven door numerous times, but let the door bang back into place...fluffy cakes became pancakes.

Although he had explained over and over what to do and what not to do, he now realized that she really wasn't interested in the job. "She simply didn't care," he told others.

"I have to let you go," he said sadly that night. "My four retired friends are all the help I need at this time."

She looked at him briefly, and dutifully continued texting. "I'm ok with it." Next, she texted herself out the door without looking back.

To her friends, she texted a different message. "Now that I'm out of a job, I really need something exciting to do."

Pop was relieved that his problems had been solved, or so he thought.


Clouds were pushing each other around in the sky lazily as Gina, Nancy and Dixie headed north on Spur Cross Road with Nellie in the back seat wagging away. All three were dressed in old jeans and tees.

"If it rains or if Berty is not on schedule with her customers, we can't leave Nellie and then return later."

Gina continued, "Let's hope it doesn't take too long. I have mounds of paper work to do tonight, and I have to call parents."

After driving through the narrow opening of the boarded compound they saw a small group washing dogs outside on a cement slab. The slab led to a roll-up door leading to a building which they soon discovered housed the main grooming facilities.

The four teens, Cory, Cortez, Susie Lee and Darlene did not see them immediately and continued antics of throwing hands of soap back and forth on each other. When they recognized the Jeep and driver, the two boys scowled in dismay and turned their backs to them. The girls noticed nothing as they led their dogs to warm tubs of water that were nearby for rinsing.

Their un-popularity did not go unnoticed among the three. Fortunately, Berty walked out of the grooming building with a big wave. Her sleeves were rolled above her elbows; she wore a grey heavy neck-to-knees apron while a large cotton bandana secured her fly away hair from coming forward.

Motioning them over, "Velcome", she said loudly above the din of dogs yelping, barking and whining. She was alone in the building containing twelve wire kennels of multi-sized compartments used before and after the grooming process and all filled with dogs of every size. "You like my washing crew?" She talked loudly above the raucous as she pointed laughingly to the teens. The girls now noticing their arrival, waved and smiled. The boys scowled more angrily.

"I love zee Greyhounds. Berty made such a loving fuss over Nellie that the three now realized Pop's fear and decided not to let Nellie out of their sight.

"We're here to help," said Nancy as she and Dixie went inside.

Near the entrance was a desk camouflaged by piles of papers and machines for handling charge cards and cash. In the back were more wash tubs and tall stands used for grooming. Odors combined stale scents of mildew and wet dog hair.

Outside, Gina decided to turn the Jeep back around facing the entrance. As she sat in the Jeep before driving, she eye-balled a circular view of the place. To her amazement, the entire compound was boarded with six foot wooden vertical fencing. On her right where the teens now worked was the dog grooming facility with outdoor capability. Behind it was a long wire-fenced dog run filled with dogs running and playing.

Looking straight ahead she was facing a large circular open area, a half-acre dirt patio that was bordered with other buildings. She assumed the main house was the one on her left, and next to the main house was a smaller one with windows and curtains, probably the guest house.

On the other side of the patio and boarded with the same kind of wooden fencing, a hinged gate wide enough for a dually truck to enter, was half open and facing the patio. In her turn-around, she decided to drive straight toward the hinged gate, back up and then follow the circle forward toward the entrance to the entire compound. This plan with the Jeep facing the road would facilitate their departure.

As she drove her Jeep forward, she was too close to the hinged gate that was swung open and outward toward the patio, so she decided to get out and close the gate rather than back-up. Since there were boxes on the outside of the boarded area, she did not want to risk the chance of backing over something with her Jeep.

While closing the gate, she could not help but see inside the entire fenced area and its unbelievable contents. To her amazement, piles of trash represented a refuse area of leftovers from dumpsters and discards left whole from dump trucks. Boxes of every kind and shape did nothing to contain the loamy mounds of papers, clothing, broken pieces of machinery, boards, pieces of wire fencing, and all things that are discarded as of no use by the general public. Pile upon pile of trash was everywhere. Stale scents of stinking, fetid stuff became nauseating as she gaped, too mesmerized to move.

Shortly, the two boys came over and silently closed the gate. Not realizing the tenseness of the situation, she jumped and let out a small scream when she heard gravel crunch behind her on their approach. Questions and expressions of doubt glued to all three faces, as each took a deep breath inward and moved away.

Gina now cleared the fenced area and drove around the patio to the entrance. She sat in her Jeep puzzled by what she had just seen. What is going on here? Some of the crates that were spilled open on the trash heaps were in Berty's truck last Sunday when she was stuck. "Treasures for donation," she had said after looking at each piece lovingly. Now they were massed in a heap.

Was this an inner city dumping area unknown to her and others? Pilfering garbage does not make sense….so what does all this mean?

As the clouds disappeared, the end of the day seemed hotter and brighter. She re-applied sunscreen on her face as she sat there pondering, watching and waiting. Looking their way, she thought that the four teens seemed innocent in all their gaiety while soaping and brushing dogs. But ugly mask thoughts played around in her head violently and she wanted to confront them with questions even though Rick said to let him handle it.

Blinded by anger and the heat of the day, she was tempted to grab the bat she always carried near her on the front seat. *How dare a creepy pervert follow me into the bathroom! What were his intentions? It had to be one of those two boys over there, now having innocent fun. They lied about playing in the game.*

Gina swung out of the Jeep in a fury with the bat in her hand and landed flat on both feet in readiness. Feeling the urge of the attack mode, she was prepared to teach someone a lesson and to get some answers.

Simultaneously, Nancy grabbed the other end of the bat and abruptly shouted, "Lose your temper and you kick yourself in the ass."

Silence everywhere.

"Stop." She now talked quietly and calmly. "Take a deep breath. Let go of the bat."

Slowly, reluctantly, Gina let go but stared glaringly in the direction of the teens; the four by now stopped what they were doing to stare back while holding dripping arms away from their bodies.

"Leave it alone. We're done. Let's say our goodbyes and get out of here."

Gina got back in the Jeep still staring menacingly at the teens while they stood gaping. She practiced counting deep breaths in-and-out to the count of five before gaining composure. This was a trick that teachers had to learn when facing drugged or alcohol infused parents in their altered state of minds who pointed long-angry fingers in their direction.

Dixie and Nancy got in after Nellie who leaped in the back instantly. She was wagging away with a new bright pink ribbon tied around her neck like a champion, her long skinny tail wacking the seat loudly. Gina leaned over and kissed the dog's forehead, sort of a spell-breaker for her. "She sure looks happy," she whispered in a collected state of mind.

Berty, who was cleaning things in the grooming compound had missed the commotion as she now came walking out to say goodbye. "Come back again any time." She waved and smiled broadly. Her clothes askew, with one sleeve above her elbow and the other at her wrist, she was a frightening figure. Thick grey hair seemed to rove in different directions as she stood shifting from one foot to another like a friendly giant waving goodbye.

"She's lonely," said Dixie as they drove away. "We need to invite her and her boyfriend over for tacos or something, someday."

"What boyfriend? What did you two learn while grooming Nellie?"

"Her boyfriend lives in the apartment next to her house. That's all she talked about," said Nancy. "I guess he works nights. And why did you lose your temper? You haven't done that in years…like the time we were having a party that you thought was a Halloween party so you were the only one who showed up in a costume…an ugly witch as a matter of fact."

They looked at each other and howled with laughter.

"Hey watch your driving," yelled Dixie as Gina drove off the edge of the road a foot.

"I need to explain." Gina then told them about the trash dump, the fetid smell, and the mysterious look on the two boys' faces. "You know, they seemed as puzzled about the heap of trash as I was. Nevertheless, the scene was ugly and reminded me of last Friday night."

"Brad is the one that we need to talk to about this. Maybe he's right when he said that she's a hoarder. He's an ex-marine you know."

They both sighed as they drove silently along. Nellie lay on the back seat tuckered out with eyes closed, twitching a dream.

"What in the F....was that all about?" Cory began ranting to the other three. "Ms. Mack was ready to attack us like a crazy person." He dumped the fetid water from the tub and started drying the big collie with a long towel.

"Something really weird is happening," said Darlene while holding the dog by his leash rope. "Mr. Cloud asked me where I got the earring that was on my mask. How would he have seen it? Why would he want to know?"

"Did you tell him that I gave it to you, and that I got it from my aunt?" He took two brushes from a nearby shelf and gave one to Darlene.

"Yes, and he said that someone has the mate to it." Action stopped as they stared at each other.

"What the fudge-cake," said Cory as everyone looked puzzled. "My aunt told me she lost it out on the desert."

"And why is my mask missing? I have to write a full description of it for Ms. Painter. She's going to help me make a new one for full credit if mine is not found," whined Susie Lee as she threw a scrub brush in the tub of water. "I want my original."

"G-good deal. You'll g-get full credit."

Susie glared at Cortez. "Ok, where is it. You only stutter when you're upset or guilty of something."

Cory intervened. "Damn it Cortez. Tell her the truth…NOW!"

A meeting was held by all in Pop's kitchen Tuesday night. Each had something to say as Dixie detailed everything again on her long yellow note pad.

Pop told how the teen's texting caused his baked goods to flop; Gina described her encounter with the principal and especially the kick to the chin; Dixie and Nancy explained the dog grooming process and while describing the facility, Gina interrupted with her description of the hidden 'dump' that she saw first hand.

Brad shook his head up and down. "I had a strong premonition; I still think like a Marine."

"What about the license plate I called in to you?" Bing looked at Rick who had been sitting there quietly listening to everyone.

He reached for his glass of beer and didn't answer for awhile, keeping everyone's attention for a full minute.

"It belongs to the Zander family."

"Hah, I knew it."

Rick looked over at Gina. "Now, let's not get out of hand. Let me investigate. There's a lot I'm working on."

"Is there anything we missed before we quit?" Pop yawned and pushed away from the table. "Tomorrow morning comes awfully early and I'm going to ask for extra help with the girl gone."

"We'll cover." The four retired friends mumbled as they got up to leave.

Everyone parted leaving Rick and Gina sitting there alone. "What's this bat business?"

"Are you going to pick on me?" She leaned back and folded her arms.

"Always." He played with his empty glass thumping it on the table a half grin building on his face.

"You and the bad guys." She leaned over and tipped the back of his hat up so the front covered his eyes.

"There is a difference."

"Prove it!"

That's all she needed to say.

# CHAPTER SEVENTEEN
Wednesday, October 19

The four teens, Cortez and Susie Lee, Cory and Darlene, arrived at seven in front of Becky Painter's classroom door, the earliest time that they could possibly get there. Cortez made the rounds picking up the other three with the black Camry--since his dad left earlier in the company work truck--but planned to return it before he got home from work to avoid a confrontation.

Fortunately, the Commercial Art's Building was opened by security at six-thirty as were all other buildings on campus. Many students arrived early for make-up work and most teachers liked to be at their desks in preparation for classes. And generally there was a large group of regulars milling around at the outdoor lunch patio, dropped off by parents leaving very early for work needing the convenience of the school as a morning sitter.

Becky was a little stunned to see the four when she arrived in the building to open her door; but thankful for having been prepared in advance about the missing mask and the mysterious earring, she kept her composure.

"Can we talk to you for a few minutes?" Susie started, "Cortez has something to tell you."

A bundle of nerves, he shifted his feet and could not stand still as he talked. The others stood anchored grabbing at their heavy back packs shifting them over their shoulders for comfort, and eager to leave when the warning bell sounded.

"I t-took Susie's mask to do some more work on it to s-surprise her and was going to bring it back the next morning....but it got stolen from my car." He looked down at the floor and kicked the toe of his boot in the carpet as he stammered.

"What? Do you have any idea as to who might have taken it?" Becky Painted was astounded by a new twist in the mystery and could hardly wait to call Gina and Nancy.

"Not at all!" He too shifted his back pack and looked at the others for support.

"You need to back-track and think of all the places you went with the mask in your car." Since Becky knew that the mask was now in a safe place in Del Rio's hands, she busied herself by moving items in the room and placing her morning mail on her desk, anything to keep from facing them.

"I'm giving Susie Lee full credit and she and I are going to work on another one today or tomorrow after school."

The four looked content as Susie said that she could meet with her today since the judging was to be tomorrow.

""As soon as I take my dad's car home, I'll be back to help. I f-feel responsible."

"It's a plan. See you after school."

127

Becky could hardly wait to talk to Gina with all of the new details and she was eager to know the results of this mystery. Next, she went to her small un-locked closet to get her white long wrap-around painter's apron. As she put her hand in the pocket to drop her room keys, she felt something. The earring from the mask was there. Had she taken it off the mask and absent mindedly put it in her pocket for safe keeping? Quickly, she walked over to Darlene's mask. The earring was gone.

With all of the commotion that happened yesterday, could she have been distracted? Seriously doubting that she had taken it off the mask, she now distinctly remembered looking at it gleaming in the sun-light under the window as she closed and locked her door before leaving school.

With the bell ten minutes away from ringing, she would have to keep this mystery a secret until later…or would she? She quickly went to her locked desk drawer where she kept her purse and put the earring in a side pocket for safe keeping. Next, she decided to go to the front office to collect her daily memos and hopefully see Gina or Nancy.

Gina arrived to a school that looked like it was in transition from general routine Western to a throbbing, exciting African continent. African drum music was playing somewhere; kids were dancing, marching or gyrating…she couldn't tell the difference…everywhere. It was group against group, a soon to be contest with many prizes.

As kids looked her way, she stomped her gold sandals on the concrete in some kind of mock dance and twirled around in her white dress. She too chose to wear long wooden earrings and matching bead sets, looking as African as possible, following the mode.

Some kids smiled, laughed and pointed while others did nothing but stare with their hands in their pockets. Not to be out-danced, they quickly circled around her, dancing to the beat. She retreated immediately a bit embarrassed. And with a wave of her hand, "You're too good for me!"

This is what took place around the perimeter of the large parking lot. When she arrived through the back doors into the office, it was a different scene.

Long faces were pushing papers at desks and near computers. A perception of heaviness permeated in the soundless office. As a scary quietness prevailed, no one looked her way in the usual cheery morning greeting so she walked over to Dixie for answers.

Dixie was busy jamming different colored office memos into teacher's mail boxes and had her back turned away from the entrance. Many wooden beaded bracelets clanged together as she gathered papers from a plastic carton to thrust into mail-boxes.

"Ok, who died?" Gina squeezed past Dixie to retrieve her mail.

"Look out the front window."

Two cop cars, Del Rio and other officers were grouped together writing notes on pads of papers and talking. Other personnel were standing around that she did not recognize.

"What's going on? Where's the principal?"

"He hasn't arrived yet. Or, as I heard, he may not show-up."

"What?"

"Just take a walk around campus and tell me what you see that's different."

129

"Gina." Becky was walking toward her on her way to the mail box. "Guess what I found in my apron pocket." She looked a little pale as she spoke.

"I'm afraid to ask."

"The earring that was on-the-mask when I left school yesterday afternoon." She spoke slowly for emphasis and stared wide-eyed.

Dixie, who was listening, quickly pulled out her large yellow writing pad from the shelf where she stood and made note of the new mystery.

"What is the motive?" Gina looked at the two women for answers. "Why would someone do that?"

"Sounds like we have a psycho playing games. But why?" Dixie kept her voice low as she spoke. "We need to share all these new happenings with the group and see what we get."

Three teachers came walking through the door mumbling.

"What a mess."

"Who do you think was responsible for everything?"

"We know why...."

Gina and Becky looked at each other, grabbed their bags of papers and left the office to walk around campus and to their rooms.

Their first stop was near the out door patio where a small group was looking stunned at the chained vending machine. VOODOO PHANTOM was printed in large, red, cryptic letters on the front and two sides.

"What about the other two vending machines, one near the gym and one over by the science building?" Gina asked some kids that she knew from her classes.

"Exactly the same. That'll teach the principal to not chain our beverage machines," said a kid with a tattoo on his forearm of un-identifiable letters and reeking heavily of smoke. A long wooden fetish earring hung from one pierced ear.

"Speaking of the principal, where is he?" asked a girl. "He needs to see what he caused." As she grimaced and grumbled with complaints, others joined in.

"The drinking fountains barely work and when they do, the water is hot."

Gina and Becky, now joined by Nancy, just stood there listening. They had mysterious secrets of their own.

"What about the beverage machine in the cafeteria?" someone asked.

"It's painted too."

"But, I thought that the cafeteria was locked. How could someone get in there?" asked another.

"What happened to security?"

"Where is security?"

"This should all be on security cameras."

Gina stood staring and shaking her head at the same time. "Nancy, what do you see that is very familiar?"

"The cryptic lettering." She looked over at Becky. "It's the same as some lettering that Gina found on a note-pad."

"Right now, that's the popular style. How can we relate it to one person?" Becky shifted her heavy bag of papers and supplies to her other shoulder.

"I can relate it to someone in my sixth hour class. That narrows it down considerably," said Gina.

As the first period warning bell rang, the three teachers left for their classes after deciding to 'keep in touch' and double checking cell phone numbers.

"Anything new, we talk after school."

The office secretaries were in a quandary wondering why they had not heard from Dr. Shieter. "I'm sure he knows about the beverage machines," said one.

"Maybe he's responsible," said another causing laughter.

At approximately ten a.m. Dr. Shieter arrived and parked in his regular spot. Dixie was the first one to notice. Because of her loud gasping noise, others came to the front of the office to gape, looking out the large glass doors that faced the parking lot.

"Uh, oh no!" A hand to the face.

"Who could have done that?" A loud gasping whisper.

"That's awful!" A negative click of the tongue.

VOODOO PHANTOM in one foot tall, blood-red lettering was legibly printed on both sides and hood of his new BMW.

CHAPTER EIGHTEEN
Wednesday, October 19

Dr. Shieter scurried in afflicted with a cantankerous attitude, his tie looking a little too choked under pinkish flab   It was noted by all that his face was as red as the lettering on his car, with the exception of the heavy white bandage on his chin. Some of the ladies in the front office became extra busy feigning paper work; some faked a phone call; some seemed to step in place, but all had time to sneak a peak.

Trailing him were Del Rio, Colt and two other plain clothed cops.  No one said a word as the door was quietly closed.

"Let the excitement begin," said Dixie loud enough for all to hear.

"Amen," someone mumbled.

As the day progressed, students were unusually quiet in classes and out.  An aura of mystery hung on campus like a low dark cloud on a rare rainy day.

Students huddling together in small whispering groups, ducked and turned their backs when teachers walked by. Different types of groups who didn't usually talk with each other, were now conversing like blood brothers.

"They know who did it," said Rich while having lunch with Gina and Nancy. "I can feel it in the air….like a voodoo omen," he taunted. "We'll all find the answer soon because of teen gossip...faster than radar. You need to ask Del Rio about all the closed door talk," he next said to Gina as he bit into his ham sandwich. "I can just see Dixie's list getting longer and longer."

"He won't tell me much." She drained the last of her bottle of Mexican coke cola and rolled the top of her bag of chips down before adding a rubber band around the remaining package.

"Squeeze it out of him," said Nancy while dumping crumbs from her lunch bag into the trash. "Colt is a good friend of mine. I'll press him for answers too or at least an attitude."

"I just can't believe Cortez's story that the mask was stolen from the back seat of his car." Then pushing away from the table Rich added, "Well, I guess I can. Most teens are irresponsible and it's been so blistering hot for too long into October that we're all afraid to roll up the windows."

"Gina, you need to try and remember the voice of the pervert last Friday when you sprayed him. Was it a young person or an older man?" Nancy was persistent.

"I know, I know. I really keep trying. It's too impossible. I think that we both yelled as I threw the spray can on the floor and turned and ran out the door."

"You should have attacked him with your bat."

"Hah!" they laughed.

"I'm missing something," said Rich looking at the two of them. "Anyway, what's going on with the four B's? Since Bing discovered the black Camry I hope he's keeping his eyes on it. Maybe it might lead us to some answers."

"Cortez and his dad drive it. Bing needs to find out who uses it and when." Gina got up to leave as the bell rang. "In my next class, I'm going to quiz Jamie and Kim about a few things. Normally, they're pretty good at telling me what's going on without giving names."

"Everyone stay in touch," said Nancy with a pointed finger, her usual last words.

Sixth hour after-lunch-bunch came jiggling in as usual from over exerting during lunch. Chatting away, they made loud noises while opening their back packs, getting their supplies ready to begin writing, and scooting their bums into their desks. Daily and weekly assignments were always listed on the board and they liked this routine.

Work for today was a questions and answers handout with blanks for fill-ins pertaining to previous African lectures with emphasis on Voodoo.

"Use your notes and especially remember to use some of these new words in your limericks. After you turn in your handout, you need to work on limericks. Don't forget to pick a number," and she pulled out her paper roll of ticket numbers from the top drawer of her desk. Next, she took out the block of wood with the nail sticking-up. Piercing the used numbers as she collected them was full-fledged amusement.

Everyone loved this method of teacher-student contact for help and especially liked to stick their paper number on the nail. "If I don't get to your number before the bell rings, I'll begin with yours tomorrow."

They pranced to the front to pick a number for her to call out in turn. "You're my special class," she always told them and remembered to lower her voice so that they would lower theirs.

Cortez, in the back of the class where he sat, had his math book open on his lap and worked problems while pretending to fill in answers to today's handout.

Gina saw him copying answers from a student's desk sitting next to him but decided to leave him alone. She needed to call his parents today after school anyway, and this would be one more item on the list.

When she walked by he leaned forward closer to his desk to hide his math book. "Are you going to work on the new mask with Susie today?" Any kind of contact was good to dampen the friction that she always felt when near him.

"Yeah." He pretended to be interested in his answer sheet.

"Good plan," and she walked on after noticing the cryptic design of his name. It was the kind of popular lettering she was used to by now considering this signature was the style of several students. She was sure that it was Cortez who wrote the word BLOOD on her note pad since she hadn't noticed it previously from the earlier classes.

Across the room Jamie Mink and Kim Rose were having a laughing good time helping each other with their limericks, reading them aloud boisterously. "I'm going to win," said Jamie tauntingly.

"No, mine's better," said Kim waving her paper in the air. "Ms Mack, come and choose."

"Gee, you two are having so much fun, we need to do this more often." She folded her arms and nodded.

"'NO!" They yelled in unison.

"Let's see what you've got."

Before she could read one, and since it was near the end of the period, the class was interrupted by the principal's announcement. He spoke slowly with tedium.

"By now, I am sure that each and every student on campus is aware of the terrible state of affairs.

Today, vandals made negative choices on campus and on my car and I am irritated beyond repair.

Indubitably, this kind of conduct can not go unpunished.

Therefore, I WILL cancel all next week's African activities, including the homecoming parade unless the perpetrator comes forward. YOU---and you know who you are-- have until Friday."

# CHAPTER NINETEEN

The students sat dazed and looked at each other in a slow motion reaction, stunned by the announcement. They stared around the room to compare attitudes. A few mouthed the word 'indubitably' in mockery and made snarly faces.

Then the commotion began.

"What about the dance and music preparations?"

"The entire town is involved."

"Long distance runners have been practicing daily for weeks."

"He can't do this to us."

"I have family coming from out of town."

"Home-Ec has been cooking African menus and sewing costumes for the parade."

They ranted and snarled for the last couple minutes before the bell rang looking at Gina for answers who just stood there with arms folded, shaking her head and shrugging shoulders.

All were actively riled except for Cortez who simply shifted in his seat quietly then leaned back in his desk in a relaxed trance until the bell sounded.

All crowded out of the room in a fury to shout down the hallway in one big commotion, pushing and shoving.

All except Jamie Mink and Kim Rose. "Well, this is a sorry predicament," Kim uttered while wrinkling her freckled nose and twisting her mouth.

"Yeah, what about the cookbooks we've been finishing in Home-Ec?" Jamie's eyes seemed rounder as she stared at Gina who was now gathering her things off the desk to make room for the seventh period teacher Jennifer, coming in to teach.

"Let's go talk in the hall." As the two girls followed her out they couldn't help noticing the anger of new students coming into the room. Books were slammed noisily on top of desks, each teen talking on a cell phone, all complaining loudly to whomever--- permissible until the bell rang.

"Ok girls. What have you seen that is different?" She started walking toward the English Office as the two followed. "My notebook----with the cryptic word BLOOD written in red----surely you can relate it to someone. I showed you the wording yesterday. Think about it. It had to have happened in my sixth hour class." And then in a whispered tone, "Who else besides Cortez writes cryptic in our class?" She stopped in the now empty hallway and starred at them for an answer.

As the warning bell rang, Gina wrote them passes to their seventh period class to avoid tardies.

Kim said as they started to walk away, "We'll work on it." They left while whispering to each other.

Gina and Nancy met in the English Office which was now vacant since all others were in noisy rooms teaching the last class of the day. With books open and papers before them untouched, they sat sipping a coke and root beer while staring in space recollecting thoughts of the day's happenings.

"Where is the connection," Nancy began, "between the spray painting and the earring?"

"Security has been breached. I want to know what the cameras caught, if anything."

"What if the vandal or vandals knew how to eliminate the security system all together? That would account for access into Becky's room."

"Get all the information you can from Del Rio and make sure Dixie makes a list of all the circumstances like she enjoys doing. Maybe we can narrow it down to the pervert."

Gina shuttered at the thought. "Remember, tomorrow we judge the masks. Cortez is supposed to help Susie with hers today after school, if he gets his dad's car. He said that he had to wait until he got home from work. Which reminds me; I need to call Cortez's dad about the low grade."


"I need to come talk to you after school in person," grumbled Mr. Zander in a low throaty voice over the phone after Gina started to explain Cortez's dilemma. "This won't do," he blurted out.

Gina rolled her eyes and frowned after remembering with revulsion the ugly encounter when he entered her classroom a few days ago with his grey flannel shorts reaching up into his butt cheeks. "But, but...," she babbled.

"I'll see you around four." Click!

Immediately she phoned Del Rio but could only leave a message while quickly recapping the events of the day ending with…"and Mr. Zander, Cortez's dad, is coming to my room at four."

Next, she decided to contact her two best friends to learn where they would be at four.

"I have a doctor's appointment at three-thirty," said Nancy. But Richard Cloud said, "I'll be here working and I'll check on you at four-fifteen."

Since the high school campus became a mini ghost town by three-thirty, she was thankful for the few others who remained around school. Teachers who had to stay late in their rooms for unknown reasons needed the feeling of safeness. They usually checked-in with others who were still around, left their doors open and kept radios playing softly for company. Most everyone else scurried out after the last bell to work in the comfy confines of home for many long hours with their computers.

However, the small few who were always working late because it was their job, kept the school humming.

Such it was with the coaches out on the fields and the few administrators in the front office who needed to talk with parents. Their after hours were late. Nevertheless, the school always seemed haunted to Gina. People were in the confines of their rooms or 'way' out on the fields.

Unfortunately, this time of the day, gates were wide open to intruders. Lone security this time of the day consisted of Tommy the non-communicator, scooting around on his quad. Generally, he hid in the custodian's garage. Dr. Shieter had been tough with him, but to no avail. "Keep your cell phone turned on at all times and fully charged!" Usually, Tommy left it some place and couldn't remember where.

Gina decided to contact Guy as a back-up plan. After all, he too was responsible concerning Cortez's football-game-playing credentials.

Easy to contact, since he had given her his cell number earlier, she was relieved that he was around. "I'll be following my cross country runners close to the school at about that time, and I'll check on you."

She had described to Guy his appearance earlier when he entered her class with Cortez's permission slip.

"It takes all types," he had said then.

On her 'to-do' list of jobs for today was to make copies of the Superstition Mountains Trail ride permission slips just in case she needed another list for referencing at home. Thankfully, the office machine was still humming, never turned off at the end of the day and she was able to complete the task in minutes.

After putting the copies in her take home bag, she stacked the originals on her desk for alphabetizing, reviewing the names and grade status of the riders and making sure that Jamie Mink and Kim Rose had completed their slips with signatures of all the appropriate parties. The district was so particular she couldn't miss a thing and ruin someone's fun.

Three-fifteen....She needed some deep-dark chocolate, and the stash behind her desk was empty. Not a good time to be without chocolate. She grabbed her purse, left her room door open, and dashed out too the parking lot to her Jeep. A convenience store was closer than Pop's bakery so she selected a quick fifteen minute round trip.

Driving a short-cut through a side street back to school, she passed Mr. Hollywood stopped on the side of the road in a roadster that she could not identify. Of course, the top was down, his chest was bare, but this time he was making out with someone sitting next to him.

In passing, she saw Berty's huge hand wrapped around his neck in a passionate embrace. The sky could fall; they wouldn't know. She too was bare shouldered in a breast covering red tunic. A long flashing earring dangled at her one ear that Gina could see. The other earring was probably tangled in his long chest hairs.

*Good for Berty!*

Looking in her rear view mirror as she drove passed, she could see runners coming this way about a half mile back. Fun view for cross country!

Pulling into the faculty parking lot she noticed a van logoed 'Security Stops Crime!' She thought this so appropriately related to all the happenings and perhaps the vandals would be found after all. She also wondered if Del Rio was in the principal's office having a meeting with security and knew that she would definitely harass him tonight for answers.

Three-thirty.... A list clicked in her head: Go to classroom, finish semi-melted chocolate, call Becky on room phone to check on the two mask makers, wait for Mr. Zander.

Her door was closed, but she had left it open when she went to the store. Maybe Tommy the custodian-security had straightened her room and closed the door thinking she had gone for the day.

She opened the door and was ready to swing it wide to catch the door peg that kept it secure, when a hand grabbed the door and a wide face reeking of alcohol smiled down at her. "Let's close the door for privacy," Mr. Zander panted, or so it seemed to her as he closed the door almost forcibly.

Dressed in a tired looking white uniform with the logo 'Security Stops Crime' embroidered on his shirt, stood Mr. Zander staring at her too long. Shirt tails hung loose over his rounded form and his pants looked a size too large as the cuffs bagged at the ankles almost hiding his work boots.

"Ok, tell me about Cortez; the little bugger not doing his homework?" He smiled at his coined cutesy remark, reeled and leaned on a student's desk for support.

She turned toward her desk to move away from him.

He came closer approaching her at her desk leaving her almost no space in which to move.

Since her desk and computer were tucked in a corner opposite the entrance, she quickly determined to station herself near the door rather than keep him between door and desk. Looking at the wall clock, she said, "You're thirty minutes early. Since I didn't expect you until four, I haven't had time to make a copy of his missing assignments. I'll go do that now." Taking the paper to be copied off her desk, she attempted to squeeze by him in a hasty retreat. Since there were thirty-eight desks in the room, she would have to maneuver around them, and him.

He stepped in front of her with a loud belch.

"S'cuse me." Now blocking her way to the entrance, he busied himself by fishing in his pocket for something. His expression was blank as he stared at her. Or, was it more of a glare, a contemptuous grin.

She backed away planning her flight.

He pulled out a handful of wadded bills. "The money for the trail ride." Handing the money to her in pieces, he made a continuous point of counting-out each amount slowly while holding her around one wrist as he put the bills in her hand. His hand was huge and his grip was tightly authoritative. She felt his fat, long fingers wrap around her wrist twice.

And twice she tried to gently pull away as her heart began to thump slowly, inadvertently feeling panic. Ready to go for the groin, she planted her feet steady. In the middle of her long skinny legs were pointy knees, one ready as a weapon.

"Relax, I'm still counting," he roughly said as he smiled wolfishly tightening his grip. Suddenly he began to sway. Staggering back he tried to pull her toward him for balance. She wrenched her arm away and was clear of him as he stepped back, leaned heavily on a student desk and toppled with it noisily to the floor.

Hustling to the entrance, Gina opened the door permanently with the floor peg. No one was around. The hallway looked ominously empty. Where was Rich?

Spooky!

Looking at the wall clock, it was only three forty-five and she needed him to leave.

Standing in the hallway she now felt safe. "Are you all right?" She sort of yelled, trying to be consoling as she looked at him sitting on the floor by the desks. Leaning on one hand, he turned toward her with a glazed stare.

"Can you come help me?" With a new lingering look, he faked a countenance of weakness, a mood that seesawed from vile aggression to that of a pup.

"No! I'll go get help." She stood in the doorway ready to run if he should get up quickly. And before leaving, "Tomorrow I'll put Cortez's record in the mail so you can review his missing assignments."

No answer.

"Helloooo Mr. Zander." Loudly making noise she pounded on the door for attention.

Like a devious cat, he jumped up from where he was sitting pretending to make a dash in her direction to scare her, stomping his feet, moving only inches.

While running without looking back, she could hear his fiendish laughter all the way down the hallway. She hit the outside doors running and didn't stop until she was near the office and saw Richard/Raquel hurrying toward her. "Rich, where have you been?" She wailed.

As the two talked, Zander stealthily left the building, got into his van and drove away.

"I'll walk you back to your room, and if you're ready to leave, I'll walk you to your Jeep." Rich added with concern, "We'll have to be more vigilant as the situation progresses. I'm sure he's gone by now, but I'm dialing the front office for security."

Driving away, she rang Becky Painter's room.

No answer.

Next, she called her cell and learned that Cortez and Susie Lee had worked one hour on the mask and had finished.

The two teachers agreed that he had assumed some kind of responsibility which was "a good thing".

"Did you discuss with them the spray painting of the vending machines and the principal's car?"

"Yes, but you and I both know how students can professionally fake innocence." said Becky. "And the earring that was moved to the pocket of my work apron, they knew nothing."

"It didn't walk there by itself." And then trying to be funny, "Maybe one of the masks is putting a 'Hex' on your room."

"Hah! That would be an easy answer."

146

"Who knows what we'll discover tomorrow when we arrive at school. Tomorrow is Thursday, and Nancy and I will be in your room immediately after the last bell rings to judge the masks."

"I'll have them all laid out for you. Keep in touch. I'm curious about all the mysteries."

After they finished talking, Gina decided that she would tell Becky later about her encounter with Mr. Zander. Enough was enough and she was too emotionally drained at the moment. But when she rang Nancy, it was a different situation.

"That was the time to lose that ass kicking temper you have," said Nancy. Then she added, "Tomorrow while we're judging the masks, be sure to tell me all that you learn from Rick. I'm curious as to what the principal thinks….and what the security cameras caught."

Among her worries as she drove home was the stack of original permission slips that she had carelessly left on top of her desk. *I hope those jewels are still there.* She trusted no one considering the strange happenings from the last six days…. since last Friday as a matter of fact, and was furious with herself for not checking before leaving. The permission slips and insurance waivers contained a special stamp from the district, a seal of approval, irreplaceable originals.

Dixie rang. "Where are you? How close to home are you?" Her voice was desperate and anxious as she now shouted, "Nellie is missing."

## CHAPTER TWENTY

"Oh no!" Was Gina's reply to Dixie as she shouted back. "When? How?"

"When I got home, I found the gate to the property open. After Nellie gets out of the doggie door in the house, you know how she loves to roam around."

Gina noted the high pitch in Dixie's voice, anxiety building to tears. "I'll watch along the roadside as I drive. Don't worry. When I get home we'll search everywhere. Alert everybody." Of course everybody included the four B's…. and their new lady friends.

After Gina quickly changed into comfy clothes…. shorts, tank, hiking boots, baseball cap…. she joined Dixie walking around the property and along the wide wash that sided their place. They carried their cell phones and walked in opposite directions…calling and calling the Greyhound's name.

Within an hour, more people were involved in the search as friends, family and neighbors became concerned. People called people for help.

Pop called all the local veterinarians and dog-lover habitats in Cave Creek and Carefree. "Yes," he informed them, "she has an identity chip in her ear."

Nothing....Two hours went by as the search became more frantic and the end of the day became hotter.

The main worry was the heat. The third week in October was a scorcher. The desert around the entire radius of the two towns was unkind...notably advancing to one hundred-five and up. The Greyhound needed water.

The men were on their cycles covering the washes slowly....everywhere.

When Gina called Del Rio for help, he said "I'll get there as soon as I can. I'm busy working on something right now with Deli...."

Great! She clicked off and decided to walk back to the property's entrance to check for any notable paw prints. She stooped down, putting her hands on her now tired knees for a good survey low to the ground. Near the corner where the gate attached to a pole, was a small yellow piece of note paper, half hidden inside a tired looking Brittle bush.

"I have your dog. I saw her roaming around your property and feared Bobcats.... Berty."

Gina was both comforted and angry. She noted that the paper had a hole in it where Berty had attached it to the gate earlier...carelessly. *Doesn't she know about the daily slow desert winds?* Immediately, she called Dixie who would relate the message, sort of start the chain reaction like a domino effect.

Pop was happy....then angry....happy.....then livid. "Is she a crazy woman or what?" He sighed from exhaustion, wiped sweat from around his neck with the huge bandana he always kept in his pocket, and became immediately more jovial. "Everybody to my house for cold drinks," he shouted. Dixie started the happy message via chain of friends.

Next, she and Gina piled into the Jeep Wrangler to head over to Berty's. They decided to keep the windows down to let the warm desert air dry their sweaty bodies and soaked hair.

"What nerve," Gina began, "to enter someone's property and snatch a favorite pet. Where is her mind?"

"Let's not complain until Nellie is in our Jeep."

"The note also said 'pictures'. I wonder what she meant by that?" Gina proceeded to tell Dixie what she saw earlier in the day when she went on her chocolate break while waiting for Mr. Zander.

The parked roadster...the two lovers...

"Good for them!" Dixie almost cackled. "We all need romance....anyway, anywhere we can get it."

"Humph..."

"Don't worry about Del Rio. He has an important agenda right now."

"I wonder if all the crazy events are connected to one person or a couple?" She next told Dixie about her 'match' with Mr. Zander after school.

"Sounds like he was more interested in his son's teacher than in his son."

"What else is new? Changing the subject, I hope the four B's will be ready to judge all the limericks that I collect on Friday...from two classes...that's seventy. I'll be busy grading the biographies from the Western Literature classes."

"Remember, they have new girlfriends that are ready to help." Dixie added, "I wonder if Shieter is going to keep his word and cancel all the African events if the perpetrator or plural...doesn't come forward?"

"Considering all the city wide publicity about the popular African week end, he wouldn't dare."


Seeing that the gates to the boarded compound were padlocked, Gina got out her cell and called Berty.

No response.

"She might be washing dogs with the radio on and can't hear her cell. Try her home phone and maybe Cory will answer."

No response.

The two decided to get out of the Jeep and look around for any action or noise. "Nellie...Nellleee...," they called.

They heard a chain rattle and a dog frantically starting to bark non-stop.

"That's her."

They called again.

Same response.

"Ok, ok, this is what we do." She pointed all fingers in the air for emphasis. "I'll drive the Jeep sideways next to the tall gate, get on the roof and climb over."

Dixie had to 'cuff-a-laugh'. "Yes, wonder woman. Are you going to throw the dog over the gate or jump back over with her in your arms? It's close to six p.m. and Berty might be coming home soon from her 'desert safari'. We could just wait for her to take the padlock off the gate."

"And listen to Nellie cry and bark? We can do this. I'll find something to stand on from the other side. She has crates of junk everywhere."

Standing on the roof of her Jeep, Gina grabbed the top edge of the gate and hoisted one leg up. She was now straddling the fence. "Ouch!"

Using her hands and arms to lift her body weight slightly, she maneuvered over the fence and jumped down on the other side.

"Nobody's here," she yelled back to Dixie. "The only light I see is one in the guest house. I think that someone is looking at me through a curtain." The cloth was drawn back a few inches with the edge of a hand.

"Get the dog and let's vamoose. This place is too weird." After waiting for only five minutes, Dixie lost patience. "Gina….Gina….Talk to me!"

Although Nellie was tethered to a heavy porch bench, she wiggled so vibrantly when she saw Gina that she pulled the bench a few feet while heading toward her.

"Hi girl! Just what I need…a bench."

"Helloooo," yelled Dixie.

"I'm crawling over. Be ready to get Nellie when I hand her to you." Not having to look far, she found a heavy wooden crate that fit tightly on top of the bench. Grunting and groaning, she pulled the bench next to the fence, crate and all. Next, she shoved it around to encourage a steady structure, and to determine the tightness of the crate.

"Ok. Here we come. Get ready."

"I'm trying," said Dixie who very gingerly crawled from hood to roof. She stood slowly, wobbling from where she was kneeling and walked her hands up the boards to the top edge where she now clung for balance.

"Don't look down." Gina yelled.

"Oh great!"

"Here we come."

Thankfully the crate was wide enough to hold a person and a dog in balance, at least for a few minutes.

With her arms around the dog's chest, she started lifting her to the top edge. "She's heavy." Gasping while bumping the gate with both of their bodies, she was able to lift Nellie to a good over-the-gate position.

From the other side, Dixie saw a snout and wild eyes cradled between two paws as Nellie scratched with her back legs climbing the wooden boards in fright.

"I've got her front." Dixie put her hands under the dog's chest, right behind her front legs.

"I'm lifting her back side." Gina put her hands on the Greyhound's back hips and helped her scratch her way over the gate to Dixie.

With a leap and a toot, the dog jumped on Dixie who held her tightly as they both fell on their sides, still on top of the Jeep. "Oomph!"

"Everyone ok?" Gina yelled from the other side.

"We're fine." Dixie and Nellie crawled down onto the hood and then jumped to the ground. "I'm putting her in the Jeep right away. Are you able to get back?"

"I can do this. I need a second crate so I'll be higher."

Since it was getting dark, she thought she heard noises way out back in all of the rubbish. *Rats!* Finding a crate nearby, close in size to the one she had stacked on the bench, she was able to position it solidly.

Crawling on top, she felt whipped with tiredness as she put one foot over the gate, grabbed the edge with both of her hands and pulled herself up...and almost over. Now lying on the top edge in a half-straddle, and too weak to jump down onto the roof of the Jeep, she started to giggle loudly as she put her face on her hands.

"I think I'll stay here all night."

153

"What are you doing?" Del Rio stood at the front of the Jeep with his arms folded.

"I'm planting flowers."

"There's one in every crowd." In seconds he was on top of the Jeep like a bear, grabbing her around her waist lifting her off the gate and onto the roof.

"My hero," she snickered.

"Hero my foot!" He jumped from roof to ground and motioned for her to follow.

While carefully crawling down to the ground with his help, she asked, "How did you know we were here?"

"Radar."

"That your patent answer?"

"It works."

"Let's get Nellie home," he continued. "I'll drive since you're shaking."

She looked at her hands. He was correct. "We had quite a difficult task that we accomplished, I'm proud to say."

He backed the Jeep a few feet away from the gate and said before getting out, "Watch this." Next, he went to the padlock, gently pulled down on it, lifted it and opened the gate wide.

"Smart ass," she said.

"Double from me." Dixie winced.

"All you had to do was check the lock."

"Well, I hope you're amused!"

"Very."

Nellie was already asleep with her head on Dixie's lap before they reached home. Pop was so excited to have his dog back, he carried her into the house and put her on her dog pad.

"I need a long hot shower followed by a foot rub," murmured Dixie as she left the kitchen with a slight limp and a waddle.

"This whole episode was too uncanny," Pop began. "The fact that Berty can come on private property and do whatever she wants, is illegal. We wore ourselves out in this heat while frantically looking for our dog. Thankfully, she was gracious enough to leave a note."

The three of them sat at the kitchen table and went over the events of the day, connecting them to the other mysteries.

Rick began, "I'll talk with Zander and warn him about coming on campus drunk."

"Is he part of the school's security system?" Gina asked.

"No."

"But, he knows how to break into any security system," added Pop.

"Maybe."

"What did Shieter say about all the spray painting? The front office girls said that you and other officers talked with him all morning."

Rick sighed, shuffled down in his chair and said, "You really don't want to know."

"Well, do you think he'll be true to his word on Friday?"

"He's determined."

"I'm going to bed," said Pop. "Tomorrow is Thursday and the start of the week end demands for bakery goods." He tiredly shuffled off.

"Berty called hours ago to tell me that the gate was unlocked so that you could go in and get Nellie easily." His face formed such a warm smile, Gina could not be angry. "The padlock looked connected but was not."

She put her head down on the table next to him and he started to rub her neck---the usual--- and then her back.

"Can we go to bed so that I can tell you everything weird that has been happening?" She muttered with her face still on the table.

"Yes on the first part, no on the second." He pulled her away from the table, half lifting her off the chair.

"I KNOW all that has happened, plus more," he quietly uttered while walking her into her bedroom with his arm around her shoulders.

She sighed as he helped her undress. Then he added barely audible, "I'll be glad when winter comes. These white short-shorts are a real problem."

"For who?"

"Me."

CHAPTER TWENTY-ONE
Thursday, October 20

As always the morning after there was a note from Rick in Gina's underwear drawer.

"Gone for the next four days to Blue Ridge. Important business. Surprise for you when I return. RDR"

She collected his notes and tossed them in a heart shaped jewelry box.  She also suspected that his trip to the Rim Country was connected in some way to all the happenings. Nevertheless, her mind was centered on the words "surprise for you".

Today, since she would be on her feet for extra hours after school judging all the masks that would be laid out, she chose comfortable flat sandals with wide straps. Next, she selected a white loose fitting dress with a hemline that fell to the knee cap.  Since the bodice was a mass of creamy colored stars, she chose matching earrings that dangled with a string of connected stars and moons.

Noting that Dixie and Pop would be gone by six this morning, their usual routine, she tended to her own usual chores. For her horse Mister in the corral closest to the house, she scooped a small amount of vitamin horse pellets for his bin. He was waiting.

She made sure that Nellie had been tended to before she filled her school thermos with the last two cups of Hazelnut decaf coffee that Pop had made earlier for her. Looking in the fridge for leftovers, she selected salty crackers, slices of Swiss cheese, and chunks of beef roast which she threw into sandwich bags before brown bagging.

Securing the house and gate after leaving, she felt like a horse with blinders, concentrating only on her list of priorities roughly listed on a clipboard next to her and not all of the goofy happenings. She gave it a heartfelt try while driving the three miles to school. Mornings had cooled down some so she powered down the front two windows a crack.

First of course was her lecture material for the day to her five classes...*Keep them busy.*

Science Fiction would be reading a short piece of non-fiction about a young boy's experiences during his escape from the rebels in Africa as they attacked his home town..... Extra time could be spent on their limericks.

*Are the permission slips on my desk?*

Western Literature classes need help with their biographies that are due this Friday.....Extra time could be spent on defining and originating brands for the African kids.

*Did Cortez know that his dad came to see me while he was drunk?*

During the free preparation-work hour, last period of the day, "need to call Berty about her nephew Cory's bad grade." She made quick note of the urgent duty on her clip board as she drove.

# BLAKELY HIGH VOODOO PHANTOM

*How is Cory involved in all the mysteries?*

Good thing that she came to a complete stop when she arrived at the intersection of Cave Creek Road. If she had rolled on to the highway a few inches, faking a stop called the California crawl, she would have been hit hard by Mr. Hollywood driving a new roadster, something she hadn't seen before. Smiling and laughing, he didn't seem one bit concerned about side road on-coming traffic. Laughing next to him this early morning was Movie-Star Gorgeous, dressed in puffy sleeve red, her elbow barely hanging over the side. In her lap, Gina could see that she held a wide brimmed matching red hat.

She was tempted to turn around and go tell Berty.

Gina learned later in the day from Guy that today's car was a 1939 Delage 120 Roadster Cabridet Convertable.

"How do you know?" She squinted at him.

"I asked him. And, we are talking mega-bucks."

After parking in the faculty parking lot, she moved slowly with trepidation, looking around her, expecting the sky to fall. As she grabbed all of her supplies from the Jeep, she wondered and half-worried about negatives for the day. What's next? Both she and Nancy had agreed that it has been a vicious circle of events since the African studies began.

They coordinated their two week African unit, planning short stories, lecture material, and hands on activities, all to culminate with ribbons and prizes next week Friday when the visitors arrive on campus.

"I have an un-canny feeling that there's a Hex attacking us from an unhappy spirit," Nancy said.

"Yeah, one with a human body….like the one I met in my classroom yesterday."

The front office was the usual…secretaries on phones…. substitute teachers signing in with Dixie at her counter after reading school rules and then their orders for the day…. teachers pulling their many different colored memos from the alphabetized bins…. personnel filling the mail box with letters, and the principal………NOT scurrying around as usual.

"Where's Shieter?" Gina whispered to Dixie.

"Locked behind closed doors. His VOODOO PHANTOM paint job is parked outside in his usual spot. He drove it today and will do so tomorrow to remind himself of his anger. A 'Do Not Disturb' sign is hanging on the door knob."

"Next, someone's going to write Voodoo Phantom in cryptic letters on the sign," Gina joked.

"I hope not.  He's in a rage as it is."

Guy in his coach's uniform came whizzing through the front office, knocking his knuckles on the long counter behind which the secretaries sat manning the phones.  They jumped. He winked.  "It's wild out there. Ya'll stay young and beautiful, ya hear?"

Seeing Gina, he apologized for not getting to her room sooner. "I always have to stay with the tail end of Cross Country runners to make sure that all the kids make it back to school."

As they walked in the same direction towards their first classes, she talked about her fright when Zander wouldn't let her go after grabbing her wrist.

"The best form of attack is not to. You wait patiently and calmly or the attacker can get riled and more violent." Guy put both hands on her shoulders and turned her toward him. "It's important."

"Great! I'll remember that peaceful bit of advice when someone holds a knife to my throat."

"I hear the big guy's out of town. There's a new band Friday night. Why don't you and Nancy come dancing?"

"I'll be afraid to leave the house."

"I'll protect you."

"And how do you know that Rick's out of town?"

"The Voodoo Phantom."

"Jeesh! Go run around the track." She waved him off and watched him go, almost in a fast sprint, in his handsome coach's uniform.

He stopped, turned, and threw her a kiss.

Students were arriving on campus. Classes would begin in thirty minutes and the hallway was crowding quickly in a faster pace than usual. Swinging the door wide as she hurried into the English Office, she noted a solemn cadence of teachers saying nothing, heads down at tables working. No one was talking and bouncing around as usual. Even the chalkboard was empty, free of Heleena's abbreviated notes.

Ducking into Nancy's room was a spiritual lift. She forever seemed cool, calm and collected. Her red hair was a denial of her calm personality, Gina always thought.

Nancy began with, "What did you learn from Del Rio? Did the security cameras catch anything?" She moved non-stop as she talked in her usual quiet voice, stacking papers on each front row desk to be passed back.

"Rick was mum…totally. I could have used my bat. If we want to learn anything, we have to figure it out for ourselves…or check with the four B's. I'll bet they know stuff."

"Yes, but we won't learn much from them. I'll pick Colt apart and you work on Bing. Since he's an ex-cop, he's got to have some insight."

"Rick's going to the Blue Ridge area for the next four days on business, and there's a new band in town. Guy said that he would meet us at Tumbleweed's. What do you think?"

"After what we've been through, we need a break. Let's invite everyone else too for a discussion."

"Good idea."

Then as Gina started to leave Nancy stopped her. "Incidentally, I found the small key to the tall cabinet where I have my mirror glued to the inside of the door. I'm keeping the door locked as a precaution. I don't want to find another ugly red mask drawn there."

"Well, perk up before this afternoon. Bring snacks to our mask judging episode. When I feed my brain, it works better."

"Ditto," said Nancy. "See you at lunch."


Stepping back into the hallway was like moving out of a revolving door from calm to chaos. The pulse of the school was frantic. Students were talking loudly and pointing fingers in different directions.

"Security was involved."

"I heard that there was no security."

The girls whined; the boys consoled.

"What if he calls it off?"

""He's not going to call it off; too many people are involved."

"The band has purchased some expensive drums and the players have been rehearsing for weeks."

"Ms. Mac what do you think?"

The students questioned her as she rushed into her room with eyes riveted toward her desk top. On the corner was the stack of permission papers, seemingly untouched. She sighed with great relief while counting them to make sure none had been taken. She hated it when unnecessary risks had been taken and decided to secure them in the small filing cabinet she kept in the English Office.

"I don't see how he can cancel next week's activities considering that the entire school, the entire town as a matter-of-fact, is involved," she stated loudly while walking out of the room clutching the permission slips. "I'll be back before the bell rings."

Returning to class, and just as she entered inside the room, Heleena came rushing toward her digging the heels of her rubber-soled loafers into the carpet.

"I hear that Mr. Zander attacked you in your room yesterday while he was drunk." She stood like a square pillar with arms folded and chin down.

She spoke loudly, too loudly and totally unaware that thirty-five students were listening. Smartly, they pretended to be busy. If a feather dropped on the carpet, one could hear it.

"I'll talk to you during lunch," Gina quietly said while accepting the paper Heleena thrust in her direction.

"This is a form, a formal complaint to give to the principal." With a swirl of her skirt, she flurried out of the room. She twirled back, and with one hand in the door frame again spoke loudly. "Forget lunch, I'm busy." She patted the door frame with authority and scurried down the hallway.

Students whispered all around to one another and Gina worried how Cortez would be victimized by the gossip....which according to Guy was faster than digital.

By the time her fourth period class arrived, Gina was accustomed to the unnatural stares and attention the students would feast on her, silently asking questions with their ogling eyes. She had attacked her snack bar twice, the half-hidden fridge behind her desk, for chocolate and a sip of soda-pop.

Jamie Mink and Kim Rose came to her desk after the bell rang and just before lunch.

"What happened yesterday?"

"We want to know everything."

They were seriously concerned and always out spoken with Gina who had known them for years.

"It was really quite simple." She walked to the board and began to erase it in a guise of down play. "He paid money for Cortez's trail ride and he had been drinking." Just as she turned around to face the girls, she noticed Cory standing in the doorway, than quickly leave as she looked his way.

"OK. What have you two learned?"

"Hand out first," said Kim snapping fingers on both hands.

"Finish it. Gina handed them the bag of chocolate chips which was more than half empty. Each filled a hand and gulped away.

"Well, we have it narrowed down to three who are taking double English as make-up for failed classes. Detective Kim and I," Jamie laughed, "think that it could be Cory, Rex, or Tom-Tom."

"Why, and who are Rex and Tom-Tom?"

Kim started, "These three are in your class and Ms. Nancy Lopez's."

"No, I don't have Rex and Tom-Tom in class, only Cory."

"Well, they write cryptic lettering on everything," added Jamie.

"And they're meannnnn." Kim had to draw it out. "Rex is the band's drum major and twirls a vicious stick…a man's long baton"

"And Tom-Tom hates people in general. Every week he arrives at school with a new piercing. Very gross," Jamie added.

"Ok, you detectives go to lunch. Keep your ears and eyes open. We don't want Dr. Shieter to cancel next week's activities…..he could you know….he's mad enough."

During lunch, Gina filled-out the proper paper work sent to parents informing Cortez's parents, and Cory's Aunt Berty of their failing grades in her English class which could keep them from graduating. Three months of school was almost finished, and the semester was over before Christmas. Wise to the fact that students confiscated the mail in these circumstances, she vowed to call the parents before the day was over. Access to telephone numbers and family life meant a trip to the school counselors.

"I need some numbers too," said Nancy during lunch. "Let's go get them during our seventh hour work time."

"And call the parents too. If they're at work, they'll be equally mad." Gina put a piece of parmesan cheese followed by beef bologna on a cracker and put the whole thing in her mouth.

"But, we can't call them at their work unless it's indicated in their files."

"Hah! I owe both Zander and Berty a karate chop for what they did."

Sixth hour after lunch bunch came pouring in, pushing and shoving, hyped from lunchtime activities. Boys hurled over desks when it was possible, like jumping hurdles.

"Aahhh, go back out and walk in," Gina pointed. "This is not track and field!"

"We have a short non-fiction piece to read and then you'll have time to write limericks." She began.

As usual during writing time she pulled out her roll of numbers from a desk drawer for them to use and set her timer to three minutes per student. They liked this procedure and felt identified and productive. "Come pick a number if you need help."

Periodically, she glanced over at Cortez who sat slumped, loudly tapping his pencil on his desk located at the end of the row opposite her desk and near the wall. When asked, he refused help.

From her podium she kept her eyes on everyone as much as possible. But, she still missed something that happened and blamed Cortez since it was closest to his area.

The bell rang and the class walked out. While straightening a few desks and walking around the room, she noticed a huge glob of tobacco spit in the corner of the room on the new carpet. She was furious.

Nancy reminded her that maybe it wasn't Cortez and it could have happened earlier in the day. "Just make sure that you notify Tommy the custodian and write a note on the board about your discontent."

Gina learned from the counselor that Cortez's mother lives in another state and Cory's, another country.

"Great situation," was her sarcasm. She used the phone in the English Office to call Zander and Berty.

"I need to come and talk with you about his grades," said Zander forcibly.

"No! I won't be here." She almost shouted on the phone thinking back to the drunken episode. "It's in the mail."

Berty was upset but polite. "I will have to contact my sister in Russia and have her talk to Co'y."

After the last bell rang, Gina and Nancy headed over to Becky Painter's room for the African mask judging contest carrying snack bags of soda-pop and two kinds of spicy-salty chips.

The masks were presented in three different groups each representing a class. "Try to pick some from each group," Becky told them as she handed them the criteria for grading. She sat and switched out her black spiked heels for simple flats, took off her long shoulder length earrings and threw them in her purse.

"What did you do with the earring?" They each wanted to know after seeing her take off her earrings and still wearing her wrap-around apron.

"I have it hidden. Maybe a student involved will ask about it. It had to have been taken by one of my art students who knew where I hang my apron. It was in this pocket." She showed them as she took off the long paint splattered white smock and hung it in a tall closet at the end of the room.

Becky continued with her directions. "I have exactly ninety for judging. Choose the top ten and each

167

will get a blue ribbon. I need to display them in the hallway cases tomorrow."

Nancy asked, "Do you want us to rank them?"

"No. They'll be equal winners. I'll be working here in my office for about an hour." She pointed to the small windowed room at the end of the large art classroom. "If you have questions, come and see me. Otherwise, when you're done bring the winners here and we'll hide them in my office. It's too weird. I don't trust anything or anyone anymore." She grabbed a handful of salty chips from the girls' bags and went into her office where she kept a small refrigerator of cold drinks.

They decided to do a quick survey before judging. Like a sore thumb was the fiendish grin of the exact mask that accosted Gina in the bathroom.

"Well, where's your human?"

"Evidently, Susie Lee remembered her mask to the exact duplicate," said Nancy.

Gina shivered in remembrance of the night just one week ago. "Ok. Let's choose a plan and get started with this project."

Working with their criteria sheets, they started a process of elimination. By the end of an hour they chose the most heinous, weird, brightly painted, devilish, ominous, roguishly aboriginal......ten.

"This judging was sort of fun," said Nancy brushing her hands together to eliminate salt from the chips.

"Yeah, one diabolical delight," added Gina who went over to tell Becky they were finished.

The three carefully carried the masks into the office room and set them out of sight on a bottom shelf which was half hidden with stacked boxes of supplies. They kicked the boxes closer to the shelf to hide the masks from sight which now could not be seen unless a person was standing extremely close.

"Just to be safe." Becky then covered all with a long cloth. "I'll put them in the lighted display cases early in the morning.....boy am I glad tomorrow's Friday." She turned off the light to the small office and locked the door as the three prepared to leave.

"Why lock it?"

"Yeah, why lock it?" They smartly concluded.

The three grabbed all their bags of snacks, school books, miscellaneous supplies they always take home nightly, and headed out the classroom. After Becky locked the door, they turned to face the long Commercial Arts hallway and the entrance at the other end.

Walking toward them was a 'tipsy' Mr. Zander, scraping the wall with one hand as he wobbled along toward them.

## CHAPTER TWENTY-TWO
Thursday after school

The three stood stunned.

He weaved a bit as he approached.

"Hey, I jush want ta apologize for the other day."

Again he was in a wrinkled white uniform. An attempt had been made to tuck the long tailed shirt into belted pants over a ball park protruding belly. Messy hair splattered across his forehead from under a company cap and his face was a puffy crimson ball void of any expression.

"You're not supposed to be on campus." Gina gasped, planted her feet stationary and scowled.

The other two got their cell phones out in a blink. Nancy called Colt, and Becky called the front office for security. Then they kept their distance, not knowing whether to duck back into the room or stay and face him.

"Ok…. Ok, I'm leaving," he stammered noting their readiness to evict him. Stumbling, he turned around and periodically leaned on the wall as he moved toward the end slowly, again scraping his fingers against the hollow boards as he walked.

They watched him shuffling down the hallway, stopping once, twice, to look in the glass cases of student art projects. Clearly, he was in a dominant mood. Near the end he turned around and faced them tauntingly, a smirking pose as he stopped and leaned full body on the wall staring back at them in their frozen state.

Richard/Raquel came hurrying in. "Hey, how's everything?" His arms and hands free of books and supplies he carried a coffee cup nonchalantly as if he were in the neighborhood with some free time. He looked a bit rumpled and tired after he had been sitting at his desk working diligently for the past two hours. Calmly directing his attention toward everyone, he fearlessly walked forward without stopping.

"Yeah, what's up?" Guy came in behind him, his shoulders raised a bit, fist clenched. He too wore his end of day look of exhaustion, but unlike Rich he walked briskly down the hall.

Although quite unbelievably relieved, the girls remained rigid waiting for something to happen while shifting their heavy shoulder bags of supplies almost in unison from one shoulder to the next.

Zander, instantly aware of the two men, clenched his jaws, sniffed, re-adjusted his cap and headed out the hallway with intermingled steps mincing left.... then right ....through the center between them. He slouched as he advanced, anger building in his slightly hunched shoulders.

They gave him room and hugged the walls.

While looking straight ahead in mockery of confidence, and without any acknowledgement toward the men, he headed expressionless out the hallway doors zombie style.

Coming up the steps from the same end and on the other side of the entrance doors, were Colt and another cop stomping loudly on their approach.

The five from inside the hallway heard banging noises outside the doors as if someone had heavily been thrust against them. More loud shouting and shuffling noises occurred before all was quiet.

Voiceless, they eyeballed looks back and forth among each other until the stillness.

"I saw him head in this direction and thought that I'd better follow," said Rich as he calmly sipped at his cup of coffee. "I remember him coming yesterday in the same condition. Sorry I was late getting to your classroom," he said to Gina.

"Me too," said Guy. "Today I was across campus when I saw him drive up and stumble as he got out of his work van."

"Nobody was late yesterday. He was early, which was his plan to catch us off guard. And I thought Rick was supposed to contact him about not coming on campus if he'd been drinking," continued Gina in a huddle with the others.

"Evidently he didn't contact him. Besides, all visitors are supposed to sign-in at the front office. He knows how to bypass every rule," complained Rich sipping from his cup again. "Security's not doing its job."

"What security?" Becky asked. "You mean the new lady that's always hanging-out in the custodian's smoke house?"

"How about Shieter who is a no-show to every circumstance….a Mr. Hide and Seek person," retorted Gina. "Tomorrow's going to be a nightmare if he cancels the parade and activities for next Friday."

"He wouldn't do that after everybody's worked so hard. I think he's just bluffing." Rich broke the huddle and everyone started following through the hall.

Before getting to the end, they heard heavy boots running up the steps. "Hey, what happened up here? I need a full report to throw at the guy." Colt looked at Nancy as he talked. "Mr. Zander gets around way too easily. We're clipping his wings and checking into the 'legits' of his business."

"I hear that someone with knowledge of the security system sabotaged the school's during the spray painting ordeal," said Guy.

"You mean we have no clue who's involved?" asked Becky.

"That's what I hear." Guy continued. "It's evident that the car was sprayed by the same person or persons."

Colt was new to the curriculum scene so had to ask, "Where in the heck do the words VOODOO PHANTOM come from anyway."

"From me. In my Science Fiction classes we're studying African cult religions," Gina offered without an apology. "It's all very interesting and the students seem to enjoy the lecture material....a little too much!"

"So, that narrows it down somewhat. It's probably one of your students," said Guy. "You're such an enthusiastic teacher; one of your students just got carried away."

He smiled at her; she punched him in the arm.

"Regardless what happens tomorrow, we'll meet at Tumbleweed's to analyze what's been going on."

Nancy and Gina made sure that Colt, Becky and Rich were aware of the meeting before they dispersed in the parking lot.

Out on the field, football players were huddling and practicing to the beat of African drums as the band marched and danced on the track around the perimeter of the field. It resembled a parade, a festive event of different groups practicing sports accompanied by music. Rex thrust his long baton up and down in a cadence while twirlers marched with their batons occasionally throwing them high in the air.

Cortez, on the edge of the practice field, watched the group heading toward the faculty parking lot verbalizing closely in an oppressive manner. He assumed and feared that they must be connected to a previous agonizing situation when he saw his dad being taken away by the police. Embarrassed beyond repair when he saw him stumble out of his work van earlier and head into the Commercial Arts Building, he knew then that there would be trouble.

He waved at Cory to hurry off the field. As they had promised, they were there watching Darlene and Susie Lee practice with the band. Now, they needed to make big plans for tomorrow concerning the principal's major announcement earlier in the week.

Since their involvement was deep, they now need to think of a distraction.

In his concentration, Susie Lee's lost mask was in his thoughts.

*I clearly remember where I last saw Susie Lee's mask. It was in the Camry when Cory and I parked it in the garage.*

174

## CHAPTER TWENTY-THREE
Thursday

Gina learned from Colt while talking to the group in the parking lot, that the town was dispatching most of its officers to act as under-cover cops starting tonight and through next week.

"They'll be everywhere on foot and cycles, on campus and roads leading to campus. Although Del Rio's out of town until Sunday night, we're following his lead on what to do," said Colt with folded arms, leaning back and forth on his boot heels while talking. Then looking over at Nancy, "I'll see you tomorrow night."

The hot sun beating down distressed the group and everyone got ready to leave, each eager for an air conditioned car. The parking lot was now a heavy accumulation of people dispersing from end of day's activities. Classified staff who worked late hours after the last bell, hustled to their cars. Students finished with sports came from the field and gym slowly, lingering at their cars talking. Like field mice, the vacant parking lot was now teeming with different groups.

Through the crowd, and in the distance, Gina saw Shieter leave the custodians' building with two women almost hanging on him, smiling and laughing. Heleena was babbling on his left while the new security lady was on his right.

She noted that a white bandage remained on his chin.

*Good!*

Before she could escape into her jeep, he waved at her to wait for him as he said goodbye to the other two. Walking toward her, he slowly looked her over from head to toe and said, "Nice sandals."

"Did anyone confess yet?" She decided to make him angry by referencing his car since he seemed too happy at the moment. Considering all that she has been going through this week, why does he get to be so worry free?

"No, and I suspect that no one will." He was too nonchalant with his simple answer as he looked her over.

"What about the campus security cameras. Was someone seen spray painting the vending machines?" She was aware of his staring and shifted her shoulder bag.

"Some how, they were turned off. We're working on it." He moved closer.

"What about your car?"

"I have insurance."

She had her car keys in her right hand and her left hand on the door handle when he leaned against the door keeping it shut.

"Why don't you and I go get a coffee or beer and talk about what's been going on. You might have some leads since you teach all these kids." His eyes twinkled and he sneaked a bit of a smile as he jingled a handful of keys confidently, throwing them up and down.

"Helloooo. You're gonna fry in this heat," Dixie shouted walking in their direction to her car.

"Any word yet?" She continued talking while taking off her long grey designer vest and throwing it over her shoulder. "What's going to happen tomorrow?"

He became smug. "We'll see."

"If you cancel activities and the parade, the whole school's going to explode."

"So be it." He shrugged his shoulders in a noncommittal attitude and walked away pissed.

Dixie took off her sunglasses and winked at Gina who quickly unlocked her door to get in.

"Ok, now I'm leaving. You arrived at a perfect time."

"See you at the house. I'll have beer and popcorn ready."

"Right!"


Driving out of campus and down the road, her thoughts were on tomorrow's big collections, Western bio's and Sci-fi Limericks. She had given them alternate due dates but hoped that they would all be turned in tomorrow as originally announced. It was especially important to secure the Limericks for the judging....by the four B's.

Nevertheless, she had told them they could turn in the papers Monday for a possible B grade and Tuesday, for a possible C grade. The boys who hated English liked this concept and felt that it was fair.

"And, if you are absent, make sure it's excused if you want the full credit for that day." She told them this over and over and in many instances, the top students who were absent, had their mom's deliver their papers to the front office.

She sighed, too much work and too little time. Fun diversions were the keys to holding this maniacal job. With this in mind she decided to turn right on Cave Creek Road and head over to Screamin' Ice Cream for a Root Beer Float.

Aware of Mr. Hollywood's crazy driving, she decided to always be on the look out for him. Sure enough, he came wizzing by in his lime green 1947 Willy's. Guy had informed her earlier in the week about his many cars and she was having a good time trying to identify them.

But most interesting were the occupants. Today again it was Berty in a flashy silver tunic. Her grey hair was flying and her bright red lipstick looked like it was melting in the hot afternoon sun. Well secured in her lap was a fluffy white dog. Berty looked happy while Mr. Hollywood, grinning and chatting with one arm waving in the air for emphasis, had her entertained with a story of some kind.

This made her decide to call Rick as soon as she parked at Screamin' Ice Cream.

The static was so bad she could barely hear him.

"What's going on up there?" stihhhhsl

"It's cool and beautiful." ssgghutjjjklk

"I'm jealous. What's my surprise?" She found herself shouting.

"Not telling."

"Is it a cat?"

"No."

"Is it a new saddle?"

"No."

"Is it a diamond?"

Sshhjgjkdlscscssss! Nothing but static. She hung up and decided on a banana split. Considering all that was going on, she could eat the entire conglomeration.

When she drove up, she saw Jamie Mink and Kim Rose sitting on one of the pink patio tables. When they saw her, they instantly got into the back seat.

"What are we getting?" Kim asked as she leaned back making herself comfortable doing her usual student gig, smiling with her hands behind her head.

Jamie, a bit more hesitant, got out as fast as she got in and stood next to the Jeep with the door open. Gina could read her like a book. Her round face and large blue eyes were on the serious side this afternoon and she knew something.....something that Gina would soon learn from her. Like a dust devil knowing exactly where to pin-point havoc---the students knew everything.

"Here," she gave Kim a ten and told her what she wanted. "Get what you girls want."

She and Jamie selected a table outside in the shade and while waiting, she questioned Jamie about any new information.

"I know nothing about the spray painting but I do know about the earring in the apron. Cory told Darlene that he took the earring from the mask and put it in Ms. Painter's apron pocket.

"How did he get in?"

"It's easy. All of the doors get unlocked when the clean-up crew arrives later in the day. Nobody watches who comes and goes."

"Why would he do that?"

Jamie hunched her shoulders up in a question mark. "Control maybe. Attention maybe."

"Spooky!"

Kim came out carrying a tray with a mile high banana split and two chocolate dipped cones. "I told them that you wanted extra whipped cream." She wrinkled her freckled nose and smiled her smarty one.

"You know me well."

The three sat licking away as fast as possible trying to beat the heat.

Soon they were surrounded by a small crowd of friends with questioning faces. They shot questions back and forth among them, questions to which they already knew the answers.

"We all strongly suspect the cryptic writers."

"But are they going to come forward?"

Gina faded out as she drooled over her 'split'.

Knowing that they were unaware of the peeking pervert, she planned to keep it that way. She wanted to blame Zander whom she considered a loose end but in the complete analyses, he was too heavy and sluggish. The bathroom invader seemed young and quick....the way he scratched her door one second, and appeared under it the next. Yes, he was fast. She would put this in her notes to Rick.

She missed Del Rio.....where was he and what was her surprise?

Kim tapped her on the back. "Knock-knock, where are you?"

Before she could respond, a short-bed faded green pickup careened around the corner, pulling off Cave Creek Road, screeching tires leaving a stench of rubber mixed with dust. Cory parked close to the group.

All was quiet.

Six boys loudly yelped African animal noises in rhythm to the beat of drums. Rex and Tom Tom were sitting in the truck-bed acting wild along with two others Gina did not recognize. Cory and Cortez exited the front seat, each with self-assurance, a cocky demeanor.

They all passed by the table group in a strut, almost brushing against them, looking straight ahead rudely. This was not their group, their clique, their cult. They didn't have to be friendly.

Gina kept a sharp eye on her Jeep. The boys entered the ice cream shop, ordered, loaded up, and pealed out before the group around her made a move.

"That's one scary bunch," said Jamie. A few others shook their heads in agreement.

Within seconds, they heard a loud screech, and a rumbling crash.

## CHAPTER TWENTY-FOUR

The screeching noise, sounding like a crack of thunder, sent everyone off tables and running out front to the road.

Now passing by and out of the ruckus was Mr. Hollywood, this time alone, music on high volume, oblivious of his surroundings.

It was learned later, and as Gina suspected, he had wildly pulled in front of the boys' pickup causing Cory to crash into a row of rustic metal horses and other Western paraphernalia, sending metal pieces into the store front and down the main road which had to be partially shut for two hours.

Although he had to veer to avoid an accident, Cory was cited for negligence. He fumed and tried to fight the accusation which only added to his lit fuse. All negative. Cortez on the other hand, remained icy calm.

"Slow down and look in all directions. You could have avoided this mistake," said the cop handling the crash who presented an example of what they should have done in this situation.

The boys riding in the bed of the pickup got tousled and thrust into the back of the cab. Pierced lip rings and others on eyebrows and ears, pushed into flesh, covering faces with fast flowing blood. Medics needed to dig out the jewelry which was deeply imbedded, and the next day at school four boys proudly wore their showy patches of attention.

Dusk was dampening the heat. Cave Creek Road now a frenzy with after work and after school traffic, came to a halt as gawkers crowded around on its surface and edges.

To hasten the clearing, most people pitched in with the road clean up. A couple store owners with note pads and pens in hands griped while listing their losses.

Cell phones chimed all around like mockingbirds.

Soon Berty arrived in her dually filled with six dogs, two in the front seat and four in the back. The bed, piled high with trash, required a tie down. Gone were her silver tunic and bright red lipstick. Now dressed in long sleeve denim work shirt, baggy jeans and heavy work boots, she thundered across the road.

"Co'y, your pickup is now mine." She shouted too loudly and showed to be totally unaware of peer presence. A ruby red face flaming with anger accented the whiteness of her scraggly hair. She didn't need an African mask to be part of the scene. "Follow me home," she repeated twice and did the unthinkable, booting him in the butt in front of his friends.

Cortez climbed in next to his furious and deflated friend, and they drove the scratched and beat looking old pickup back to Berty's place on Spur Cross Road. A fender hanging low and badly needing repair, loudly scraped the surface of the speed bumps.

Gina stayed put, watched the happenings with astonishment, and feared repercussions from Berty's irate scene. Tomorrow they would all pay.

Berty, while driving off, knew that she had over stepped the boundaries of repair between her and Cory. Why had her sister sent her only son to America to live here, on this hot, barren desert in the first place? What was she thinking? Now her ill sister would have to learn about his failing grades and his bad attitude, information she had not wanted her to hear considering he has been her sole responsibility for these many months.

But, today she had lost it and in her remorse knew what she would do to feel better. She would go to the guest house and talk to the man, like always, to feel composed and together. After all, she had saved him from decay out in the desert two months ago, and he was now surviving, thanks to her.

While she talked to him he would listen in agreement, always making her feel better. They were a team.

He was her man.

They had tea together.

He didn't talk much

She would go to him later tonight, as always.

## CHAPTER TWENTY-FIVE
### Thursday, late afternoon

Gina worried about the entire scene and wondered how she and Nancy could counsel Berty about her anger and also teach her the psychology of peer pressure, especially among teens.

Nancy would definitely have to be involved. This was heavy stuff, the kind for which she depended on Nancy's expertise.

Once she had a bad student who had the meanest mom in town. When she called her to carefully complain about the boy's behavior in class, the mom shouted at her, "Don't call me. Call his psychiatrist".

Nancy to the rescue. "Put the boy in the desk next to you and give him special things to do….hand out papers…erase the board…etc."

It worked.

Now, they would have to go lightly with the uniqueness of this situation.

Driving home and wishing that she could get school off her brain, she thought about all the people that needed calling for one reason or another.

She clicked off a list in her head.

185

Pop….Bring home some chocolate éclairs.

Rick Del Rio…When was he coming home?

Bing….Tell the group about our Friday meeting.

Back to Rick…What was he doing that was so important at Blue Ridge? What was her surprise?

Mr. Hollywood….Who is he? Where does he live? Is he a retired race-car celebrity?

Guy….What does he know about him?


Thinking back about the accident and the dangerous Mr. Hollywood, she reminded herself to look out for him. She had seen him driving too fast down this popular three mile stretch that led to her home.

Call it premonition, she inadvertently looked in her rear view mirror and there he was coming up fast, too fast down the bumpy, curvy road.

"Race-car driver nut," she said aloud.

Moving her Jeep to the far right rim of the road was her strategy to give him all the room he needed.

Expecting him to pass, she was totally surprised when he didn't. Instead, he slowed and pulled next to her, shouting with a broad smile.

The smile worried her.

They were coasting at a 'run-along' speed and his unbuttoned orange plaid short-sleeve shirt was flapping in the wind. A gold tooth flashed adding to his façade. Hair too thick for his age was plastered down with drug store gunk. She noticed these physical features for the first time considering he was looking straight at her.

"Want a ride?" He motioned to the empty space next to him.

"No."

"Wanta' race?" He smiled broader.

"No."

"You will when you see my next car." He waved, raced away, and soon became an orange speck in a lime green Jeep.....before Gina sped home.

She called Dixie to tell her to watch the road when driving home at any time and told her why.

"That's a hoot," said Dixie laughing. "We need to introduce him to Zander. They're a pair."

During the last mile Gina recalled today's mishaps:

Tobacco spit on her carpet in the corner;

Zander's attack in the Commercial Arts hallway;

Dr. Shieter's invite for coffee or beer;

Cory's crash into the curio shop;

Berty's attack on Cory;

Mr.Hollywood's lurid offer to ride in his Jeep.

Tomorrow will be unbelievable.

She shivered, looked at the late time and called Pop before he left the bakery.

"Bring home lots of goodies...double the éclairs."

She called home again and talked to Dixie. "Pick out a good movie for tonight. I'm not working. I'm snacking."

"Super!"

# CHAPTER TWENTY-SIX
## Friday, October 21

A close crack of thunder Friday morning awoke Gina quickly. Simultaneously, her alarm rang and she wondered which one of the two was in control. It was a 'hex' sort of thing, and she was now in a good mood.

To her, the rain today would bring happiness to every situation, negatives gone. The extra long-hot-dry summer lasted too long into October and like gasping fish in a dry pond, desert people were ready for a change.

Thick dark clouds hung low. Scents of wet Creosotes painted the corners of her bedroom after she opened the windows, a scent matched only by orange blossoms in the Spring down in the Scottsdale, Phoenix valley.

In the kitchen, Pop, Dixie and she put a little extra jive into their steps while going through their morning routines of coffee cups, toast, and egg flipping.

"How long do you think it'll last?" She asked while walking outside with her cup.

"We'll take what we can get," said Pop joining her. After they talked out their schedules for the day, he said, "Stay close to your friends. We don't need a repeat of last Friday. And remember our new rule; the last person to leave, locks the gate. We don't need Berty coming on the property to take Nellie again."

Since she was always the last person to leave, she made a mental note about the gate.

Today's outfit would be all about comfort. The night before she selected a brightly flowered blouse that gently flowed three inches below her waist, continuing below the belt of form fitting denim jeans that stretched with each movement. A short light pink vest accented the tulips in the blouse. Comfortable sandals finished the look.

A quick shower, swipe of make-up and she felt prepared for the chaos of the day after looking in the mirror. "Let it come."

The rain washed away lonely thoughts of a week-end without Rick. And the dance tonight would be on her mind as a 'happy' emergency retrieval when there was a bad moment in class. It was all part of the 'survival' instinct.

Tonight she would meet with the Family Farm group of four B's to discuss the criteria rules for grading the two class sets of Limericks, roughly about seventy of them...give or take those students who are always absent on Friday.

Luckily, they volunteered themselves plus their new girlfriends. Gina could never be happier since she had two class sets of Western Literature biographies to carefully read and grade. These needed to be presentable and cleanly readable to the African students visiting next Friday.

The parking lot, puddling in the same areas she knew to avoid, contained only a few cars this early in the morning and she found a place close to the sidewalk.

Upon opening her umbrella, she shook out the cobwebs and dust before getting under it. Then locking her Jeep, she hurriedly headed off to her classroom to dump her supplies. After leaving her lunch in the English Office, she checked on Nancy.

"Any surprises on campus from last night?" She clung to the door frame to talk to Nancy at her desk.

"No, thank goodness. Colt and crew will be very active until this next week is over."

"Let's get our mail and quickly swing by Commercial Arts to check on the displayed masks. I'm so curious about the students' reactions....winners or not."

"Keep in mind we'll be seeing most of them in our classes today because Becky's handing them back."

On their way up the stairway, students ran by them taking two steps to their one, zig-zagging from one side to the other avoiding slow movers. Some had notebooks on top of their heads to ward off the steady rain which was now coming down harder. Others acting cool and totally soaked, shuffled up slowly.

It started out a happy day.....the rain breaking the monopoly of the bright sun day-in and day-out accenting six months of intense heat starting from last May. Now, a giddiness prevailed. Gina hoped it stayed that way and looked forward to a weekend break.

Quickly they walked through a throng of students staring and pointing at the mask winners. A silence bounced of the walls as the winners savored their talent. Each seemed to know which mask belonged to whom. They muttered names with a relish. All was good.

Becky had done a superb job of displaying them in a decorative way among scattered African artifacts that she had collected through the years. Bright oranges blending with pinks, reds, and blues surfaced from the illumination of the flood lights inside the four foot tall glass cases. All was eerily gory, eerily beautiful, a riveting opulence that knew no other competition.

Becky was standing inside the door-way of her room with fingers crossed as she looked at her two companions. "So far, so good!"

They nodded, chatted a bit, then hurried away with, "See you tonight."

The beat of the day laced both with fun and somberness as everyone waited in fear for the principal's announcement. Kids were suspicious. Periodically, Gina rang Dixie during classroom breaks to learn the latest news from the front office.

"No news from behind closed doors. He hasn't been seen all day and we know that he's in his room."

Not good. Gina had the urge to entice him to change his mind if she needed to do so and day dreamed a scenario, a plea bargain to just let it go as scheduled....so many units already prepared...so many students. She would meet with him every night for coffee or beer in a crowded place. Should she yes, should she no?

During lunch, she would confer with her two buddies, Nancy and R&R. They would give solid advice. A plan could be schemed concerning acting as spies when they would meet with Shieter. They would make it work for a week; that's all time needed.

Tapping her pencil on her podium nervously through her first four classes as she collected Bio's and Limericks caused Jamie and Kim during fourth hour to check on her attitude.

"Ok. What's up?" They stood in front of her during the last five minutes of the period with feet firmly planted and arms folded.

"What do you know that we don't?"

It always made her laugh when they read her mind so well. They would get in her face and since she could never fool them with a lie, she would turn her back to them and pretend busyness.

"Don't turn your back to me," Kim playfully teased.

Gina couldn't help but chuckle. "Let's have some snacks." She went to her small 'fridge behind her desk and got out root beer, Mexican cokes and chocolate chips. "This will ruin your lunch. Get going. I've got a meeting during mine."

They each took a root beer and a handful of chips. Jamie stopped at the door. "Cory was absent today." She seemed worried.

"Yes, I know."

"I bet Cortez isn't here either." She said a lot with this statement "What do you think the principal is going to decide to do?"

"It's a mystery," was Gina's reply although she felt a vague foreboding of disaster.

Lunchtime was the calm before the storm. The doors at one end of the English Department hallway were purposely propped open and the peaceful sounds of a desert rain were like surround-sound. Scents perfumed the walls beyond freshness.

Gina, Nancy and Rich ate silently, interrupted only by Heleena popping in to loudly announce, "Brace yourselves! Dr. Shieter is going to make an announcement soon and I fear it's not going to be good." Her hair needed combing and large brown rimmed glasses tilted askew on her nose.

Coming from the large custodian's building meant that she was in the know. This group always knew the politics of the school before all others.

## CHAPTER TWENTY-SEVEN
Friday afternoon, October 21

Gina was thankful that sixth period was her last class of the day even though it was her 'after-lunch-bunch', wild from too much play, or sleepy from too much food. This was her science-fiction class; limericks were due, and of course Cortez was absent as were about five others.

Although masks had been handed back throughout the day, no student decided to wear one in class. Instead, students would proudly show Gina their creations, thrusting the crafts with the multi-colored fiendish grins in her face. By this time of the day, she thought all of them appeared with a predatory roar, more and more devilish.

The bell rang and an undertone of suspicion fled with the students as Gina gathered her supplies and the limericks. Stowing away in the quiet English Office during seventh hour, the last period of the day, was always a treat, a restful work time which she looked forward to enthusiastically.

She and Nancy had the room to themselves and the time was usually productive.....with the exception of today.

During the middle of seventh hour, the intercom cackled with preparation for an announcement...THE announcement.... And later during the big debate at Tumbleweed's, it was never decided when all of the havoc commenced.

Was it in the middle of Shieter's announcement or with the first word, "Unfortunately......"

Students all across campus spilled out of their classrooms twenty minutes before the last bell of the day, unable to be contained by shouting teachers.

In the English Building it all began with a noisy din. Provoked by the announcement and like rats running after spilled oats, a catastrophic wave of students, most wearing masks, ran bellowing down the hallway. Attached to ears, the disguises fit stunningly and diabolically well, hiding faces disillusioned and angry.

In pairs they opened closed doors to shout in the classrooms where some teachers cowered, waiting for the anger to subside. The boys pounded loudly with fists and feet on the walls as they ran and jumped through the throng of friends.

Having to wait for buses and rides home, the students crowded together in the large outdoor patio pounding on drums and yelling as they rallied, provoking newsworthy ramifications. Teachers gathered around the masses to form some kind of civil order, calmly talking to them.

The rain had subsided to a drizzle.

"We will all work at changing his mind."

"Starting with tardies, maybe we can earn a reprieve?" This was Heleena talking. "Remember, the daily tardies triggered this domino effect." She walked through the different groups fearlessly spinning her umbrella as a distraction. Drizzled rain spit off the edges.

Students came to her bravely shouting complaints, than less loudly as she stood her ground listening.

But Friday was Friday, and like no other day of the week, students were eager to let go of the week's tensions by making an extra loud exploitation and display of their disapproval. But, they were stopped from acts of visual vandalism as all the teachers were watching them.

Security.... where had she been hiding.... called 911. Soon two, three, news 'copters hovered over head extremely low with cameras perched like hawks.

Shieter locked himself in his room while all staff and teachers mingled around and among the students gaping at all the action, hoping there would be no accidents.

Time was on their side. Soon the end of day, punctuated by the bell and the arrival of the buses, scattered tensions as students fled quickly to their own cars to drive away through the now un-padlocked front gates.

Teachers grimaced, shook their heads and moved away slowly, chatting in groups and complaining loudly. "He'll change his mind," whined a wrinkled and gray haired teacher. "He better," added another.

Cop cars were parked around the school's circular perimeter, purposely within view of all drivers.

"Students are eager to vent," said Gina to Nancy and Rich as the three walked away from the scene. "We need to explore creative ways to change his mind."

"He sure is a stubborn man....very set in his ways," said Rich.

"Wait a minute. I have a plan." Gina stopped in her tracks, put her hands on her hips, and slyly continued with a positive nod. "Nancy and I will visit him Monday after school wearing our low-cut short dresses and talk him into a compromise.... with an idea he can't refuse."

Nancy looked at her wide-eyed. "Not me!"

"I'll do all the talking. You just look alluring."

"You serious?" Rich asked.

"Of course! We can handle him. During class time we can wear tops that flatter our dresses and cover our low-cuts. It'll work. Trust me. Tonight at the dance, that's one more thing for us to talk about....a scheme."

Nancy added wryly. "Our list is getting longer and longer."

"We'll get Dixie there with her long yellow note pad." They laughed....a much needed emotion.

"If you need, call me at home for some suggestions to add to yours. We have to make this work." Rich's age was almost double theirs and he could not help but chuckle at their youthful naivety.

Gina and Nancy went back to their classrooms to gather supplies and lock up.

"This hallway seems solemnly evil now. Too quiet after the fiasco," said Gina.

They parted in the parking lot after discussing what they would wear tonight to the dance....tight black jeans tucked into knee-high boots, short sleeved silk blouses, and buckled belts.

Guy was leaning on Gina's Jeep reading a piece of white note paper in his hand, the kind all students regularly used. "I don't think you should read this," he said gravely as she approached.

CHAPTER TWENTY-EIGHT
Friday afternoon, October 21

Printed in bright crimson cryptic lettering with drops of blood ghoulishly drawn to perfection and splattered here and there on the paper was the following limerick:

**"The Prince of Darkness met a blond Bitch**
**Who thought that she was such a cool Witch**
**All went to hell**
**When she cast a spell**
**And now she lies deep in a Ditch"**
**THE VOODOO PHANTOM**

"Well, he/she certainly has the correct rhyme scheme." Visibly upset, Gina quickly folded the paper a couple of creases and put it in her purse.

"I'll call Colt; you call Del Rio. This is a genuine threat on your life." Guy leaned back on the Jeep and folded his thick arms.

"'Cast a spell' probably has something to do with grades," she said squinty eyed.

199

"Get with the program!" Guy flamboyantly said as he opened the door to her Jeep. "Give every student a grade of an "A" or "B" and live happily ever after."

"It sure would eliminate all this nonsense," she said as she drove away. "See you tonight."

Immediately she called Pop who reminded her that an open threat is made by someone calling for help, whatever the consequences.

"A death threat goes unprinted, unannounced. It just mysteriously happens."

"Jeesh! Thanks a lot. I'm not sure that your expert analysis helps."

"I don't want you to worry and lose sleep over it. It should be easy to run down the printer. It's got to be one of your students that's failing."

"One more mystery. We'll get the culprit." She hung up to put two hands on the wheel while driving down the long winding Spur Cross Road to home.

Coming towards her, whipping around the turns too fast was Mr. Hollywood in an older model Chevy Corvette with bright yellow historical license plates. Next to him this time was Delilah, Movie-Star Gorgeous, laughing and having a good time.

Gina, knowing that he was a maniac on the road, drove off the edge onto a smooth surface thankful for no outcropping of boulders. She gave him lots of room to pass.

He drove down the center line. Neither occupant was aware of her Jeep as they looked at each other, seemingly entranced in conversation.

She would definitely be on the lookout for him from now on and also needed to talk to Del Rio about this long stretch of winding road becoming a speedway. After all, this was her twice daily route and she didn't want to honor the last sentence of the eerie Limerick and become a prediction.

Just as she drove into the carport, Dixie came to meet her with the house phone.

"It's Del Rio. He says that he has a good connection for a few minutes." She handed Gina the phone.

"Hey!" She said.

""Hey blondie, I miss you. What's been going on? Are you staying put until I get back?"

"Well...sort of. Tonight we have a meeting at Tumbleweed's to discuss all that's been happening."

"Why don't they meet at your house? It's safer."

"No place is safe. My tires got stabbed, Nellie got stolen, someone is writing cryptic notes at school....One got left on my car."

"What? Who found the note and what did it say?"

"Guy found it under the windshield wiper. I'll read it to you when you get back."

"Stay home! I'll be back tomorrow or Sunday."

"With my surprise?"

"Yep! Gotta go."

After hanging up, she talked to Dixie to remind her to bring the big yellow note pad tonight "so that we can sort things out from all angles."

Dixie added, "Friday night music, snacks with good friends, what could be better?"

"Until we find answers, nothing will work."

## CHAPTER TWENTY-NINE
Friday night

Cory and Cortez worked all day helping Berty with chores, particularly dog grooming ones. They needed to get on her good side…keep her happy and trusting.

"Why you not in school?" she asked earlier.

They sneezed, sprayed vinegar water in their eyes to fake illness when she wasn't looking.

"Everyone at school has been absent from colds."

"Something is going around and we caught it."

She didn't pursue the questioning. A day's labor was greatly needed because she had much to do and looked at her list longingly before putting the boys to work. "Help wit' de' dogs for now. Later, we sort my collections."

They knew these to be pilfered junk from backs of restaurants, coffee shops and desert debris.

After discussions with her, they shook their heads in disbelief and talked quietly to each other.

"I'm sorry about your aunt."

Cory took the last puff from his cigarette, threw it on the ground and stepped on it with the sole of his boot, two, three times sideways. Then he picked up smashed pieces and put them in his pocket. His aunt must not catch him smoking again. She had busted his lip once and he was in fear of her. "Tonight's the night," he said while slowly shaking his head up and down in confirmation. "We check out the guest house and talk to the 'boyfriend'. I have never met him and he's been locked up in there since August. Something is weird."

"Go over your plans again. Let me remind you, your Aunt Berty is twice our size."

"Are you being a chicken-shit?"

"No, no. Let's not get in trouble. What if he's a gangster with the mafia or something?" Cortez took a step back and put his hands up in his defense. "It's just that Cave Creek is such a good hideaway for bad people from other places."

"Well, maybe we just might find one. Anyway, trouble finds me. After the accident today in my truck, I need some fun….a daring exciting event. My aunt loves her Vodka. We make sure that she gets plenty of it and then we sneak the keys away."

"Where are they?"

"Always on a big ring that hangs on a cupboard next to the kitchen door….or around her neck. That could be a problem."

The boys worked diligently all day doing what she asked working to perfection. They knew her routine well…times when she left to drive away for junk and what she did when she returned.

"Aunt Berty, break time." Cory shouted periodically enticing her to drink her Vodka while they drank root beer and orange soda.

She brought them a tray containing hard cheese, canned sardines and a variety of crackers. Her staples.

They shook their heads in awe noticing her tilted walk and slurring voice as the day escaped into the night. Their goal was to wait until she passed out in a deep sleep. But they had to keep working harder and harder to hopefully tire her out first. They were determined to have some fun and nothing would stop them. Rex, Tom-Tom and the girls were waiting for them to help "tear up the town" after today's announcement.

"We'll be in touch later," the two groomers said. "We're working on a project," and did not elaborate.

Tirelessly, the boys kept going, relentlessly committed to their plan. It was a late ten before Aunt Berty fell into a chair at the outside table. Down went her head with a thump on one arm resting there while the other one hung loosely near the ground. She snored immediately. Her big, dirty apron hung around her ankles as her feet turned inward.

Promptly the boys began their quest. It was an especially black, dark night.

With thumping heart beats they stealthily began. Cory retrieved the big ring of keys, thankful they were not around her neck, turned off the outdoor lights that focused on the guest house and shut the door behind him so very quietly.

Almost tiptoeing, Cortez followed, bug eyed with fright. He watched Berty sleeping as he passed by the porch and outside table. With genuine fear he stepped closely behind Cory who now walked briskly toward the guest house.

Now and then, a curtain moved ever so slightly in the small window next to the entrance. Because of this, Cory decided to knock…softly….his ear at the door listening for interior sounds.

Cortez kept looking around like a scared thief.

No answer.

Cory turned the key slowly, trying not to jingle the ring of other keys. With the 'click' of the lock, rats scurried out back, dogs barked and a cat hissed.

The boys held their breaths.

They stole a look toward the house…no movement from Berty.

Stepping in, they heard the quiet whirring of a fan that was aimed toward the curtain causing it to stir.

In the room was a table for two containing a floor length lacy cloth and a tea service of a dark blue pitcher with two matching cups. A short table lamp sitting on a tall bench along the wall was dimly lit. It was enough to filter the shadows of the small room. A refrigerator and large chest type freezer were against a flat wall. Except for the small curtained window in the front by the door, the room was windowless.

"Helloooo" Cory said in a modified voice.

Cortez clung close by.

No one was there.

They looked carefully in every corner, scanning the small room.

"He's not here." Cory whispered.

"No", Cortez answered.

"Boys!" Berty whispered loudly as she entered the room through the open door.

They jumped grabbing at each other, almost falling. "Whoa!" Eyes bugged.

She shuffled lop-sided towards the freezer, opened the lid, looked down, looked up at them and softly stated with a thick tongue, "Meet my MAN."

## CHAPTER THIRTY
Friday night

The boys gulped, paled, felt their knees knock and actually had to hold onto each other in a reaction of shock.

On top of boxes and boxes of frozen food, lay a man, a frosty-crumbling-swollen Zombie. He lay under the surface of the lid, looking like a body in a coffin.

Immortalized in the freezer was a cadaver.

Cory shook free from Cortez's firm grasp and looked at his aunt.

Her eyes were glazed over as she stared passionately at her 'man', now the repulsive disfigurement of a body. She looked at him lovingly and then started to waver on tired knees.

The boys grabbed her and walked her to the house, one gigantic arm over each boy's shoulder. She stumbled and mumbled as she walked.

"Found him on the desert…..saved him…..he's mine….all mine."

They walked her to the couch in the living room and placed her there. Cory put a pillow under her head while Cortez took off her heavy hiking boots. They needed her to sleep while they could do some thinking.

Some very creative thinking.

Outside, Cortez stood around with weak knees as Cory paced up and down the patio for ten minutes while smoking a cigarette. He removed his cap, two, three times and replaced it again after running his hand over his sweaty head. Although it was getting late and they had worked extra hard this day, adrenaline was rushing through every nerve of his body in renewed energy as he finally originated a plan. He clapped his hands together once in a decisive gesture. "Aha! I've got it."

It would be a wickedness like no other.

He said to Cortez, "If the principal was upset about his car, wait until he learns about what's going to happen next." He rubbed his hands together, slammed a fist into his open palm and got out his cell phone to make some calls.

"You call the girls," he said, "and I'll call Rex and Tom -Tom. We'll tell everyone to come here."

Although it was late, it was Teen-Time for them. This was the time for mischief and fun, regardless of good or bad.

"Bring your sharpest knives," he told the two boys. "And hurry. We're going to paint the town."

Squeamish at first, the boys soon rendered the adventure as a group. By now, others had heard of the plan and got into the act.

Girls stonily stood around while a prolific flow of body parts were bagged and sacked for the final plan.

Now twenty to thirty students were involved as they stealthily planned their next move.

"Hey," said Cory the leader, "we're doing nothing wrong. Isn't this the missing body the cops have been looking for? And isn't he the bad guy who was part of the porno ring back in August?"

They all shook their heads in agreement. Now acting with uncanny, part bestial feelings, they continued their morose adventure. Guilt was gone. "He has it coming!"

Most everyone became involved in the finality of the plan. No one wanted to be left out. The accelerated students, the gifted, the music department, football players.....it was like 'Who's Who at Blakely High'?

This was a form of retribution against Shieter. How dare he spoil their long...long...hours of hard work! Everyone was enthusiastically involved in the final plan for African week and enjoyed the change from the ordinarily drab curriculum. Also, they had been eager to meet the foreigners from Africa..... And he had to go and make adverse changes.

Everyone whispered. Rex, the drum major and parade leader, met each new arrival at the gate. "Shhh-shhh-shhh" was heard through out the quiet night.

The girls from the Spirit-Line kept watch over Berty, making sure her snoring was constant.

The girls giggled and the boys smiled devilishly as they schemed. Among them, they knew about hidden keys, busy shopper hovels, popular places that flagged newcomers entering Cave Creek and Carefree from either direction.

They compiled a list, and worked tirelessly through the night secretly moving about town in pairs with the bags of goods.

Meanwhile, a very large group was meeting at Tumbleweed's trying to be problem solvers. They were tired as it had been a terrible week with ridiculous happenings, all listed by Dixie.

Before them on the long rectangular table were two pitchers of beer and one of root beer for the non-drinkers. Two large platters of nachos were dispersed at each end with small plates and napkins scattered about.

The live band was the valley's best and of course, most everyone danced. Colt and Nancy were hot on the floor as were Guy and his partners…..he danced with each of the Family Farm's new lady friends. Since the four B's did not dance, they were obliged that Guy was there.

"Hey we would rather listen to the music," Bing stated.

"Why does that not surprise me," laughed Dixie. "You're Pop's friends!"

"Yeah! And we need to analyze your list," Bob added.

"Grab us for the slow ones," Brad and Blake said to their dates almost simultaneously while sipping on mugs.

Dixie, Gina and Becky Painter read the list from the note pad, over and over.

"We've narrowed it down to a possible father and a couple students," Dixie said to those who were listening as she tapped away on the pad while indicating clues gleaned from the teachers.

"It's cryptic!" They all agreed.

Becky questioned the significance of the earring being moved. "What was that all about?"

"We learned that Cory moved it, but is it a real gem or a piece of glass?" Gina continued with, "Maybe it's worth a great deal of money and came from Russia!"

They yawned. It was getting late and Pop called for extra help at the bakery so that he could get home early for once.

At 10:30 they pushed away from the table and went their separate ways with everyone agreeing to "keep in touch".

The four B's were anxious to meet with Gina "tomorrow morning at ten" to learn how to grade the Limericks.

The four look-outs were attending to their dates and not really paying attention to what was currently happening around and about town.

Although it had been a harrowing week, it was no match for the one to come.

CHAPTER THIRTY-ONE
Saturday

Gina had no idea what time it was when she heard a noise out back. Exhaustion had set in and as Nellie barked, Gina covered her head with a pillow assuming it was Pop and Dixie coming home later from the bakery.

It had been after midnight when she finally drove home barely awake but enough alert to watch for the crazy driving of Mr. Hollywood. Fortunately, she didn't see him. Unfortunately, she didn't see the secretive movement of others which by now had become quite abundant.

It took three sets of cell phone rings before Gina finally awoke and answered. Since everyone knew not to call the house phone and awake Pop after a long night at the bakery, she assumed this call to be personal.

It was eight in the morning and Nancy was on the line.

"The unthinkable has happened! Colt just called me. Body parts are showing up all over town!" In

211

hurried speech she shouted in her excitement causing Gina, now fully awake, to sit up quickly.

"What?"

"Ohhhh yeah! And they're all signed 'THE VOODOO PHANTOM'."

"Meet me at Greasy's in one hour for breakfast."

Gina made sure that she put a note on the round table for Pop and Dixie, telling them what was happening and she would be calling.

She let Nellie out who was jumping around at the back door excitedly.

"Hey, what's up with you?"

The Greyhound ran out the door unusually fast, sniffing everywhere with her nose to the ground, and then vigorously over to Gina's Jeep, barking non stop.

"Sorry, you can't go." She gave the extra anxious dog a pat on the head.

Gina opened the door to her Jeep and stood gaping at the steering wheel for a full minute while Nellie jumped up and down and barked.

A large clear baggy was duct taped to it. Sealed inside was a garish looking hand with all five fingers dripping a wet glob as the fingers spread out like an attacking spider two of which were purposely manipulated to wrap half way around the steering wheel.

She didn't scream, nor jump around in fright. Instead, she felt her heart beat in anger when she read the attached red signature taped to the bag.....THE VOODOO PHANTOM.

"Nancy, can you come and get me right now? There's a hand duct taped to my steering wheel and I know not to destroy evidence." She couldn't believe the pedantic and quiet sound of her voice. Enough was enough!

"Be there in a few."

"I'll be out front on the road by the gates. We don't want to wake Pop and Dixie.....and watch out for the crazy man using our road as a speedway."

Next, she added a sentence to the earlier note she had left on the table now telling Pop and Dixie about the 'present' attached to her steering wheel.

It was mid-morning before the two teachers arrived to a very changed town. Brown suited local police and not so local navy ones were everywhere, parked on the sides of roads entering from the north and south, and driving up and down Cave Creek Road, the only main thoroughfare. Five news helicopters were hovering noisily at no particular place.

Helmeted cops dressed in tight navy, wearing knee high black boots, rode cycles up and down the streets. Serious expressions were masked by large dark sun glasses shielding the pitiless blazing sun. They were an assortment of short, tall, lean and mean, ready to perform, all young looking men and women.

"Wow! Let's park and walk around," said Gina.

After parking in a coffee shop lot, they started walking on the northwest side of town joining a large crowd gathered there in front of a popular metal works place talking loudly and pointing. The shop is famous for its unique metal conglomeration of life sized animal figures, colorful metal flowers and Mexican pots.

In the jaws of a fifteen foot metal Tyrannosaurus Rex, was a decapitated head, un-bagged and tightly tucked between serrated teeth. The spiked fangs pressed together tightly in revulsion as melting flesh rolled out between them and globs of liquid dripped on the sidewalk. Written on a piece of cardboard attached by a looped string to a bottom serrated tooth, were the words... THE VOODOO PHANTOM.

This unprecedented event was one of many spread all over town, some openly visual and some in hidden places. For each find, the same three words were printed or written differently. Forensics noted later that the signatures were dissimilar each time, meaning many were involved. Most importantly, the numerous misspellings clued them to possible student involvement. In many cases, PHANTOM became FANTUM, PANTUM, and PHINTUM. "Who else do we know who doesn't give a dang?" They said.

Much later, dogs were brought in to sniff out the pieces and parts. Locals, however, beat them to it when the frozen parts melted in the heat and the fetid odor wafted about town like a curse. People literally followed their noses like a plague. "It's around her somewhere," was heard throughout the day's uncanny search for a heinous prize.

Cops answered calls long into Saturday night as new parts were found. Sunday was an exhausting equal.

The town became crowded as curious participants from down in the valley arrived to join in the festival of search. It was later said that the local saloons took bets as to where the next body part would be found. Because of this, mobs began exploring everywhere, walking from one shop to another. Business owners became excited as new cliental thickened their cash registers.

This Saturday morning, 'Movie-Star Gorgeous' was talking wildly to men rushing out of cars clearly marked C.S.I. Stunned, they pointed and stared like all the others at the dinosaur and its morbid contents.

The words of the day were, "Don't touch, don't cover and don't damage clues. Just call us!"

Forensics was in control.

The re-known members of 'The Family Farm' cycle group rode around town helping spread these directions for forensics. They felt important!

Next door, in an adjoining lot of crafts and metal statues, stood a Texas longhorn bull with head slightly bowed, ready to trample. Hooked on one pointed horn, and also un-bagged, was the milky white fleshy palm of a hand. A few fingers were missing which led them to the scary thought that these would reappear in another mysterious place. Attached were the same three words.

After Gina told Delilah about the bagged piece attached to her steering wheel, the forensic team decided to start there with identification of the cadaver.

Beginning with the DNA found last August from remnants of the missing body out on the desert, they discovered immediately that "this is the missing photographer, the bad guy who died from venomous bites."

Instantly, this good news was spread around town in seconds with the important fact that each piece tested came from the same body. Ease and calm now invented new discussions. Questions evolved. "Where has he been kept all this time?"

Later, they pointed fingers in every direction as they speculated who initiated this entire disgusting affair. A big debate developed everywhere with half accusing the principal and the other half defending him.

"Since 'The Voodoo Phantom' is written on each ugly piece and it's very African, he invented this monstrosity last August."

"If so, where did he keep the body, and how could he lacerate it in about a hundred pieces and spread it around town all by himself?"

"He's too much of a dandy," said one.

"How would he have the time, or interest?" noted another.

In the meantime, Dr. Shieter, as he liked to be called, remained incognito while forensics had to test each new piece that was delivered to the temporary station they set up at the local sheriffs' office. As a matter of fact, it was learned much later via the teen network that he sat at home in a dark house with shutters closed pretending to be out of town.

Cave Creek carried on without him.

A toe was found in a jar of honey that was from a heavily locked, wheeled kiosk on the outskirts of town. The honey man discovered that the lock had been broken and the contaminated jar of honey had been purposely set aside without a lid. He was thankful the numerous other jars remained sealed.

Shop owners in the two adjoining towns of Cave Creek and Carefree, scrambled to find similar bags of flesh each time a bagged piece was found in a store. Could there be others? As they worried, it became the scourge of the town's business owners as to where the swollen, raw cadaver meat would next appear. They soon became un-impressed with the wagering and the search that continued all weekend. If it had not been for new customers coming in while jingling coins in their pockets, owners would have locked their doors. Instead, they fed the anxiety by adding temporary help.

Pop and Dixie were furious when a dripping bag contaminated a fifteen pound container of flour. Feeling like everybody else, if it had not been for the out-of-towners spending money everywhere, they would have closed the bakery for the night. Dixie had to make an emergency mad dash down in the valley for more supplies for tonight's work. They would double the batches of whipped cream pasties and popovers. 'The Family Farm' four were extra helpers.

"My disgruntled teenage employee did this," Pop said as held a piece of paper in his hand for his pals to read. "She was the only other person who knew about the hidden key....and the note signed voodoo phantom is her handwriting."

The same recognition occurred with other business owners. Soon 'Mean Teens' were the two popular words spread about town and glued to the tongues of all the local gossip groups.

By late Saturday night, Heleena had a long list of possible student suspects connected to the devious adventure. "They will have to pay in one way or another," she adamantly announced all over town as she skirted around in her flowered knee length baggy pants from one discovered bag to another. "I can hardly wait until Monday!"

By late Saturday afternoon, Gina, Nancy and friends announced they were finished searching and all went to Gina's house to grade the Limericks as planned.

Gina spread the large round table with snacks and drinks to everyone's pleasure. They devoured a variety of chips and dips together with the popular small burger-sliders all washed down with bottles of Root Beer and pitchers of iced tea.

Nancy graded her own bag of stuff.

Gina graded her bag of stuff....the Western Biographies, but not before she handed the stack of Limericks to the four B's and their girlfriends. Not having graded before, they found this task to be a fun adventure after Gina discussed the criteria and related grading scale.

"All Limericks will receive an 'A' or 'B' or re-write if incorrect."

"Hah!" They each scoffed with the same attitude. "I wish I'd had a teacher like you back in my days."

"Well, I want this to have been a fun activity. Trust me. They'll have many other difficult assignments."

They all agreed that it was a pleasure to grade papers among a group of friends, especially since they kept talking about the affairs of the day. Time flew while talking about all the body parts that were found.

And, they all knew that Bing's analysis was the best. "The kids were upset with the principal's announcement cancelling the week-end's festivities. This could have easily happened back in New York. Teens get upset when you pull the rug out from under them."

"Actually," continued Brad, "it was the last domino to fall, a kind of retribution. The first one was the chaining of vending machines. He could have handled the tardy situation better. A marine learns about consequences and how to avoid the negative."

"We need to grade together more often," Gina noted. "Nancy and I can always use extra help." They winked at each other.

"Just feed us," the group almost said in unison.

Watching the time, Blake said, "We need to leave to help out at the bakery if everyone's finished."

They left after handing Gina a stack of Limericks completely graded....a task which would have otherwise taken her eight hours to complete.

"Wow!" Gina sighed.

"We've been doing this wrong for the past five years," Nancy added .while looking at her 'to do' stack which was taller than the 'done' one. "I need to hang on to Colt and train him as my assistant.  His after-hours' bonus can simply be…me."

"Super idea!" They high-fived.

Rick called while they were working.

"So what's been happening?"

"Nothing!  It's been a boring week-end."

"I've heard otherwise."

"What have you heard?"

"Someone was very busy during the night."

"When are you coming back with my surprise?"

"Give me some details of what's happening."

"Let's just say that your missing corpse is spread all over town…and not by Pack Rats!"

## CHAPTER THIRTY-TWO
Saturday-late

Nancy left to go home with "I'm done for the night," and bagged her supplies with a yawn.

"Let's do breakfast again tomorrow. We need to relish the excitement," said Gina as she waved goodbye and continued to chat away to Rick on her cell with the details of the day…. "and at the saloons they're placing bets as to where the next body parts will be."

"With the heat, that should be easy."

She laughed. "They just follow their noses."

"Colt's placing a stringent curfew in town this entire week until we have more details."

"Curfew?" Her question sounded like a complaint.

"Teens have to be off the streets after ten."

"Good luck with that one. How about old men?" She told him about Mr. Hollywood's wild driving.

"I'm on top of it?"

"Good! He's been using Spur Cross as a speedway. We think that he's an ex-racing champion and that's why he drives such expensive cars."

"Maybe."

"What are you doing up there at Blue Ridge anyway?"

"You'll soon find out."

"Back to the body parts….They were frozen you know."

"Yes, I know."

"You know everything."

"And more. But, I need to find the person who placed that threat on your windshield."

"Who tells you everything?"

"That's my job."

Gina flopped down on her bed, kicked off her shoes and felt the coolness of the pillow under her head while still talking. When the conversation changed to the weather and undressing from the clothes they were wearing, she couldn't believe that she fell asleep. A sharp click from the other end prompted her to hang up and quit.

She was exhausted.


Berty awoke late Saturday morning feeling sick as she pulled tangled hair away from her face and very dry mouth.

How much vodka did she drink? In a daze, she tried to remember some of the events. It seems that there was a crowd around her…but was she dreaming?

As she started to move around, she wondered why she was still on the couch. This was very unusual and her suspicions dictated a search.

First, she called for Cory to feed all the barking dogs.

No response.

Considering it was late Saturday morning, he must be out with his friends which she allowed him to do on weekends.

But, he always fed the dogs and cats in the morning. This was one of his main chores.

Standing, she winced at the pain in her head, grabbed a small bottle of water from the counter and downed two head ache pills. She felt extra clumsy while fumbling her way through the kitchen and bathroom where she splashed a great deal of water on her face.

As she thought of Cory again, his truck entered the gated compound and two boys jumped out. The dogs squealed during feeding and Berty was contented that he had come back with feelings of responsibility.

The truck left as quickly as it had arrived.

She wanted to talk to him, but it was too late by the time she opened the door to leave the house.

While standing there clinging to the door frame for balance, she surveyed her beloved compound. To the right, the dogs were in their large fenced dog-run eating happily. Straight ahead was the tall wooden fenced area that contained her treasures. Slightly to the left was the guest house where she had daily tea with her friend.

The door was open. Why?

Twisting to the left she could see the large ring of keys hanging there just inside the kitchen. The special key was there.

Had she in her drunken stupor visited him and carelessly forgot to close the door and lock it?

She drank the small plastic bottle of water dry, threw it in the large barrel on the porch with her other collections, then shuffled to the guest house.

Her friend would be upset with her carelessness, so she decided not to tell him as she opened the lid for their visit.

Horrified, she stared a full five minutes with a pounding heart.

In the yawning empty space above frozen old packages which had lifted the now gone cadaver to easier eye viewing, was a ragged piece of cardboard with the words, THE VOODOO PHANTOM.

# CHAPTER THIRTY-THREE
Sunday   October 23

Pop and Dixie left early for the bakery knowing today would be a money-maker. They had worked extra hours late into the morning with the help of their cycle friends in preparation for the predicted larger than usual town crowd; also, the extra help that had been hired manning the sales needed directions. Like all others, they were at peace with the horrors of yesterday because newly hired police descended on the town like fleas. Brown suits, navy suits and under cover cops were out and about. The latter were stand-outs with their sloppy clothes and beards.

Movie Star Gorgeous was seen running around town from one end to the other with her pasted on jeans. Her crowd of followers grew as she inspected each site.

Although curfew had been set at ten for teens, none showed last night. An uncanny feeling of emptiness was felt by all the locals. Out-of-towners noticed nothing unusual as they raced about from one end of Cave Creek Road to the other end. They were impressed the way the road curled through town, beginning in Cave Creek and ending somewhere between Carefree and Scottsdale. By day, it was an easy, walkable three to five mile scenic loop. By night a busy stream of motorcycles, trucks, and BMW convertibles flowed from one bar to the next. Considering the lively and unique happenings, the vibrations of the little towns shook the pavement.

But, an unusual amount of teen employees called in sick Saturday night and this morning. "Guilty", was the word of the day as locals speculated about who, where, why, when…..was the cause. Family volunteers reluctantly worked as fill-ins.

The October heat seemed to go unnoticed with the new excitement of a never before mystery that stirred the town like an end of summer wild dust-devil. Aware of the heavy flow of traffic, local coffee shops, bars, and eateries extended hours, opening extra early and closing much later.

Gina and Nancy sat in the patio at Greasy's enjoying a late breakfast of biscuits and gravy while watching the unusually busy street traffic. Soon, Mr. Hollywood drove by with Berty as his passenger. To their disgust he was wearing an African mask which did nothing to flatter his open shirt bare chested appearance.

"He either borrowed it from one of the students, or purchased it from the school store where they're on sale to help finance next Friday's events," said Gina sipping her coffee.

"What next Friday's events?" Nancy questioned sarcastically.

"Did you notice Berty? She was not her smiley, happy self."

"Actually, she looked grumpy and depressed. She usually covers her frizzy hair with a hat."

As the two sat discussing Berty, Mr. Hollywood, and all the happenings from the past week, Dixie called to bring them up-to-date with the newest findings of putrid flesh. Her voice was extra feisty.

"Are you eating?"

"Yep!"

"O.K., I'll save my list for another time. Incidentally, Rick's back in town. He stopped by the bakery earlier." She hung up abruptly with, "See ya later."

"And here he is." Gina sparkled looking up at him as he sat a box of pastry on the table.

"For my ladies!"

"Ahah! My surprise!"

He moved her curls away from her face, curled his palm around her neck and gave her a quick kiss.

"No, that's for later." He pulled two chairs next to the table and waved at a man who had accompanied him into Greasy's and who was now standing at the counter reading a menu.

"This is Dickie from Blue Ridge."

A man of medium height limped over, extended a thin hand to each of the girls and reintroduced himself repeating their names with a slight wheeze. A square short sleeve cotton shirt hung just below his belt line and over slightly baggy denims. Because of thin shoulders acting as a hanger, Gina thought him to be quite gaunt.

Reminiscing to last August Gina quickly said, "You're the person that helped save our new teacher after she was kidnapped."

"I did my best." He didn't smile as he clasped his hands together near the edge of the table, leaned back in his chair and squinted at her.

"My turn," said Rick while opening the box of pastries. "You might as well know that we think his cousin 'the chief' is here hiding out in town somewhere."

"You mean the porno king that was the cause of all the trouble last August?" Nancy questioned with surprise as she continued. "And wasn't he connected to the photographer who is now being spread all over town?"

Rick grimaced.

Dickie sniffed clearing his throat.

Gina cut four chocolate eclairs in half.

Nancy doled out napkins.

New coffee was served as the four sat in silence eating éclairs.

Gina began, "Maybe he was the masked peeking pervert."

"Nope, he wasn't." Rick was too quick.

"Ahah! You know something." Gina leaned into his face.

"I know a lot!" He did his half smile and added three mini tubs of half and half to his hot coffee.

Out front on Cave Creek Road next to their patio, a steady stream of traffic flowed bumper to bumper both coming and going. Among trucks and expensive cars were intermittent groups of cycle riders, the mom and pop kind.

Expensive cars included an abundance of refurbished Corvettes and Chevrolets, all bearing historical license plates.

But most notable was the string of convertibles and the drivers; each person behind the wheel was wearing an African mask.

"I guess the look is catching," said Gina.

Nancy added, "As long as they're being purchased from the school, it's money for next Friday's parade."

227

"I heard it was called off," said Rick.

"Hah! How little you know." It was her turn. "We have a plan. Remember tomorrow!" Gina looked at Nancy and winked.

Rick stared at Gina as the corners of his mouth slowly formed a smile. "This has to be good."

Just as Gina said, "It's a secret," Dickie quickly sat forward in his chair intently watching movement out on the road.

He sat quietly staring, moving his head slowly with the flowing traffic out front. Squinting in thought, he rubbed his chin smoothing out the untrimmed whiskers. Someone of particular interest caused his notable reaction.

Although the girls were oblivious while finishing the last pieces of éclairs, Rick caught the movement.

He nodded slightly at Dickie who nodded back without moving his hand from his chin. It was their secret.

Out front, a parade of convertibles with masked drivers moved along oblivious of any investigation.

## CHAPTER THIRTY-FOUR
Sunday Evening


Gina planned her glittery-sexy outfit for school tomorrow as discussed with Nancy earlier in the day before they parted.

"Deep v-necks and thigh-high skirts," was the look they both agreed on for their meeting after school with Shieter.

Now she was getting clothes ready while talking on the speaker phone with Nancy. "I have a red top and red skirt that I can camouflage for the classroom with a short bolero cover-up and knee length black tights."

"I'll dress the same with black colors. We'll take off our tights after the campus is empty."

"I made the appointment for three thirty."

"I'm excited. That gives us time after school to choreograph our meeting. Tell Dixie to warn the secretaries who are still there to help us out in any way needed."

"Will do and see you after school."

"Hot dog!" Dixie exclaimed after Gina told her their scheme. "I'll make sure to keep him in his office; he's such a 'scatter-head'." Then she turned to Pop and shared her plans for tomorrow afternoon about prepping the secretaries for the girls' meeting with Shieter.

Rick Del Rio arrived on his Harley before dark.

"Here, put this on and ride with me." He handed Gina a pearly white helmet. "It matches your white short-shorts."

"Ok, ok. I'll go put on long pants."

"You're fine. We're just going two miles down the road." He pushed her hair back, helped her with her helmet, than smiled broadly.

"Cute!"

"What's up?" Gina asked while securing her left foot on a pedal and eagerly swinging her long right leg over the back.

He didn't answer.

At dusk, her favorite time of the day, the soft navy blue of the early evening highlighted a pleasurable mood, an urge for a different adventure. Shadows of tall Saguaros lay like circular sticks on the brown earth as cotton-tailed rabbits hopped away from stagnant brittle bush freckling the yard out front.

Nights during the last week of October were perfect with temperatures hovering slightly into eighty, and Gina was dressed in the costume of all desert people for this time of year, cotton shorts and top.

Slowly, he pulled away and down the road.

"Watch out for the maniac in the convertible."

"I know."

"I forgot. You know everything." She didn't see his half smile but felt his chuckle with her arms around his middle. "A six pack." She tickled him and squeezed thick loose flesh near his middle with both of her hands.

He squirmed. "You're going to get it. Don't molest the driver."

Dusk to dawn lights were starting to twinkle out in the distance in no particular pattern as they pulled into a gated driveway that led to a medium sized stucco house. A dim porch light glowed near the front door which was set back about five yards from the edge of the patio entrance. Interior lights were few.

He parked and secured the 'cycle.

"Wait here."

She took off her helmet and hung it on the handle next to his. Looking around, she noted that the acreage, sided with rusted pipe fencing, was near neighbors. At a short distance away, they too were set back from the front of Spur Cross Road allowing for some privacy.

"Hey," she yelled as Rick scooped her up while her back was turned and carried her to the closed front door.

"Your surprise." After setting her down, he took something from his front pocket and put it in her hand. "A key to my new house."

She found herself holding her breath, than finally letting it out with a long "Ohhh."

"It's a start….a key to my heart. No one else has a key to my house," he proudly added with assurance.

"Wow!" Was all she could say in an undertone as she turned it around in her hand fingering its heart shaped head. Next, she opened the locked door and turned the handle swinging the door open.

"Oops." Again he picked her up, shut the door with his heel, walked her through a stylish great room and into a large bedroom where he gently placed her on a king sized bed. Curtains billowed at an open window.

"Hey, you can come and go as you wish, or move in. I get embarrassed sleeping with you at Pop's house." His green eyes glistened while he quickly removed his form fitting black tee exposing a firm, darkly tanned frame and joined her on the king size bed. Moving closely he grabbed the top of her leg, slid his hand down to her bony knee and pulled a long slender leg over him so they now lay facing one another.

"Wait!" Fearing she would lose the key out of her pocket as her shorts came off, she had to roll on top of him to reach the nearby Oak dresser.

"Super," he breathed hotly, sucked in his breath and rubbed her back then her buttocks, grabbing each cheek with his hands.

Startled by a soft cough from a nearby room, she raised on her elbows. "What was that?"

"Dickie is staying with me for about a week. And, when I go back, I'm not going without you this time," his voice now a passionate whisper.

Considering the extra monstrosity of events yesterday and today, she was not terribly excited at the moment and needed to slow things down. She rolled next to him, stared at his lips and rubbed her forefinger over them in slow motion, a feather touch….a long, long thirty-seconds. "I can't stay. I have a big day tomorrow. Special plans."

"So I fear."

A welcoming breeze from the open window did nothing to help cool their passion.

Out on the road, Dickie wheezed while leaning his thin frame on the gates waiting for a particular car to come by.

## CHAPTER THIRTY-FIVE

Dickie did not have to wait long. Lights in the distance raced his way, than slowed upon approach.

As planned, the driver switched to parking lights only, moved slowly off the main road and approached very near the gate stopping a couple yards from his boots.

"Dickie, is that really you?"

"Take off the mask and quit playing the part."

He didn't move. "What part?"

"It's been about thirty years, but I recognize the voice."

The Jeep convertible hummed as the two men stared at each other in the semi-darkness of a half moon. From a combination of desert sand and rock, the ground flushed a pale iridescence offering a dim view of the night.

Dickie wheezed and coughed.

"Same old problem."

"You should know all about it. You gave it to me." He spat on the ground and wiped his mouth with the back of his hand.

After a long pause, "Get in."

Dickie didn't move. "You take me for a fool?"

"What do you want? You contacted me.... Surprise!" Flamboyantly he waved his arms in the air as he talked quietly, just above a whisper. "How did you do it? But wait! You always had your mousy ways of getting info." He spoke with his hands moving back and forth to his stationary mask, an eerie scene because the silvery painted odd shaped lips did not move.

Small Kangaroo Rats scurried about in the quiet night jetting from bush to hole escaping the piercing eyes of night owls.

"You're such a show. You owe me." He shifted his weight off his handicapped leg but remained leaning on the gate, his sharp eyes watching every hand movement coming from the Jeep.

White knuckles caught the buffered gleam of the moon as the man grasped the steering wheel tightly with both hands. In the pocket of the driver's door was his gun with a silencer attached. Although he was quick, he knew Dickie to be quicker, and he noticed that one hand was always out of sight, tucked near his loose shirt. He had to think. A tricky move to open his door where the gun was handy would not work because his cousin, highly trained and aware of every gunman's trick, would be faster. He remembered him well and knew the look of deserving hate staring at him now in the dimness.

"Can we be friends?" He raised his left shoulder to indicate calmness as he took his left hand off the steering wheel raising it with palm upwards as he spoke.

"Don't move!" Dickie's words were so abrupt the driver slowly put his hand back on the wheel.

They each heard a door close in the distance back at the house, an indication for the driver to move on.

"We'll meet again soon," he uttered while slowly pulling onto Spur Cross Road and not looking back.

Dickie's heart was pounding, not from fear, but out of hatred for the man who tried to kill him thirty years ago in another state, so far away.

Rick had urgently told him to stay away from his cousin. "Let me deal with him my way with mounting evidence. Your job is to simply identify him."

Although he had made a solemn promise to Rick who had become a new good friend, he was prepared to defend himself and would carry his favorite gun while in Cave Creek.

Unfortunately, he now needs to watch his back from the man who used to be a childhood playmate but has become a devious and conniving killer while 'faming' his way in the business of porn.

No other person knew him so well.

Behind the mask was the king of terror.

## CHAPTER THIRTY-SIX

As Rick and Gina started to drive out of the yard they saw Dickie walking back to the house.

Rick stopped. "Out for some fresh air?"

"I needed a little walk after today's long trip." The darkening night masked feelings of annoyance from a few moments ago. Not one to change quickly from one mood to another, and never a good liar, he simply flipped a quick hand wave and looked down at his path being careful not to stumble.

"Snakes are out in October in abundance," Gina warned. "Watch your step."

He frowned and moved on.

Rick drove slowly for the next two miles with Gina clinging to his waist, her head resting on his back. Warm night air added to the tranquilizing effect. It had been a perfect night, but now he began to worry with thoughts of Dickie out walking this late and believed he had met someone at the gate. Why else would he dip his head in guilt while greeting them?

He would have to keep him close.....encourage him to help with the mysteries of the town. Because Dickie was coming from a rough and knowledgeable crowd, Rick had shared the town's weird happenings with him while in the peacefulness of the Blue Ridge. Drinking coffee and then beer on the front porch near the tall firs, they solved everything.

Walking Gina now to the door, he warned her about the enormity of the bizarre events that could yet happen.

He hugged her and kept talking. "It's not over yet. Tomorrow is huge. Will the culprits show their faces in school? What's the principal going to do?" He spoke in a quiet manner and looked around suspiciously. "How dare someone climb over the fence and puncture tires on your Wrangler."

He looked at her as he held her at arms length. "It's got to be a couple of your disgruntled students. But the peeking pervert thing puts this over the edge. It's gone beyond simple pranks of cryptic threats and moveable earrings. Something is wrong about all of this and you're the innocent victim."

"Students are capable of doing crazy things without thinking of the consequences," she began. "A select few can be quite notorious for one reason or another."

It was Rick's turn. "It usually involves family and sports. This is what they live for...family relationships and social approval."

She unlocked the door and before he stepped away to leave he said again, "Tomorrow is going to be heavy. Watch everything that goes on around you and don't leave school late....especially don't leave alone."

After they said their goodbyes, he began to worry about Dickie at home alone and roared the 'cycle down the highway full speed.

CHAPTER THIRTY-SEVEN
Monday-October 24

Gina pulled into the faculty parking lot her usual six fifteen, a favorite time to get prepared for the daily five classes. Pop had always told her, "Preparation eliminates exhaustion," so she fell into the family motto early in life. Besides, today was a special day and she welcomed the excitement.

Only a few cars were there, including Nancy's.

While stepping out of her Jeep Wrangler with a big bag of graded papers, the biographies from her Western Literature classes and Limericks from Science Fiction, Guy pulled in next to her.

Following a wolf whistle he asked, "What wild plans do you have for the day?"

"It's a secret! Hey I have a bolero over my v-neck and red tights under my dress." Walking next to him as they headed to the front office for the mail of the day, his fresh scent of soap and after shave was intoxicating.

239

"Not enough! I have four sisters and I can see right through your escapades." A usual gallant smile spread over his tanned face.

"Lucky you! You arrive everyday dressed in Blakely High sporting goods."

"Comes with the job! I'm going to stop by the room of 'little red' to see what she's wearing. I bet you two have a plan as usual."

"Comes with the job! Hey where were you this weekend? I didn't see your racers running anywhere."

"We had an early morning run from Bartlett Lake to the school on Sunday, ten miles up hill. Fortunately, their parents supported their early bedtime Saturday night." Opening the door to the English Department Building he added, "These kids are committed and plan to do their best against the African long distance runners.....if events are not called off by you know who."

"Keep them practicing," she said with confidence while unlocking the door to her room. After laying her things on her desk she went two doors down the hall to Nancy's room where Guy stood staring at Nancy.

"Ahah!" He said. "Stand up; turn around."

Nancy sat there with folded arms. "Am I in a contest?" She wiggled her shoulders in a flirty manner.

He pointed back and forth between them. "You two are up to something....Gotta run; keep me informed." Hurrying away he almost crashed into Heleena coming out of the office.

Gina said to Nancy, "Let's go see Rich and tell him our plans. He's our supportive anchor."

Heleena met them in the hallway as they walked out of Nancy's room. "Wow! What's the occasion?" She asked after eyeing them from head to toe.

"Nothing special," said Nancy.

"Nope! We decided that Mondays need to be dressy days to brighten the week ahead." Gina twirled around and her thigh-high dress flared."

"Bright idea," Heleena said surprisingly, then added, "Make note of suspicious acting students today to possibly add to my list that's growing longer and longer. We're positive that the Saturday spread of body parts was done by angry students." She took off in a hurry, her hands in the pockets of her ankle length gathered skirt heading towards the custodian's building for her early morning usual. Fingering the pack in her pocket, she often told others that she was quitting, next year.

"Hey Rich!" The two young teachers entered his room strutting in model run-way style.

"Ok, what's going on?" Slouched down over his desk and barely visible behind a stack of papers, Richard Cloud, looked up and readjusted his burgundy tie. "I hope I'm presentable for the likes of you two," he joked.

"We'll tell you about it at lunch!"

"I can hardly wait."

It was now a hallway of whispering faces as Gina walked to her room. Everyone acted mysteriously and in a suspicious manner grouping together in small circles of cliques. She could read them like the cover of a book and would be extra alert as the day progressed.

Students in the room passed notes around while pretending to be listening to her lesson of the day. Some mouthed quiet messages.....a known fact that students are able to read lips. A few years back when she did her student teaching, she had been told that "they are part of the bat family and move by radar." This truth she witnessed as the day progressed.

Today's job was easy. Hand Limericks back and discuss them.

Hand 'bios' back and discuss them.

During the class before lunch, Jamie Mink and Kim Rose were a little too quiet. Walking over to talk to them with a few minutes remaining of the class period, she was approached by Heleena who scurried in through the room loudly. "Here is the list of possible student involvement," was all she said as she put the list on Gina's desk and hurried out.

Every student all of a sudden became a giraffe.

Jamie and Kim hurried over to her desk to talk about their limericks.

"Thanks for the good grade. Which one is better?" Now they were their silly selves.

"Twins! I gave them each an A+" She made sure she had read and graded these two when she culled them from the stack before handing it to the four B's for the grading process.

"Gotta run to lunch!"

"See ya later!"

As always, they became hand waves in the door frame when leaving.

Gina puffed a loud sigh, sat in her desk chair and swiveled around to her small fridge for her usual glass bottle of Mexican coke to take to lunch, her Hazelnut decaf long gone earlier this morning. The small fridge idea was one she had copied from an old retiring teacher named Colonel Redbird. However, his fridge contained a bottle of soda enhancer.

Frowning at her desk top, she noticed that the list of student trouble makers was gone.

"Jamie and Kim took the list that Heleena gave me.  Do you have a copy?" She spoke matter-of-factly to her lunch time friends.

"It's quite extensive," said Rich chewing on his salad.

"What proof does she have," questioned Nancy cutting her sandwich in half.

The loud speaker crackled as the principal began to speak in a louder than usual monotone: "Those students who have been involved in the horrific caper over the weekend better come forward or there will be NO off-campus-lunch passes starting tomorrow."

"Oops, that's not good," said Gina.

"Wow! We better bargain a fantastic plan when we see him today at three thirty," said Nancy.

"See me after school," added Rich.  "I'll help you think it out."

During the last two classes of the day, Gina determined that the principal's announcement was a further jinx to the student body atmosphere. The gravity of the afternoon spiraled into a tornado.  Students glared and whispered back and forth.

They were just plain nasty when they tried to argue about the proper usage of the words "hang and hung" during a lecture she gave in Western Literature concerning the killing of horse thieves.

"They were hanged by the neck," she said.

"Hung." A number of students interrupted.

"Hanged."

"Hung." Another group repeated angrily without looking up.

"Ok.  Look it up in the dictionary or on your computers when you get home. For this week only,

243

every time you find these two words written properly in a magazine or newspaper, bring in the article and I will give you five points extra credit with a maximum of twenty-five possible."

They were pleased.

She was pleased and moved on.


The students and teachers became more "testy" as the day progressed, and she was thankful the last period of the day was her free prep time. While walking through the hallway passed the open doorway of a full classroom of freshman she heard:

"This sucks! That sucks!" The teacher waved his fist in the air at them. "The next time I hear that word, I'll give you something to suck on," he shouted red faced.

"Whew! It's a good thing he waved his fist," Gina told Nancy during their prep hour as they drove to Greasy's for planned snacks. Dixie had told Gina earlier what Shieter liked for munching after school, plus his favorite coffee drink. "Feed a man…fill him up," was her catty statement as she handed Gina the list the day before.

They settled in a table out on the patio near the road watching the movement of tourists while waiting for their order.

Sunday traffic was gone but the usual half dozen older men driving expensive convertibles or motorcycles still existed on the main road fronting the restaurants and bars. Soon, the thick gold chain around Mr. Hollywood's neck glistened in the afternoon sun as he drove by in a shiny new convertible, this time alone. His extra dark sunglasses and shiny gold beret were always part of his costume.

"Where are the women?"

"You mean his two followers." Nancy added, "I saw Berty this weekend doing her usual desert search."

They took their time, planning to arrive after the last bell rang when the campus was empty of most everyone except the secretaries, administrators and few coaches out on the field.

On campus, they carried the food to Rich's room for the meeting as planned.

"I'm donating my Golden Pathos trailing plant as a gift to Shieter." Richard/Raquel Cloud bragged. "You want to have numerous reasons for your meeting to help confuse him….drinks, food, a plant."

As always the girls followed his wisdom after tying a bow round the pot.

Dixie rang and said, 'The office is ready."

## CHAPTER THIRTY-EIGHT
Monday afternoon

With hearts thumping vigorously, they slowly walked towards the office building with Gina leading the way. Every time Nancy lingered to pull down her skirt, arrange her v-neck top or check one of her high heels—taking it off, then putting it back on—Gina stopped too and did a below the waist hand wave.

"Come-on. I'll do most of the talking but just be sure to pitch in when you can."

They opened the office door to the scent of vanilla candles so strong, they had to turn around and look at the label of the door again assuring they were in the right place. Overhead lighting was off, and dim lights from small desk lamps sent shapely shadows on adjacent walls, changing the cheap grey carpet to rich smooth velvet.

They stopped and stared, afraid to move while listening to the soft sounds of jazz playing in the background.

Dixie came sneaking around the corner and motioned with her fore finger for them to move forward. "Come on. He's waiting."

They followed her passed staring secretaries, all smiling in connivance, one with sparkling glasses as she stood next to a lamp, her hands covering her mouth to hide a giggle.

The small group of six followed them to the principal's door, acting as if they had been wined and dined waiting for this encounter.

When Gina asked Dixie later what the heck that was all about and did they have some wine at the office since they were so happy, she replied, "I'll never tell."

Dixie motioned for everyone to get back to their desks and nodded for the two young teachers to knock on the door. She skirted away around the corner.

"Come in," Shieter crankily ordered.

"Snacks for our talk," Gina purred as she handed Shieter his favorite drink, an extra large vanilla latte with half the pumps of vanilla and extra espresso. She adjusted the long straw towards him.

"Do you mind if we join you? We've had such a 'horrrrrible' day," said Gina while pointing to the chairs next to his desk. Nancy just shook her head up and down speechlessly, eyes dilated.

As previously choreographed by Dixie, they pulled the two roller chairs next to him, putting him in the middle. All three sat together behind his larger than normal desk. The two girls closely positioned their chairs facing him and leaned their elbows on the cherry wood surface. They crossed their legs showing bare bony knees and smooth thighs where their skirts fell in soft, short waves.

Speechless, he looked from one to the other.

Acting oblivious to him, they made an issue of mouthing their straws, showing extra bright lipstick and sighing one after the other:

"These are Soooo Good!"

"And after such a Hard Day!"

"We love curly fries. Do you want some?"

He cleared his throat a couple times. "Those are my favorite."

"We brought extra sauce."

"Your favorite," said Nancy. Gina gave her THE look.

He didn't get it!

The girls made an issue of playing with the fries, curling them around their tongues before chewing. "MMMmmmmmm."

He glanced at them briefly before taking a handful.

Nearly finished with their drinks, they needed to move on.

"We're forgetting our plant, a gift to you," said Gina.

Nancy shook her head up and down.

Gina had purposely set the plant on the floor in front of the door when entering and now she made a show of bending over and picking it up slowly.

"Here Nancy, put it over there with his others if it is OK with Dr. Shieter."

"Good idea. It's remarkably beautiful," he added while watching Nancy reach up to the very top shelf in her short-short skirt.

He wiped his lips with his hand and didn't know what to think.

"We are here with a possible solution to this entire campus mess." Gina began extra softly while raising her skirt above her knee and rubbing her leg for no apparent reason.

"More fries?" Nancy asked shoving them under his chin.

248

"These are good," he said smiling at her.

"How would you like to be a hero?" Gina began looking him in the eyes closely, speaking very slowly, almost cooing.

"Such as?"

"Well, I know for a fact that the big parade this Friday needs a Grand Marshal."

No response. He sipped on his Latte.

She began to worry. "Many, many big news stations, even national ones, will be in Cave Creek covering this 'verrry' rare event." She played with her skirt as she emphasized her words.

No response. He chewed briskly on a curly fry.

She and Nancy did an under cover eye contact of emergency.

Suddenly, Nancy's cell phone rang a loud and very popular Western tune. Instead of answering it, she got up and started dancing, twirling around too fast showing black lacies and butt cheeks for an instant. She laughed, the fake one known only to Gina, as she flopped back in the chair.

Shieter's eyes got larger as he nodded with the beat.

With his back slightly turned, Gina got up and faked a stumble, falling on his shoulders with her head close to his.

"I'm so sorry," she whimpered in her half voice so very close to his lips, "I reached for another fry and my heel caught under the chair leg."

She quickly moved back in place as he moved forward.

"Who sent you two?" He asked abruptly squinting one eye.

"The student body president.  He said that they need a Grand Marshal for the parade and recommended you."

"Why didn't he ask me?" He shifted in his chair.

She leaned closely over him.

"He was afraid, considering all the trouble that the student body has caused lately.  And, I might add, he is positive that the spray painting of your car was done by pranksters from another school. You know how nasty these school rivals can act."

It was Nancy's turn.  "He's in my class and said that he'll preach to all the student body to respect the tardy policy if only you will rescind the order of no lunch time passes and re-instate all the African events." She didn't mess around.

"He said that?"

She shook her head up and down.  "He said that today!"  She clasped her hands together in prayer.

"Well!" He got up and pranced around with his shoulders back. They said nothing while he strutted slowly around the room. "Well!  I am so fortunate that you two brought this to my attention."

Nancy began talking again hoping to put a positive cap on his decision. "And, later in the day there will be a big Western dance at Tumbleweed's honoring you, the Grand Marshal, and all our African guests."

Gina could have hugged her. Later she bragged to all their friends, "Our hero found her voice!"

"Thank you for coming to see me and…."

Dixie knocked loudly on the door as planned when her phone buzzed via Gina's cell.

She opened the door without waiting for an answer and walked halfway into the room. "We are all leaving now!"

Gina got up. "Oh, oh, my, I need to get going. I promised Pop that I would help him with the pastries tonight."

"Me too," said Nancy looking at her watch. "My dog's at the groomers."

Dixie and Gina glared at her instantly. She didn't have a dog.

"Again, thanks for coming to see me. Tell the Student Body President, what ever his name is, that we need to meet tomorrow during lunch." His nod up and down was pleasing as he pressed his fingers together in push-ups.

They left, all three 'high-fiving' with success. "Whew. I really have some work to do. Actually, the president is in my first hour class and I'll talk with him immediately....better yet, I'll call him tonight. Maybe he can stop the tardies for Tuesday morning classes. We've always said that student cell-a-thon is faster than digital."

"This is going to work. Nancy, you saved the day!" They all hugged and did a goofy laugh while walking in the parking lot.

"I need to hear every detail at dinner tonight," said Dixie.

Although it was close to five with a lingering heat of ninety-nine, no one felt it.

\

## CHAPTER THIRTY-NINE
Tuesday

"Unbelievable," was the popular word of the morning transferred from teacher to teacher, department to department, then front office to principal.

"It's mid-morning and there have been no tardies across campus," Dixie announced to the front office secretaries. "No student has come in for a late pass either."

"Astounding," someone said as the secretaries sat dumbfounded by the rarity of 'no tardies'. "If it persists, we'll have some of that toasting liquid at the end of the day before we leave," winked another

"Voodoo magic," said Dixie. "The table has turned!" She stood before them playing with the long loose ends of her concho belt, pacing back and forth watching through the office glass doors for the arrival of Andrew Chang, the Student Body President.

Chang walked into the front office during the middle of the class period just before lunch and received an immediate hand shake from Dixie.

"Go do your thing," she half whispered. "Dr. Shieter is waiting for you in his office."

Andrew nodded hesitantly, clamped his teeth together and sucked in air.

The secretaries in the area encouraged him with hand waves and positive nods. One pointed to her mouth and did a fake smile for him to copy.

He complied with the same, still gritting his teeth walking in. Without saying a word, and as he had smartly planned, he opened the gold and white banner while slightly into the principal's room and thrust it very close in his face. Smooth as silk, the satin banner shimmered as if alive.

Shieter's eyes became brighter as he took it so gently in his hands and read aloud, "Grand Marshal. Is this for me?" He held it at arms length in admiration.

Chang could only nod, still clinching but looking better with lips closed in a half smile.

Shieter threw it half over his shoulder and strutted in front of a floor length mirror near his desk; feeling its smoothness and re-adjusting it a couple times, he stared in the mirror.

Finding his voice after clearing his throat a couple times, Chang began. "It would be an honor if you wore it for our big event this Friday." And then with great diplomacy he added, "The students all voted on it."

"Yes! Yes! Of course!" He paused and strutted in front of the mirror again. "Absolutely." He threw his shoulders back.

Dixie walked in and said, "Just a reminder; did you want to make an announcement?"

He hesitated in thought.

She waved a piece of paper in his face. "Hurry before the bell rings; you've got ten minutes."

Shieter walked over to the front office intercom and read from Dixie's paper:

"Because of no tardies today, off-campus lunches are now possible. Also, many thanks to the student body who voted for me as Grand Marshal for this Friday's festivities, parade, and dance." He emphasized the last three words loudly because Dixie had purposely underlined them.

Immediately, his face looked puzzled and questioning until the surrounding staff clapped, yelled loudly and patted him on the back with praise.

The bell rang.

Andrew Chang and the front office staff did a thumbs-up signal as he walked by. It was learned later that his mom was the seamstress who, after a long day at work, toiled all night and into the early morning sewing the brightly, shimmering satin banner. They owed her big time!

"You should have seen all the puzzled faces during the announcement about voting for Grand Marshal," Gina said to Nancy and Rich during lunch.

Nancy added, "Those blank faces disappeared quickly when he followed it with lunch passes and renewed festivities."

"You girls saved the day. Toast?" Rich held up his can of diet Coke and they all 'clunked' together.

"To the teachers who hexed the principal yesterday!"

Heleena walked in and stopped in the middle of the room next to their round table. "What did I miss?"

"Nothing." Rich stated while stirring his plate of spaghetti, "We're all going on the trail ride in December and we're toasting to a great adventure."

"Me too! I'll drink to that." She took her can of root beer out of the department 'fridge and asked Gina, "When can you start riding lessons for me? I've never been on a horse before." She positioned a loose chair at the round table, flopped down and grinned cheerily tilting her head side to side which was one of her silly habits.

"Well...."

"Let's not worry about it until after the African events." She waved her can of root beer in the air as a simple fact and left.

"And here's a second toast to that hefty job," said Rich.

"Amen!" They clunked.

The entire school became an instant spark plug of events opposite of yesterday's lame, dragging with hope, attitude. Like a domino effect, everything fell into place.

For the remainder of the week and long into Friday night, drums of all shapes and sizes were tapped and pounded in campus corners and around town. Replicas of originals constructed of wood, goatskin, and cowhide, were bought from down in the valley. The most popular was the Nabita, a conical drum made of wood and antelope skin from the Congo.

Music, dance and foods were the three areas researched and practiced every day by the different departments. Lunchtime vibrancy became exotic as news people from down in the valley of Phoenix joined the sampling of traditional soups and breads, all to the beats of different drums.

Principal Shieter, immersed with redemption, strutted around campus with renewed friendliness. He even stood and watched the repainting of the vending machines after unchaining them.

Digital orders were: "Be nice to the principal! Be nice to the principal!"

And they were.

When the cowboys walked by, they touch the brim of their caps, "Hi".

Spirit line girls and boys put authentic looking wooden beaded necklaces over his collar.

"Oh," he smirked a bit tongue tied as monkeys, lions, tigers, and giraffes hung half way down his vest, covering his tie.

Home-ec students pinned hand sewn badges on his jacket.

It finally got out of hand when the Gardening Club came to school one morning, each student carrying a different potted plant. "All for his room," they said.

In order to find places for approximately one hundred plants, the staff spent two hours positioning them everywhere. The front office became "The Green Room".

"Quit brown nosing" became the new order on campus.

Everything went well for the next two days.

Home Economics sewing classes put together a lunch time fashion show of colorful, strapless, ankle length tunic dresses. Since the entire town was invited to take part in the festivities, everybody wanted one. Models were short and fat, tall and skinny. It really didn't matter because 'strapless' was the magic word.

Male students didn't get too carried away with the African theme until the 'strapless' dresses started appearing on all the girls.

"Alluring" was the word. Even the most callous of the tattooed-pierced groups got involved when a girl presented a 'lei' of African wooden beads around their necks.

Along with making masks, Arts and Crafts invented and designed necklaces of shiny, painted wooden animal beads, like the one presented to Shieter.

Becky Painter was in her glory with all the creativity manifested by her students.

"Let's wear them all week," she said to everyone.

All agreed.

Since parade workers had such a short time to build homecoming floats, the town curfew was eliminated so students could work until midnight.

Most clubs and groups had only two days to prepare, so entire families pitched in as a workforce.

Because of the good natured merriment, Heleena's lists of bad students who were involved with the 'body-parts-terror' kept disappearing. Someone mysteriously erased the list from her computer too.

With the extra lists from each department gone, and the one from the computer erased, she finally admonished, "We'll work on it next week, after the activities."

Even the secretaries in the main office shook their heads a negative in pretense of innocence.

"What list?"

Nevertheless, Rick, Pop and the four B's memorized the names of the few bad ones and kept watch around the clock taking turns calling each other from their particular stations.

"In a few more days, we'll solve it all!"

"This merriment around campus is scary," Dixie said at the dinner table Wednesday night while ladling steaming beef stew into her bowl.

"I'm afraid that it's too good to be true."

And it was!

## CHAPTER FORTY
The day before

Thursday was the busiest day of the year, a twenty-four hour circus.

Tubs of ice containing bottled water were in every corner on campus, donated by the local businesses well aware of the publicity the festivities would bring to the town this weekend among the populace down in Phoenix, the Valley of the Sun and the surrounding towns.

Five main news stations had been broadcasting the unprecedented events highlighting the two Arizona Western towns. And not to be out done, each newscaster wore a hand made student mask during the broadcast telling where they could be purchased.

Definitely, a clever eye opener!

"Hosting young African students is a wonderful exchange of cultures.....very educational and fitting.....come and join the fun!"

They filmed students cooking, dancing to the beat of African drums, wearing tunics and beads.

Most impressive was the band practicing a dress rehearsal out on the field being led by the very statuesque Rex, the drum major who could throw the

258

baton famously high. Ostrich plumes on his headdress added to his height and the drama of it all.

Glass beaded straps were attached to the girls' tunic dresses as they marched and gyrated with the loud and crazy beat.

"It is a strutting affair like no other," bragged a newscaster.

The campus was so busy with parents coming and going as parade float helpers, security was lax and for this one day only, 'guest passes' were exempt.

"You don't need one for today," said Principal Shieter wearing his over the shoulder banner proudly as he met on going traffic at the front gate.

Cops would have to suffice as 'look outs' for trouble.


Although *he knew* that undercover cops were around town, stationed in the coffee shops, saloons and especially on campus, *he decided* to sneak into the school's temporary store to buy beads and another mask. He too knew the ropes on how to dress undercover. And, since he carelessly lost the first mask last week in a show off escapade that brought him fun and satisfaction, he needed a replacement.

*All I need to wear for the parade is a mask.*

Dixie Hoot as the school's 'go-fer' was manning the temporary store along with three senior girls and two parents. All were busy with customers because the word was out that profits supported the badly needed extra curricular activities. Sales were plentiful and quick.

Much later when she had to describe the customers for the day, she saw nothing out of the ordinary. "There were business men in suits, cowboys in boots and straws, and moms with babies. We were exceptionally busy because it was the day before and most people paid with cash."

Nevertheless, Rick and his group examined the credit card receipts and checks but saw no names matching their danger list.

Half the student body and teachers were in the gymnasium setting up activity booths and decorations, while the other half were in class as usual. These teachers were teaching short periods so the entire student body would be getting out of school early to help with a massive list needing to be done.

It happened while Gina's fourth hour class was working quietly on a handout due at the end of the period. She stood before them at her podium intensely grading papers in a room so quiet that a dropped feather would be heard. Five minutes remained of the class period.

Suddenly, her body buzzed a tone from head to toe, a numbing effect with simultaneous ear throbbing.

Puzzled, she slowly looked up and saw the last person in the row next to the wall staring at her.

Cory squinted back a hateful, malingering look, a stare, more of a jaw clinching malicious glare, slouched down at his desk doing nothing.

Neither looked away.....five....ten....fifteen seconds.

She stood taller at the podium straightening her shoulders, thinking.

Voices vanished around her as her temples beat rapidly in rhythm with her heart. Taking in a deep breath and sighing loudly didn't help.

She now knew!

The bell's ring seemed extra loud with the students leaving rapidly in excited flurry while putting today's work on the table by the door as usual.

Paled, she sat quickly down on her stool and grabbed the edges of her podium for steadiness.

In a daze she put her head down on her arms and sat there for a full three minutes before someone came in and started rubbing her neck.

"Are you all right?"

Rick massaged the top of her head, pushing back the natural curls that had fallen to her wrists on the podium. She loved it.

Looking up with watery eyes she quietly said, "I know who it is."

"Cory."

"How did you know?" Gina was stunned.

"Just doing my job. If I told you my tricks, you would want to trade jobs, and I don't want to be a teacher." He now massaged her shoulders.

"Well, now what?"

"Let us handle it!"

"Who's us?"

"My crew, my gang, the Family Farm." With this they both smiled and puffed out a short laugh.

"He's bad, but he's not the peeking pervert. You can relax about that," Rick continued.

"Oh great! Now I feel better. Who is it?"

"I can't tell you…yet!"

"And you know who it is?"

"Yep!"

"But you're not going to tell me?"

"Nope!"

Heleena stormed in vocalizing loudly. "I saw you come in here. We have a drunk on the school grounds. We need help!"

CHAPTER FORTY-ONE
The day before—continues

After Heleena swirled out the room with only the hem of her dress slapping the door frame, Rick put his arms around Gina.

"I have major duty tonight and tomorrow. We'll have a special date this weekend when possible, at your place or mine." He held her at arms length. "You haven't lost the key?"

"It's in my special jewelry box." She lied and worried for the remainder of the day where in the heck she had put it.

He hurried out.

After gathering the finished handouts at the door, she looked through the names while walking to her desk. Of course, Cory did not turn in today's finished assignment. Instead, his was the 'no name' with the mysterious cryptic red lettering. Checking off names in her roll book, all others had been completed.

Looking at his paper, she breathed a sigh of relief that he had not included a nasty limerick like the one she found under the wiper of her Jeep.

His cryptic signature was identical, and she would save it for Rick to compare with the limerick he now has in his possession.

It was a nasty threat, and she shook as she collected her thoughts.

Gina, Nancy, Rich and Becky walked around the grounds together taking it all in.

In one area and far out on the track, was the group of five particular floats being decorated by hoards of community volunteers and school club members.

Each class had a particular flat bed to embellish with painted signs and crepe paper streamers. The senior's float, being the largest and most lavishly decorated, would be second in position followed by the Junior's, Sophomore's and Freshmen's. The most important float and the one chosen to lead the parade carried the Homecoming Royalty.

The procession would begin here, proceed north toward the towns and then on to Cave Creek Road to the center of town where bleachers and speakers were massed. It would then circle back to the track by noon, at which time the festivities would begin inside the gym.

The field crew sweated away dressed for work in denims, caps and sneakers, the major order in yesterday's announcements; fortunately, the weather couldn't be more accommodating with a cloudy eighty degrees.

Dixie in a bright orange wide brim hat was on the walkway of the bleachers over looking the track making announcements for the workers below who needed materials or an extra hand.

She loved talking on a microphone and apologized every time there was a 'squeak' or 'squawk'

After workers came to her with a list of needs like supplies or extra help, she was in her glory, pointing, reading notes and bossing.

"I felt so important," she would tell Pop tonight during dinner. "I was like an orchestra conductor."

But, in the early afternoon as she looked their way, Gina and her group ducked and hurried toward the big gym where they would be anchored tomorrow.

"Let's run before she puts us to work!"

Inside the gym, Heleena was another Dixie, doing much of the same, pointing, talking on the microphone when needed, then rushing here and there checking on the booths that had been constructed by school groups and community sponsors.

With her big red plastic cup always in hand, she checked for debris on the gym floor and made sure the garbage cans were in designated places for the Welcoming Club who volunteered for cleanup duty.

Purposes of the booths were two-fold: to show school activities to the community and to introduce the African students to typical American culture.

Gina's booth covered horsemanship with photos and literature concerning the yearly trail rides. In particular, were brochures and pamphlets for sale about the mysterious Superstition Mountains and the gold miners lost in its hills and vast canyons.

Nancy's booth next to Gina's covered the literature taught at Blakely High, all in stacks according to each of the four grade levels. Varieties of used novels were for sale, mostly dog-eared paper backs from the school library. "I'm keeping the price low to get rid of them," she said while piling books on the tables from boxes below.

Becky's booth was the largest and would be the most popular because of hand-made arts and crafts from her classes; all on display and all for sale. Rich crated the left over 'goods' from the book store sales and helped her organize them.

Rich's job for tomorrow will be handling the cash flow and charge cards. "I have the easiest job, the money booth."

Food booths of popular American snacks and African delicacies were arranged by Home Ec inside the cafeteria with emphasis on American popcorn, pizzas and Indian Fry Bread. The African coordinators would arrange their foods, after arriving, in booths provided for them.

Town sponsors prepared booths with donated and discounted Western wear, candies, and Western trinkets.

It would be an affair like no other.

Africa was coming to town!

After the parade, the band would perform periodically during the day on the stage at one end of the gym. As planned, an adjoining stage for the African performers was elaborately decorated by foreign language students.

Shieter was in charge of everything with 'no sweat'. Office secretaries carried out the orders and duties, making contacts, setting up time lines and listing activities with the foreigners. It would have been better if someone listened to them, but no one did....everyone was too excited to think clearly.....until it was too late.

Today, Shieter merely walked around with his shoulder banner and his hands in his pockets from gym to field and back again with his usual half smile and lips pursed.

Tomorrow would be a different scenario.

Gina, Nancy, Becky and Rich walked out of the gym at around seven. Even though it had been a long day, they were thankfully finished and prepared for tomorrow.

"The parking lot's packed!" Gina noted. "And cars are parked along the road."

"And as soon as we leave, someone will be taking our parking spots." Nancy waved. "See ya."

"The entire town is volunteering today and the band is practicing late on the field." Rich waited for Becky and Gina to drive away before leaving.

Words previously exchanged were: "Call if there is something we need for tomorrow."

Driving home, Gina wondered who the drunk was out on the field and made a mental note to call Rick later.

Having worked late at school, and considering the busy activities ahead, she decided to leave all grading for next week and brought home no papers. Instead, she would talk Dixie into joining her for a good comedy movie from their stack of DVD's.

"A de-stressor is needed."

Along the three mile route of winding road, she expected to see Mr. Hollywood and was always ready to run into him, coming or going.

This time, he was coming fast from behind and very close...too close...honking about a yard from the back bumper, again in his lime green 1948 Willy's Jeep.

She slowed, almost to a stop.

Since the road straightened ahead, he and his passenger, Delilah again, pulled up parallel both grinning ear to ear.

"Hey, we're heading up to Elephant Mountain Trail for an early night hike. You want to come?"

"My day is too busy tomorrow," she said after shaking her head.

"Mr. Hollywood acted extra friendly and did all the talking while movie star gorgeous seemed smug," was Gina's description to Dixie and Pop later at home. "Then he sped away like a bull out of a chute!"

"What's the connection between those two anyway?" Dixie wanted to know.

"I'm sure we'll find out soon," was all Pop offered while rubbing Nellie's belly with his bare foot. The dog rolled side to side with all paws in the air.

"Where are you going to be tomorrow?" Dixie asked him with her hands on her hips.

"Locked in my bakery, hiding out!"

"I thought so. Keep your cell on!"

"You expecting trouble?"

"Africa is coming to town. What else can I say?"

CHAPTER FORTY-TWO
Thursday, the night before


After a quick chat with Rick, Gina was relieved that the drunk on campus was no one she knew.

"Some out-of-towner wanting to cause trouble came for a look around, then left with a designated driver." Rick stated with a sigh. "Under cover cops got there first. Heleena and others aren't aware of who they are so she came for me."

"See ya tomorrow."

"Keep your fingers crossed."

"Whatever it takes."


After selecting her colorful strapless tunic dress....combinations of red, orange, and green.... with matching beads, bracelets and sandals, she called Nancy.

"What are you wearing tomorrow?"

After Nancy's description, Gina slyly said, "Something's not right about all this."

"What do you mean?"

"Well, why are WE dressing like Africans? It seems awkward."

269

"Don't you mean 'back-ass-ward'," Nancy snickered.

"You amaze me sometimes." They both started unstoppable laughing their usual, Nancy snorting and Gina tearing. "It's got to be nerves."

"I'm checking with Dixie to see what she's wearing."

"Probably something stupid like us."

That set them both off again. Gina laughed her wall slapping lose control, eyes watering, nose dripping ridiculously foolish noise so loud, Dixie had to come into the bedroom.

Soon, the two of them were rolling on the bed out of control.

Nancy on the other end of the cell was laughing her hardest. "It's got to be nerves," she repeated before saying, "See ya early in the morning."

Pop filled the door frame with one shoulder leaning on one side and a big hand on the other for balance. "I'll be glad when this is all over."

He sat down on the edge of the bed and joined them while examining his hands. "I've been so busy at the bakery I think flour under my nails has turned to concrete." He got the words out between laughter.

"It's got to be nerves."

Finally in control, Dixie described what she was wearing and added, "But, I'm not wearing a damned-dumb mask like Shieter wants the office personnel to do."

This set the three of them off again. Nellie came in and did her happy dance, bouncing against the bed with two front paws then turning circles on the carpet.

"Crazy dog."

"Wish we could bottle-up this laughter for tomorrow."

"We might need it."

## CHAPTER FORTY- THREE
Friday, the BIG day

Chaos began much too soon.

Not able to sleep well the night before, and waking too early, Gina decided to go out front to the mail box at the edge of the road since no one had retrieved the mail yesterday.

Bright red letters on the small clock next to her bed was an electrifying four.

She grabbed the small canvas mail bag from a kitchen shelf and slowly walked the short distance towards the front gates.

A pale dawn of buffered blue allowed her to be on the look out for snakes along the road, and she knew to step away from dark sticks stretched here and there which could easily come alive in a snap.

She yawned and made a mental note to come here in her bikini this Sunday afternoon, pick up sticks to avoid future menacing confrontations and throw them against the fence line.

As usual, the mailbox was packed with junk made for recycling, and she filled the bag.

Before heading back, she looked north down the road in admiration of the wide open spaces towards Cave Creek Mountains in the background. The air was clear and the visibility, picturesque.

Far, far down the paved road she caught an image....perhaps a person walking, tilting from one edge of the road to the other on the straight away.

She squinted.

Not able to discern whether it was a person or a very large dog, she stared for a full minute.

After seeing arms flailing, she figured that it was a person, someone who now lay unmoving along the edge of the road in the dirt and desert sand.

Running quickly to the house, she called out to Pop and Dixie that there was someone down the road in great trouble. "I'm heading out in my Jeep."

Grabbing her cell phone, she slammed the door behind her.

Expecting no other cars on the road this early and this far out of town, she sped north faster than usual toward the dark figure lying on the side of the road.

After parking off the edge near the body and with her cell phone in hand, she hurried toward the victim now curled in a lump.

Delilah moaned. Matted dirt and cactus thorns were stuck in her long brown silky hair glued with coagulated blood.

Hurriedly, Gina dialed Rick Del Rio knowing that he could make the calls for the quickest help.

Within seconds, Pop and Dixie were there and all three consoled her in gentle tones.

"Water,....wa...." she mumbled thickly before passing out. In a daze, she tried to open her eyes periodically.

"We're here. Help is coming......breathe deeply......" They knelt close.

Within minutes, sirens.

Then two emergency vehicles and a cop car arrived followed by Rick and Dickie.

Gina was amazed at the expertness of the professionals. She stood back and watched keeping an eye on the time, while Delilah was put on a stretcher, and lifted into the ambulance but only after her wounds were emergency wrapped and fluids needled into her body.

For future reference, Gina made note of the hospital where Delilah was headed. An overwhelming sting of melancholy set in while standing there watching them drive off.

With the time ticking away, Gina and Dixie pulled themselves together and headed quickly home to get ready for the big event; they desperately needed to replenish their mood to a positive.

"She was giving them orders as they administered help."

"That was a good sign," they each hoped.

Rick and Dickie headed north to search the desert.

It was five thirty.

As planned, Gina, Nancy and Rich carpooled per the principal's orders. They personally agreed that "there's confidence in numbers."

Since it was a few minutes after six, they easily found a parking place in the faculty lot near the Hondas, Accords, and BMWs of the administrators and secretaries who had already arrived.

The day's schedule began early and would finish late.

At Eight: Teachers, students, city officials, business sponsors, out of town media, moms and dads, and numerous under cover cops....would all be at their stations preparing the booths again, and last minute parade essentials.

The band had been practicing since five.

Guy's runners had been stretching since six.

All were dressed in African attire "to make them feel welcome," was Dr. Shieter's reasoning. His staff, refusing to wear masks, painted their faces with stripes and circles like the pictures they had seen in books, magazines and on the internet. No one wore a serious face this morning while mingling with coffee cups in hand and eating donuts provided by Pop's bakery.

Students needed to check in with attendance at the front office before going to their designated places; since there would be no classes held today, they were extra giddy.

Boys wore specialty tees of African designs painted by art students, and leis of wooden necklaces. Cut-off jeans and sandals completed their casualness. A few painted their faces.

Television media people, unusually younger than normal, were the only ones in regular clothes. Strutting around, they were seen interviewing different groups, important or not. It was a good day to practice.

Of greatest importance to them, was their planned interview with Guy's cross country runners who, along with their African competitors, would start the parade with a designated ten mile run.

Start and finish would be on the track in front of the bleaches, which by the end of the run would be filled with a myriad batch of students, parents, locals, out-of-towners, and media.

275

"We're ready."

"We've been practicing since August."

"We've got it nailed!"

At eight, Gina got the call from Rick who was stationed at Sky Harbor Airport in Phoenix, forty-five minutes away, saying that Continental Airlines had arrived with the guests. "Africa is coming to town," he said cheerfully. Then he added quietly, "Uh-oh!"

"What do you mean 'uh-oh'?"

"Nothing!"

"What do you mean 'uh-oh'?"

"Nothing!"

Knowing him well, persistence wouldn't help.

She changed the subject. "Hey, what happened to Delilah this morning? The last time I saw her, she was with Mr. Hollywood."

"So I heard."

"In his lime green Willy's Jeep."

"Yep!"

"Well, where's the Jeep?"

""Flipped over at the bottom of a ravine."

"And Mr. Hollywood?"

"NOT around!"

"What?"

"Disappeared!"

"What?"

"Can't talk now. My men are on top of it. Colt's in charge at the moment."

"But, it doesn't make sense?"

"Incidentally, for your own peace of mind, Cortez and Cory are being shadowed by a number of under cover cops. Talk to you soon."

Not soon enough, she thought. What the heck was "uh-oh" and why did he abruptly change the subject?

CHAPTER FORTY-FOUR
The BIG day, continued…..


Gina found the four B's walking around and invited them to go to the Home Ec 'chop house' for snacks to settle their nerves while waiting for the two bus loads of students to arrive at nine. Steps were livelier than normal. She wrung her hands together, did finger-spider push-ups to release nerves then started pushing back her cuticles.

Band members played more loudly than usual with the beat of special drums in the background. Twirlers were twirling and marchers were marching out on the grass.

The ground shook in merriment.

Five colorful snow cone machines provided and paid for by the Parent Teachers Organization were stationed around campus offering free ice treats for any one interested. Cops helped replenish the ice from the supply trailer.

All were costumed African.

Everything and everyone was in place.

Bright ruby red welcome banners and purple directional signs were placed appropriately.

Blake, since he was the retired cook and restaurant owner, had special interest in the tasty bits of African snacks, flat breads and corn paddies. They joined him.

"Corny."

"Salty."

"Spicy."

"Delicious"…..they all agreed.

"So" began Gina, "you four and the media are the only ones dressed normal."

"This is our costume," said Bing, coffee mug in hand, tugging on his biker's cap.

"We're bikers don't you know," Bob teased turning his back to Gina to show the special eagle emblem on the back of his tee. "This is why we retired."

Brad added, "We're leading the parade too so we have to look the part." He carefully wiped crumbs off his mustache and pointed to their bikes with the attached poles on the backs from which colorful African flags waved representing the different nations. "We're ready!" Small American flags fluttered in the slight breeze from each handle.

"Fun," she sighed. Then after getting a tube of hand cream out of her fanny pack, she creamed her hands and pushed back cuticles again.

"Share." She felt a shoulder bump.

"Time to share." In her face were Jamie Mink and Kim Rose.

"Catch." She threw them the tube.

"We're your favorites you know." They began rubbing lotion on hands, arms and legs.

"How can I forget? Have you seen Cortez or Cory around?"

"They're with Darlene and Susie Lee," Jamie said.

"Trying to be men, they're being followed by under cover cops," added Kim.

"How do you know that?"

"Every one knows."

"Jeesh! I have a necessary job for you two. Man the bleachers that are ribboned off for us teachers and other celebrities." She raised one shoulder and cracked a slanted half smile.

They laughed. "Celebrities?"

"Just keep the kids out of that area."

"You owe us snacks on Monday."

They parted after several high fives, and slapping hands.


Nobody noticed the black Camry parked across the street as anything out of the ordinary; after all, varieties of vehicles were in every available nook and cranny. Three windows were cracked two inches for air circulation, and a man sat waiting.

Tapping his fingers on the stirring wheel in rhythm with the sounds from the drums beating far out in the field, he bobbed his head and hummed along.

Today would give him great pleasure. He stopped for a minute to scratch his watermelon belly and re-adjust the Velcro that held his African skirt tight on his circular form. Noting he would blend in with some of the other men who chose the same kind of costume, he felt secure for when the time came for him to get out of the car.

However, he would have a 'little' surprise for the stuck-up bunch….or should he say 'big' surprise.

He laughed aloud and poured more whiskey in his coffee cup, which by now, was only a small amount of caffeine.

Looking over at the new mask he purchased from the book store, he decided to keep it in the shade and on the floor of the car in case someone came walking by close to the sidewalk. A few minutes ago he had to duck when a group of six kids came brushing by his car. Fortunately, they were so mesmerized with the noise of the current happenings they paid no attention in his direction.

With the printed list of events in hand, he waited. Timing had to be perfect.

At nine thirty on the dot, Rick escorted two large commercial buses into the school parking lot, his siren on low. Forming a semi-circle as they entered the patio area for de-boarding excited the particular meet-and-greet group as they stood quietly staring and pushing forward in mincing steps.

Dark tinted windows allowed for no peeking at the passengers.

A small special welcoming school band stood ready to start on signal.

'Hissing' and 'swishing' sounds accompanied the bus as it stopped and the doors slowly opened.

The audience held their breaths in anticipation.

A coordinator stepped out of each bus with a list of students' names on a clipboard, one six foot African male and one African female a bit shorter.

Each wore dark sunglasses.

The clean shaven male was dressed in a three piece dark navy suit with white shirt and beige tie.

With the addition of small white pearl earrings, the female was identical, only in a knee length skirt, nylons and two inch heels. Her tie was short and feminine. Dangling from one wrist were three pearl bracelets.

Both mayors in their African costumes and painted faces lost their bounce as they came forward to acknowledge the two. The mayor of Carefree pushed the one from Cave Creek forward and lingered a bit behind examining his feet. To distinguish themselves as mayors, they selected to be barefoot for the greeting with ankle bracelets purchased from Arts and Crafts students. Without any doubt, each felt exceedingly naked for many reasons.

Dr. Shieter was suddenly not around. As a matter of fact, he had locked himself in his office earlier.

Heleena stood silently gaping, her belly protruding, sandaled feet turned out....with red socks. She played with her two wooden necklaces then quickly pulled dark sunglasses from her fanny pack and put them on being careful not to smear her white face paint.

Each group gaped and gawked for a full minute with the Africans timidly mumbling while reviewing their clip board of names with each other.

Then extending their hands politely, the two coordinators stepped forward with subdued professional smiles to shake hands.

After a few welcoming words by the mayors, and with a signal, the band began to play a chosen medley of American and African songs as the students started disembarking.

The 'twenty something' young, restless media personnel representing the five major television channels from down in the valley, stood around chewing gum, tapping their toes, and filming everything as a norm. What did they know!

All the students were tallish. This was not the shock. Each slender male teen was suited in dark navy dress pants, with white shirts tucked in and meticulously belted. The thin girls wore belted skirts, nylons and black wedges. Most outstanding were the red, white, and blue small ties that each wore.

This was the shock!

With elegance and grace, twenty-five students unloaded from each bus, leaving all personal possessions behind for the moment.

"America has arrived," Rick whispered to Gina who was standing back but watching closely from under a shade tree. Surprising her, he took one of her hands and held it tightly while watching.

"Now I know your 'uh-oh'," she whispered.

Stunned were the grin-less Africans as they stared in bewilderment at the gauche and clumsily dressed Westerners.

No one spoke!

The band finished playing and milled around silently, petting their instruments out of embarrassment.

Suddenly feeling duped and mislead, the two opposite groups stepped back from each other and began mumbling among themselves re-thinking a plan.

Richard Cloud, Dixie Hoot and the front office secretaries were watching all the proceedings together and decided to take action. They came walking gallantly forward in a group.

Speaking loudly Rich began. "Welcome! Well, did we get it right?" He was now almost shouting as he grinned exuberantly, spinning around and pointing to all the unusually dressed Cave Creekers who were standing there feeling like imbeciles in their fake face paint or masks. He clapped his hands together two, three times making his statement.

The office personnel and Dixie followed his lead speedily walking through the crowd of fifty students and clasping each hand in both of theirs.

"Hi, how are you?"

"So good to see you."

"Welcome to Cave Creek."

The barrier broke.

Towners, teachers and students glowed in the welcoming pageantry and the Africans, speaking perfect English, laughed and grinned profusely showing the whitest teeth ever. Tension was over.

Continuing their lead, Guy stepped forward with, "Grab your gear and follow me to the locker rooms." He shouted louder than normal since everyone was now gloriously smiling and talking.

Scrambling to the buses, the students came out with suitcases; stepping lively, they followed the lead of Blakely High kids who were surrounding each one, all talking at once to gentle back slapping and double hand grasping.

Because of the initial slow greeting, the parade would be thirty minutes late, now starting at ten thirty.

The short delay added extra income for the food and drink booths out on the patio which became suddenly very busy. Indian fry bread, hot dogs, hamburgers and of course pizza were the main edibles. But, and it was a winning argument much later, the Spanish Club's chicken tacos were the Africans' favorites before the day was over.

With the parade in proper formation, everyone milled around waiting for the Africans to come out of the locker rooms. Each float was crowded with riders listening for the starting whistle from Rex the leader of the band and of the parade. He and the band immediately followed the Family Farm Motorcycle group who would clear the street with tooting horns.

Plans are for the majority of the townspeople to watch the parade as it flows through Cave Creek and/or join the students in the football bleachers for the finish. The entire Valley of the Sun south of Cave Creek is invited to watch or participate in the sporting games and other festivities inside the gym.

Heleena and the front office had done a remarkable job correlating bicycle races around the track, volleyball games and basketball tournaments on the field, and of course, dance activities inside the gym.

At ten, Dixie was alone in the front office watching over the phones and front door when she heard, "Pssst! Dixie, come in here!"

Shieter had his office door cracked, waving at her to come in. "I need help!"

Now in his three piece suit, he was rubbing his face raw trying to scrub off the paint with a dry towel. His mask and African garb were slung over a nearby chair.

"Just a moment; I'll get the special cream." Jars were stacked on the office counters available for everyone's use. She took one, a box of tissues, and went to work on all the bright, colorful whites, reds and blacks.

"How's it going out there?"

"Everyone misses you!" She lied.

"Ok, you look good!" She lied again as she took his face in her hands and roughly shoved it from one side to the other pretending to look for left over smudge.

Then 'whack' she slapped him on the cheek hard, smiled and said, "You look great…... all gone."

Another lie.

She helped him manipulate his gold and white Grand Marshal banner topping one shoulder and reminded him to wear his two wooden necklaces over his vest.

"The parade is getting ready to start at ten-thirty so you had better get out there," she said with a smile.

"Thanks. I'm leaving now."

Turning her back, she left feeling naughty and knew that she would catch hell later. She had purposely overlooked the ruby red paint that splattered his nose and had avoided reminding him to change out of his flip-flop sandals.

At ten-twenty, fifty Africans in authentic costumes and face paint, excitedly high stepped out of the gym to get in the proper line-up on the track.

"WOW!"

"SENSATIONAL!"

Everyone gawked and showed total fascination at their major transition from suit to native.

They are to follow the floats except for the long distance runners joining at the very front with Guy's Blakely High runners who, after looking at the natives, now 'gulped' and shook each leg nervously in warm up.

Looking Olympian in running shorts and numbered tees, both groups shook hands and smiled cordially while shaking their legs and doing knee bends.

At ten-thirty, three things happened.

First, Guy shot the gun to start the race.

Second, Rex blew his whistle to march.

Third, Brad got a call from Del Rio.

"I know you're in formation, but we've lost sight of Zander. Tell the group to be on the look out and report to me when he's sighted."

Brad relayed the message to the other three who lined horizontally, in front of the procession, with a good view of the populace both at school and the soon to be Cave Creek Road.

It would be an easy ten mile stretch for all.

Everyone looked well prepared:

A flat-bed trailer followed at the end of the sequence to gather any tired marchers; half the student body was in segregated areas along the route with water bottles; Gina and her group monitored the on going sporting events in which the other half of the student body were competing; and Grand Marshal Shieter escorted the two coordinators around the school yard with great pride, occasionally patting his satin shoulder banner feeling its silkiness.

Driving his Ford pickup, Guy led the runners making sure to stay a short distance ahead. Pop, acting as monitor and watching for injuries, sat in the front beside him. "I need an important job for tomorrow," he had said to Guy the night before, calling from the bakery. Since the four B's girlfriends were in charge of bakery sales during the day, he decided that he could take a day off. "I need to party!"

All the while, a sneering Zander was watching the time while 'hunkered' down in his Camry.

## CHAPTER FORTY-FIVE
The BIG day continues---

Gina, Nancy and Dixie stayed within sight of each other and very near the Central Information Booth. Each tended a special interest and task.

Dixie was in contact with Bing learning the flow of the parade; "It's at the half-way mark, in front of Screamin' Ice Cream," she announced on the 'mic' for everyone to hear.

Nancy talked to Colt periodically pertaining to his task of searching for a missing person north of town. She learned nothing. "He plans to be at the dance tonight regardless of lateness," she told Gina.

Gina knew that talking to Rick more than once was a waste of time because he never told her anything he was doing. Today he was in charge of everything, but for tonight, "I'll be at the dance, sooner or later," he had said in a steady voice resonating stress.

Walking around checking on booths gave her free time to worry......

How is Delilah?

Why hadn't she seen Berty around town?

And Mr. Hollywood....where did he go?

Really, who the heck is Dickie?

At one end of the field and abutting the parking lot, the Horsemanship Booth was being finalized with the construction of three portable corrals for six horses. Riders' Club members and their parents arranged the gear, bales of hay and watering system.

Richard Cloud asked to be in charge of this event. "Horses love me. They don't talk back!"

An extra large short sleeve 'Cowboy Hardware' checkered shirt hung below the belt of his loose baggy denims. Choosing his favorite old black and purple Diamondbacks' cap and weathered tennis shoes, he was in his comfort zone. Gone were his Oxford shirt, tie and black belted slacks.

Students didn't recognize him. "Is that really you Mr. Cloud?" Then they would 'high-five'.

Coordinating with him was the Roping Club which had brought a couple of steer dummies for participants to rope at no charge. Food booth tickets would be given to competitors with the least amount of misses.

Pro ropers in the Cave Creek area donated their time and were ready to help the African students who had E-mailed ahead indicating this being a favorite.

Ten sparkling silver buckles logoed 'Arizona Cowboy' with specks of garnets were among the prizes donated by local businesses. On display, they still gleamed and glittered in the now muted sun.

All were ready and waiting at their stations.

At twelve-thirty Dixie's announcement was heard for at least a quarter mile circumference.

"The parade is a half mile away."

To get a good seat, everyone rushed to the bleachers to join those who were already there. Out-of-towners, locals, students, teachers, sponsors, and media vied for favorite seats. Those milling around the food booths hurried over with drinks and pieces of pizza in hand.

It was a lucky, lucky day for all because the weather still co-operated with a nice seventy-five degrees. "Could easily have been ninety-five to one hundred," chatted the natives throughout the day.

Coming down the side road with flashing lights and slowly entering on the track was Guy's Ford pickup containing Pop and two tired looking Blakely High runners sitting in the bed.

As soon as Guy's truck ran over the finish line, he parked on the side out of the way and at the end of the bleachers before running back with Pop to hold the winner's tape.

To extremely loud cheers and claps came the finishers.....six out of six African runners ran across the finish line. Not in sight yet were Blakely High's.

After the winners were ribboned with over the shoulder banners, they lay on the grassy carpet to cool off while others misted them with water. They grinned profusely, so impressed.

Cheers began again as four strung---out---runners entered the side road and onto the track. Or was it five?

"Huh?" Everyone gawked and couldn't believe what they were seeing..... Silence.

At the end, a nude heavy set masked man jogged zig-zaging onto the track very near the bleachers and waving his African skirt in the air.

"A streaker!" Roaring laughter, whistles and cheers could be heard a mile away.

He waved at the audience with a blatant grin.

Shieter threw up his hands, grabbed his cell and became unglued.

The two coordinators smiled with composure.

Action on the field began with a story to tell for life. It even made the national news, played over and over on all the stations for the week.

Two top ropers, Grant and Jeff, saw the man enter the track and they immediately sprang into action. Grabbing their ropes and mounting their horses in seconds, they galloped after the streaker who now saw them coming.

He put his thumbs in his ears and waved his fingers at them in mockery while preparing to dodge their twirling ropes.

With the audience un-contained, he zig-zagged successfully feeling the wave of their laughter.

Two more tries….one missed and the other caught the edge of his mask which came off and dangled at the end of the rope, headless. The streaker was now running and dancing out to the middle of the field where a string of about ten plain clothed cops chased him……one way…..then another.

"It truly is a fiasco," one television media person stated while filming live for the afternoon news. All the five media stations compared footage later to 'paste' together the best of show.

The streaker's 'little' surprise was a circled blur.

It was a long five minutes before Zander was wrestled to the ground by the cops. Six piled on top of him in desperation but not until Zander had mooned the audience. His dropped skirt with the Velcro waist band was found on the field and again attached around his circular frame.

Teenagers in the audience intoned a fake "Boo" when he was wrestled to the ground. Then they clapped.

Cortez and Cory walked off campus to hide in a stretch of desert before hitching a ride to Berty's spread on the other side of town.

The un-planned free entertainment restored the hard working festival workers to a new vivaciousness as they laughed and joked about the embarrassing event. Some of the old timers reminisced about streakers in their past.

"My cousin………"

"My neighbor….."

"The school drop-out…."

Also, because of the 'surprise' un-planned sneaker, no one made note of the fact that the Blakely High runners were last in the race. Hugs and pats were plentiful and their participation ribbons were colorful.

Gina called Rick. "Guess what!"

"I heard."

"No fair. I'm done talking to you."

"Does that mean less talk and more action?"

"Hah, you're in a better mood."

"You'll find out tonight."

The parade which had stopped on the edge of the field due to the unexpected entertainment, now marched forward following the Family Farm, each and every participant swollen with pride as the over flowing audience yelled and clapped.

Rex, the senior drum major, lifted his knees to new heights with the beat of the school's song, leading a very animated band and five floats. Homecoming Royalty and flat-beds of grouped Seniors, Juniors, Sophomores and Freshmen, ferried after him.

Last, and the most popular in the school parade, were the students from Africa in full costume dress, dancing a Zombie Jamboree, pounding on weird looking drums made of wood and different animal skins. Kettle drums, conical drums and hourglass drums were put on display later in the gym for everyone's amusement.

All followed Rex to the grassy middle of the football field for their planned exhibitions before dispersing and joining other festivities in the gym and also again on the field.

Most headed to the Horsemanship Booth.

It was a gala like no other, ending before dinner so the town could rest and regroup for the big Western dance tonight at Tumbleweed's.

Cory and Cortez waited inside Berty's chained and locked compound for Rick Del Rio's arrival. Hands in pockets, they shifted from one leg to the other, playing with the sandy gravel, drawing lines with the points of their boots.

Berty and her Ford truck dually were missing.

## CHAPTER FORTY-SIX
Friday, continued……


"Where's your aunt?" Cortez began

"I don't know. She left before dawn this morning as usual, heading north." He checked the time on his cell. "It's already six. She's always home by now." Cory motioned for Cortez to join him on the wooden porch where a table and four chairs sat anchored, handy for waiting guests preparing to pick up their well groomed pets.

They slumped in a chair looking out at the fenced dog run where Berty's dogs now chewed on snacks. The boys had fed and watered them and cleaned their long dog pen while nervously waiting for Rick and ultimately, the results of their demise. Each held a cold bottle of root beer.

"Did you take Susie Lee's mask from the back of the Camry when I parked it in the garage last Friday?" Cortez's voice ended with a down word note. He really didn't care at this point. He was failing classes; he wouldn't play in the homecoming game tomorrow night; his father was a jerk; his mother was gone; he helped about a hundred others cut up a dead body.......why?

"No!" Annoyed with this question he continued with a glare. "Why would I do that? She's Darlene's friend." He played with his bottle on the table wiping at the accumulated sweat.

"Then, what happened to it?"

"Your dad probably took it so he wouldn't have to buy one."

"Makes sense." Cortez hung his head then spit off the porch sending a small spiral of dust in the air as it hit. He stood, put his arms around a square pole at the end of the small veranda and looked toward the closed gates behind which were piles of boxes, crates, loose papers, junk, and trash.

"What's wrong with your aunt? Why does she collect all of this stuff....this junk?" He grimaced and pointed toward the compound with the bottle in his hand.

Cory shook his head. "Don't know. She's lonely...sentimental....I don't get it."

"Is your mom like her?"

"I wouldn't know. I haven't heard from her in years." Cory stood and angrily threw his empty bottle towards the closed gates hitting a corner sending broken glass everywhere.

"Hey, you're in the wrong sport. You should go out for baseball."

They tried to smile.

"I don't want to go to jail," Cortez continued with a whimper switching weight to the other foot.

"Don't worry. They can't prove anything. We weren't alone spray painting the chained vending machines."

"Who sprayed the principal's car?"

Cory ducked his head in guilt.

"And," Cortez continued, "who wrote the threatening limerick to Ms. Mack and put it on her Jeep?"

"I thought it was extremely creative," was Cory's cocky reply as he leaned back in the chair and crossed his ankles. After looking towards the guest house, he suddenly sat straight in his chair. "Did that light just come on?" He nodded toward the building.

"Is it on a timer?"

"No," he whispered as they both stared toward the dimly lit window and the moving shadow behind the curtain.

With mouths open, they squinted in the semi-darkness for a full minute.

"This is crazy!"

"Doesn't make sense!"

Both boys jerked out of their spookiness when they saw lights at the main gates and heard the roar of motorcycles speeding towards them.

## CHAPTER FORTY-SEVEN
Friday…early evening

Rick opened the large wooden unlocked gates and swung them inward, wide enough for traffic following him. After driving in he parked his brown sheriff's car facing the dog run. A few other cars marked and unmarked, parked near. Four motorcycle cops in tight navy blues, and the four members of the Family Farm parked near the porch facing the two boys who were now shaking.

Rick's friend Dickie had ridden with Bing on his cycle and lingered back from the others.

Cory and Cortez sat on the wooden porch with hands in pockets too stunned to move.

A dusk to dawn light came on lighting the entire compound emphasizing the early evening slight October breeze that sent swirls of dust to the east and towards the fenced trash.

Each in the entire group took off sun glasses and put them away in pockets or cycle packs, then marched to the porch. Wearing their most official faces, they waited for Rick to lead.

297

"Someone's in the guest house and we're scared." Cory babbled with fright.

Cortez stammered, "W-we saw movement."

Leading the way, Rick walked towards the guest house with Dickie and the four B's following.

Others stayed back whispering with occasional mystic nods towards the guest house.

"You need a key," Cory yelled as he went into the kitchen to retrieve it from a hook.

He couldn't believe his shaking hands while handing the key to Rick.

Cortez joined him walking behind the group.

Rick opened the door slowly and stood back on the small wooden veranda while cautiously peering inside.

Berty sat at a small table grasping a tea cup in both hands. Expressionless, and disheveled, she stared back at him in a daze. Uncombed tousled hair almost covered her tear stained face, and it was apparent that she had been here for hours. Depression replaced her usual vibrancy.

Rick went back to the door entrance and motioned for the female cops to come forward to help.

"Bring some water."

Next, he dialed paramedics.

The room soon became crowded as others shuffled in hesitantly, slipping inside the door frame and becoming motionless.

The infamous room had quite a reputation.

All stared at the fresh blood that stained the large box freezer sitting next to the wall and close to the tea table.

Bloody hand prints covered the edge of the lid.

Coagulated blood spotted the floor as it had dripped from the latch earlier.

Cory and Cortez turned white from memory of a few nights ago and moved hesitantly a few steps back behind the cops.

Berty still didn't speak or move, only occasionally blinking.

Someone handed Rick rubber gloves.

Gingerly he lifted the lid.

The dim table light sent shadows along the walls and into the now open cavernous box.

There lay Mr. Hollywood, bloodied and crumbled, his thick gold chain pasted to his collar bone.

No one stared too long at the bestial sight, but all came forward to see. Frosted bits of ice clung to the hairs on his pale chest, tanned no more.

"Step away and take deep breaths," Rick ordered after about two minutes.

"Dickie made the sign of the cross then clasped his hands together in a quick, simple personal prayer, "To my cousin, the chief."

Paramedics arrived, tended to Berty, than placed her in a cop car for further assessment.

"She needs medical help," Rick said.

"Will do!"

A coroner arrived and determined the cause of death was most likely the car accident that happened in the wee hours of the day. "You found your missing body," was his only statement.

"Again!" Rick's tone was one of disgust. "The fact that Delilah got out alive and crawled back to the road was a miracle."

Bing, reversing back to his New York cop days, took over at this point explaining the accident in full detail. "....and probably showing off, he drove the

Willy's Jeep too near the edge and flipped into a canyon that abutted the road."

"Then along came Berty." It was Brad's turn.

"Why?"

"How?" Two young cops from the big city to the south were perplexed with the situation.

"Is this related to the body parts episode from last week end?"

Rick pushed everyone out of the guest house and into the court yard where Bob and Blake explained what they knew. "The chief here was the missing porno king who collaborated with the deceased photographer."

"The one spread all over town," quipped a very young cop trying to be funny.

Everyone grimaced. A few spit while others shook their heads and sucked in their breaths.

"Cory and Cortez, do not get out of my sight," demanded Rick as he and Colt cordoned off the small tea house with yellow tape.

"Come with me." He waved at them to follow as he opened the wide gates housing the trash area and Berty's multiple crates of junk. Tucked in a far corner was the dually with doors open. Blood almost covered the front seat cushion and head rest.

"She belted him in the front seat next to her," Bing sadly uttered as he examined the scene without touching a thing.

Cortez walked a few yards away and vomited.

Cory ducked his head and coughed over and over.

"We need more tape over here," Rick yelled.

By now a few more official cars had entered the compound and the yard was getting overly occupied as security lights that had not blinked for weeks were now coming off and on. Dogs were milling about

300

uncomfortable with the excitement, poking their noses through the wire mesh.

Rick shouted and pointed out a few more orders. "You, keep everyone away from the guest house. You two, guard the front gates and don't let the media in."

He continued on a roll. "Now, you seventeen year olds are going to be in our custody over night to give us all the details starting with a missing mask, spray painting, and body parts." He thrust a forefinger in their direction.

"I've never seen Rick this mad," whispered Colt to the four B's who were grouped waiting for orders of any kind….after all, they were family.

"And," Rick told a newly arrived lady cop who had been standing there favorably eying him, "take the boys to jail but bring them back tomorrow morning to take care of the dogs and do other chores." He softened but the boys still shook with fright. "Before leaving, I need to see the list and some kind of timetable."

Two helicopters hovered high above in the darkening night while media crews set up stations outside the padlocked gates. They were pumped with every juicy detail they had heard from the town's people….basically tourist…and everything else they half invented. Their favorite word which they touted the most was 'allegedly', which they used in the beginning of each sentence. This got them off the hook for wildish reporting known as 'misinformation'.

"It'll be a long, long detailed story," offered Dickie. "They'll never get it straight."

The little town of Cave Creek made the national news, again.

## CHAPTER FORTY-EIGHT
Friday night

Gina and Nancy had secured a long table the day before at the now amply packed Tumbleweed's Saloon. Pop and Dixie guarded it and its 'reserved' sign from mischievous others who felt cantankerous enough to remove the sign and move in. It was only eight and a crowd was pushing through the entrance non-stop.

Extra tables and chairs were numerous on the wooden porches surrounding the exterior of the dance hall. And as planned for larger than normal events, a fifty foot tent adjacent to the wooden patios contained its own bar and dance floor. Music was piped at all locations from the main dance hall where performances by the 'Cave Creek Cowboys' and the 'Superstition Miners' would be topped only by short segments from the African drummers in full costume.

When finished, the Africans would don western clothes for the 'hoe-down' at the high school. Presents of bolas, straw hats and colorful neck scarves were given to each of them and they would probably choose something from this array of gifts. They were ready and hyped.

Dixie told Pop..."The girls took a large bouquet of mixed flowers to Delilah at the hospital but will be here soon." She checked the time on her hand tooled one-of-a-kind silver bracelet while straightening it on her wrist. "Are we dancing tonight?" She teased Pop knowing he would never dance.

"Sure, you and many others." He ordered a pitcher of beer from the passing waitress then turned back to Dixie who sat close now with her head on his shoulder. "Clue me in," he continued. "What's the agenda for tonight?" He thumped his thick fingers on the table impatiently. "And where is everybody?"

She yawned, put her elbows on the table and cupped her head in her hands. "It's been a long, long, long, long, day."

Massaging her shoulders with his broad hands, he circled under the shoulder blades with his thumbs stopping only when a pitcher of beer arrived on a tray with two frosted glasses. He filled both.

She continued. "The adults are here at Tumbleweed's and the high school teens have a big dance at Blakely. After the African drummers perform here, they're headed to the school for the remainder of the evening." She put her head down on her now folded arms.

"When everyone arrives, let's go home and put on a Western movie. I'll make the popcorn and you won't have anything to do," he whispered sedately in her ear.

She mumbled and shook her head up and down. "Nellie needs us."

Gina and Nancy, feeling their youth, came bouncing in smiling like a commercial for white teeth.

Matching, they wore black tight jeans and one of a kind leather belts containing engraved names on back and specialty jeweled silver buckles. Each wore tight v-neck, short sleeved tops with sparkling sequins. Gina's was red and Nancy's emerald green.

They dressed alike. No one was surprised.

Gina's short blond curls bubbled unruly touching her shoulders only when she dipped her head to the side. As usual, Nancy's red hair was straight and long, sweeping down front below her collar bone almost as long as salon extensions.

After waving, smiling, and talking to everyone they knew on the way in, they finally spotted Pop and Dixie, looking very much ready to leave.

"You're here; we're gone." They hugged and said their goodbyes. Dixie only shook her head, too tired to talk.

"Finish the beer if you like," Pop said pointing to a half full pitcher on their way out.

Dragging behind the two bouncing teachers and looking beat and tired, were Bing, Bob, Brad and Blake. "I'm staying for only a short while," Bob began. "I want to hear the results of today's horror story."

"Same here," the other three mumbled. Blake yawned.

Gina asked, "Where are your dates?"

"They're working at the bakery giving Pop a breather," Bob offered.

Brad said, "They're done in an hour."

"We each have our own plans," said Blake. "And it includes being gone from noise and excitement." He ordered a pitcher of root beer and one of ice tea while they sat and waited for Rick.

They all sat through a display of African musical talent. To the beat of conical and kettle drums, ten African youths danced in full costume and sang while the audience clapped along to the beat.

"Unbelievable talent," said Nancy.

"It's too sensational. I love the bright colors of orange, purple and reds," said Gina.

"Yeah, one look and you're wide awake." Guy moved up to the table and sat. "A person doesn't need coffee," he said with his widest smile.

"Hey, what are you doing here?" asked Gina. "I thought that you and the entire athletic department volunteered to help at the school dance."

"I'm heading out with this group." He nodded toward the stage. "I'm escorting them back."

She pinched his cheek. "You're such a good boy!"

He grabbed her hand and kissed it. "Don't get carried away now."

Andrew Chang, the student body president, was next at the microphone. "All of this week's events would not have been possible without our wonderful principal, the first Grand Marshal for African week, Dr. Shieter." He waved a welcoming signal and began clapping.

Everyone clapped as Shieter came forward from the background.

It was the four B's turn for exclamation points as they stared in awe.

"Just a minute!"

"Hold the phone!"

"Stop the music!"

"And play it again Sam!"

Principal Shieter strutted on the stage in a knee length tunic style skirt. Thankfully, a wide silky banner over one shoulder that read Grand Marshal, and numerous beaded arm and ankle bracelets took attention

305

away from his near nudeness. Around his head a red beaded stretch band shimmered in the overhead light.

He smiled.

People clapped.

Preparing to talk, he pointed to the ten piece band which took it as a cue and began pounding and singing loudly. He was drowned out.

People clapped.

Guy got up from the table. "Time to go," he said and escorted the now finished band and the speechless Dr. Shieter out.

The group at the table chatted about all the events that had occurred the past two weeks while a new band was setting all their gear in place to start.

Finally, Rick and Colt walked in nodding in their direction immediately. "Is this week done yet?" Rick looked disgusted while Colt was all smiles in Nancy's direction.

"Are you crabby?" Gina looked up from where she was sitting.

"No, I need a steak." He waved at the waitress. "How many do we need? I'm buying."

"We're out of here as soon as you tell us some stories." Bob said.

Bing added. "The girls are working at the bakery and we're leaving in about twenty minutes."

"Ok. Four steaks."

"No, we're going to the movies," Colt said.

"Ok, Two." He finally had to smile at the break down. He waved their waitress over who was nearby and ordered.

"Start!" Bing said impatiently while yawning.

He sat in the chair behind Gina, poured himself a glass of beer and began. "Zander was the peeking pervert two Friday's ago and the streaker earlier today.

He said he didn't know why he did it, but was disgusted when the school district didn't honor his security business and renew his contract. After he was jailed as the streaker, forensics ran some DNA and found a match with the mask he wore as the pervert. He's in big trouble."

"Ball and chain," added Gina sarcastically.


He looked at Gina, pulled one of her curls, than continued after sipping from his glass. "Cory's and Cortez's problems are all parental. We're keeping them close until relatives come to town. They were not alone with the dispatching of the body parts. About one hundred others were involved. Cory's in the deepest trouble for writing that threatening limerick to Gina and leaving it on her Jeep."

Blake asked, "What about all of the spray painting?"

"They were the leads. To repay the principal for the damage done to his BMW, I know that the judge will make them work it off. In the past, one year of daily street 'scaping' in both Cave Creek and Carefree has been the punishment. You know, the maintenance, clean-up problems, landscaping needed everywhere."

"But why did they pick on me?" Gina asked.

"You were like a mother figure to them. Because of failing your class, they could no longer play football. They also thought that puncturing your tires would relieve their frustration. And of course, the fact that Shieter initially chained the soda machines because of tardies, this brought on the spray painting, which caused the cancelling of the African festivities…A domino affect. He followed this with his short smile.

"Tell me. What did you and Nancy do to change the principal's mind......all the details."

Gina and Nancy looked at each other. "We'll never tell," Gina teased shaking her head seriously.

"Nope," added Nancy leaning back into Colt with her arms folded.

The waitress arrived with a big tray of two plates of steaks. She set a bowl of pinto beans on the table between them and a large salad.

"We're all leaving," said Blake.

"And we'll be late for the movies. Call me with more info' tomorrow," said Nancy while getting up to leave.

Now that the table was empty, couples from the standing-room-only crowd asked if they could sit at the almost empty table.

"Help yourselves," Rick said.

While eating their steaks, the 'Superstition Miners' began playing in the background.

"This is my favorite tune," she said. "Listen carefully to the words."

"Did you write it?" He mocked seriousness as he cut a piece of steak without looking at her.

"Yes, just for you."

I want a handy dandy super man
Who'll trim the trees, pull the weeds
And mow the lawn at early dawn
Spray the bugs, look for slugs
Check tomatoes on the vine
Rake the leaves, cough and sneeze
WHILE I GO POUR ME SOME MORE WINE

He'll fry the eggs, toast the bread
Answer the phone and make the bed

Dust and polish mop and scrub
Wash the windows and unplug the tub
Keep at it darlin' you're doing fine
WHILE I GO POUR ME SOME MORE WINE

Don't want a handsome man who flirts with everyone
Nor a rich man with an all day job
He isn't any fun
I want a plain man who's handy dandy all the time—
when it rains and pours
I need some help as a mean's of escape
From these never ending household chores

"You forgot the bit about searching pack rats'
nests out on the desert."
"You remembered."
The waitress came, gave Rick a couple side
glances and cleared all the dishes in slow motion.
"Come here. You're too far away." He pulled
her over to him setting her on his lap, hugging her
tightly. "Where have you been these past two weeks?
Are you coming to my house or am I going to yours?"
Then he added with another short smile, "Pop and Dixie
love me you know!"
"Ha! Your mood has changed. I'll follow you
to your house."
Rick studied her face for ten seconds as she
began her crooked smile.
"What?"
"You lost the key."
"No…..I misplaced it."
"So some other girl could find it."
"Speaking of other girls, I saw Delilah at the
hospital today and aside from bumps and bruises, she's
going to be fine."

"Amazing, considering the Chief's ultimate end….morbid."

"Morbid. I feel sorry for Berty!"

"We all do. Basically she's a good person who needs help." He yawned. "Today started too early."

"And is lasting too long." She got up and pulled him off the chair. "Let's go to your house."

Dickie's there. I need to take him home to the Blue Ridge tomorrow and you have to go with me. We could spend the night at Hannagan's Meadow."

"Romantic."

She followed him to his house north of town near the foot of the Cave Creek Mountains where coyotes howled nightly in the nearby low canyons. Again he swung her off her feet on the patio, carried her through the front door closing it with his heel and put her on top of his king size denim quilted bed.

"I thought you were tired. What happened to that yawn earlier?"

"Yeah," he said taking off her boots. "What happened to it?"

Moon shine and starry sky lit the half dark room as they peeled off each others clothes, laid them together on a nearby love sofa, than pulled back the cover folding it like an envelope at the end.

"You're so meticulous," she said facing him on top of the cool sheets with her head on the bicep of his folded arm.

"Takes one to know one." He pulled her very near with one hand on her buttocks, then slowly ran his hand up the contour of her spine before playing with the curls on top of her head, springing them in and out. He crushed them gently as they fell between his fingers while cupping the back of her head drawing her near his lips.

All events of the past two weeks faded.

## CHAPTER FORTY-NINE

Cory and Cortez paid for their crimes in more ways then predicted. Daily they scrubbed customers' dogs that had rolled in stinky rotten flesh not found previously even though about one hundred students searched for body parts at least one hour weekly for an entire month as punishment.

This was all done 'free of charge' and took weeks considering that numerous Border Collies were the bulk of the canines owned by horsemen. These dogs, as part of their gene pool, loved to roll in anything stinky and dead to mask their own body odor from by-gone predators.

Berty's hoarding batch was openly dispatched to all who came and 'looked and took'. Trash was cleared away, taken to a nearby dump. With humanitarian overload, townsfolk helped Berty's dog grooming business survive and took turns taking her to counseling sessions.

"She is the best there is!!!" They touted.

The Africans went home, each with an armful of souvenirs, chattering excessively, all smiles with many wild stories to tell while boarding buses. The two coordinators riding the buses shook hands over and over with the office personnel before leaving, giving each secretary a jeweled trinket.

Shieter encased his silky banner in a specially made lighted glass case attached to the wall above his cherry wood desk for all to see immediately upon entering.

And it rained, and rained, and rained sending rivulets of water down the canyons, into the parched washes filling deep arroyos, washing dust from lowly bushes welcoming the fall, and erasing the horrors from the last two weeks.

And, Gina found the lost key.

# *Coming Soon:*

# BLAKELY HIGH GHOSTS OF THE SUPERSTITIONS

## *By: Dot Jay Gomez*

A December trail ride in the mysterious Superstition Mountains of Apache Junction, Arizona becomes one of chaos and terror when uninvited guests appear.